GHETTO SKETCHES, 2021

Odie Hawkins

authorHOUSE®

AuthorHouse™
1663 Liberty Drive
Bloomington, IN 47403
www.authorhouse.com
Phone: 833-262-8899

Published by AuthorHouse 08/27/2021

ISBN: 978-1-6655-3582-3 (sc)
ISBN: 978-1-6655-3585-4 (e)

Library of Congress Control Number: 2021917217

Print information available on the last page.

Front Cover by Tony Gleeson
http://www.tonygleeson.com/

Author's Photo and inserts by Zola Salena-Hawkins
www.flickr.com/photos/32886903@N02

Zola Salena-Hawkins, Head Researcher

CONTENTS

PROLOGUE

"Ghetto Sketches" was my first Protest Novel. As an optimist I hoped that it would be my last; but the history of Life in our country prevented that from happening.

"Ghetto Sketches" was originally published by Holloway House Publishing Company in 1972. It was not seriously promoted, but it sold well. I can say that because my in-house sources gave me documented evidence of how well the book was selling. I can't say that my royalties were honest reflections of those sales.

Fast forwarding – Holloway House sold its assets to Kensington Press in the 1990's (including "Sketches"). I petitioned, via my unions – the Author's Guild, the National Writers Union and the Screenwriters Guild, West, for a reversion of rights for all of my originally published works by Holloway House.

Subsequently, "Ghetto Sketches" was re-issued with a new cover. I felt that some of the circumstances, the subject matters in the book were too dated to merit further marketing.

Fortunately, it seems Zola Salena-Hawkins and several other "Lobbyists" agreed that I was partially correct; but squashed my attempt to place the book in retirement. "Look, man, it may be an antique, but as you know antiques gain value with age. We think that the 'Sketches' fits that category"….

So, as they say, my protest fell on deaf ears, ergo, The "Ghetto Sketches, 2021".

Odie Hawkins

PREAMBLE TO "GHETTO SKETCHES, 2021"

"Ghetto | Definition of Ghetto at Dictionary.com
Ghetto – [get-oh] SHOW IPA
See synonyms for: ghetto / ghettos on Thesaurus.com

---

noun, plural **ghet·tos, ghet·toes.**
a section of a city, especially a thickly populated slum area, inhabited predominantly by members of an ethnic or other minority group, often as a result of social pressures or economic hardships.

(formerly, in most European countries) a section of a city in which all Jews were required to live.

any mode of living, working, etc., that results from stereotyping or biased treatment:*job ghettos for women; ghettos for the elderly.*
adjective

pertaining to or characteristic of life in a ghetto or the people who live there:*ghetto culture.*

Slang: *Often Disparaging and Offensive*. noting something that is considered to be unrefined, low-class, cheap, or inferior: *Her furniture is so ghetto!*"

It's more than a Black thang yawl. It's a White, Black, Brown & Asian…thang.

The "Ghetto Sketches" was written in 1962, published in 1972. The ghettos in Chicago (North, South, Westside) provided the foundation for the novel. As you read these pages, keep in mind, The "Sketches" happened in a time frame when there were few community programs to help people with drug issues, alcohol addiction, racism. We've come a long way, but we still have a long way to go, as indicated in this "Ghetto Sketches, 2021".

Bright Moments,
Odie Hawkins

GHETTO SKETCHES, 2021 - PHOTO GALLERY TABLE OF CONTENTS

PHOTOS By ZOLA SALENA-HAWKINS - *www.flickr.com/photos/32886903@N02*

* "https://islamexplored.org/what-is-jihad
Jihad is **a struggle to do good and to remove injustice, oppression and evil from oneself and from society.** This struggle is spiritual, social, economic and political. Indeed, the concept of jihad is one of life, and it is vast, not limited only to armed conflict."

"SAY THEIR NAMES!"
"Ghetto Sketches" – Murdered Folks

https://www.fbi.gov/services/cjis/ucr/use-of-force
"National Use-of-Force Data Collection: The FBI created the National Use of Force Data Collection in 2015, in partnership with law enforcement agencies, to provide nationwide statistics on law enforcement use-of-force incidents..."

No.	NAME	AGE	LOCATION & YEAR
001	Hunter Brittain	17	Beeba, Arkansas (2021)
002	Stanley Howard	64	Phoenix, Arizona (2021)
003	Leneal Frazier	40	Minneapolis, Minnesota (2021)
004	Andre Hill	47	Columbus, Ohio (2020)
005	Manuel Ellis	33	Tacoma, Washington (2020)
006	Daunte Wright	20	Minneapolis, Minnesota (2020)
007	Rayshard Brooks	27	Atlanta, Georgia (2020)
008	Daniel Prude	41	Rochester, New York (2020)
009	George Floyd	46	Minneapolis, Minnesota (2020)
010	Breonna Taylor	26	Louisville, Kentucky (2020)
011	Atatiana Jefferson	28	Fort Worth, Texas (2020)
012	Aura Rosser	40	Ann Arbor. Michigan (2020)
013	Stephon Clark	22	Sacramento, California (2018)
014	Botham Jean	26	Dallas, Texas (2016)
015	Philando Castile	32	Falcon Heights, Minnesota (2016)
016	Alton Sterling	37	Baton Rouge, Louisiana (2016)
017	Freddie Gray	25	Baltimore, Maryland (2015)
018	Tanisha Fonville	20	Charlotte, North Carolina 2015)
019	Eric Garner	43	Staten Island, New York (2014)
020	Michelle Cusseaux	50	Phoenix, Arizona (2014)
021	Akai Curley	28	Brooklyn, New York (2014)
022	Gabriella Nevarez	22	Sacramento, California (2014)
023	Tamir Rice	12	Cleveland, Ohio (2014)
024	Michael Brown	18	Ferguson, Missouri (2014)
025	Tanisha Anderson	37	Cleveland, Ohio (2014)
026	Who's next?		
027	Who's next?		

It didn't begin with **George Floyd** and it didn't end with **George Floyd**. No it didn't…**SAY THEIR NAMES**….

Available names, ages and locations of the 229 Black people killed by police since George Floyd:

1. Tony McDade aka Natosha McDade, 38, Tallahassee, FL
2. Modesto "Marrero Desto" Reyes, 35, Marrero, LA
3. Ruben Smith III, 35, North Little Rock, AK
4. Jarvis Sullivan, 44, Yulee, FL
5. Terrell Mitchell, 34, Philadelphia, PA
6. Momodou Lamin Sisay, 34, Snellville, GA
7. Derrick Thompson, 46, Fountain, FL
8. David McAtee, 53, Louisville, KY
9. Tyquarn Graves, 33, Brooklyn, NY
10. Kamal Flowers, 24, New Rochelle, NY
11. Lewis Ruffin Jr., 38, Orlando, FL
12. Phillip Jackson, 32, Tunnell Hill, GA
13. Michael Blu Thomas, 63, Lancaster, CA
14. Rayshard Brooks, 27, Atlanta, GA
15. Cane Van Pelt, 23, Crown Pont, IN
16. Donald Ward, 27, Phoenix, AZ
17. Brandon Gardner, 24, Beach Park, IL
18. Terron Jammal Boone, 31, Rosamond, CA
19. Derrick Canada, 43, Giddings, TX
20. Skyleur Toung, 31, San Bernardino, CA
21. Robert D'Lon Harris, Vinita, OK
22. Rasheed Mathew Moorman, 26, Roanoke, VA
23. Aloysius Larue Keaton, 58, Little Rock, AK
24. Kevin O. Ruffin, 32, Sheboygan, WI
25. Ky Johnson, 31, Kansas City, MO
26. William Wade Burgess III, 27, St. Louis, MO
27. Joseph W. Denton, 35, Milwaukee, WI
28. Paul Williams, Houston, TX
29. Malik Canty, 36, Paterson, NJ
30. Erroll Johnson, 31, Monroe, LA

31. Richard Lewis Price, 49, San Diego, CA
32. Hakim Littleton, 20, Detroit, MI
33. Vincent Demario Truitt, 17, Austell, GA
34. Aaron Anthony Hudson, 31, Syracuse, NY
35. Darius Washington, 24, Chicago Heights, IL
36. Vincent Harris, 51, Baton Rouge, LA
37. Jeremy Southern, 22, Sacramento, CA
38. Name withheld by police, Detroit, MI
39. Chester Jenkins, 60, Stockton, CA
40. David Earl Brooks Jr., 45, Roxboro, NC
41. Darrien Walker, 28, Detroit, MI
42. Ashton Broussard, 30, Houston, TX
43. Amir Johnson, 30, Ventnor City, NJ
44. Julian Edward Roosevelt Lewis, 60, Sylvania, GA
45. Salaythis Melvin, 22, Orlando, FL
46. Jonathan Jefferson, Bossier City, LA
47. Rafael Jevon Minniefield, 29, Moreland, GA
48. Kendrell Antron Watkins, 31, Tuscaloosa, AL
49. Anthony McClain, 32, Pasadena, CA
50. Adrian Jason Roberts, 37, Hope Mills, NC
51. Trayford Pellerin, 31, Lafayette, LA
52. Damian Lamar Daniels, 31, San Antonio, TX
53. Julius Paye Kehyei, 29, Houston, TX
54. Name withheld by police, 43, Dearborn Heights, MI
55. Michael Anthony Harris, 44, Daytona Beach, FL
56. Robert Earl Jackson, 54, Thorsby, AL
57. Dijon Kizzee, 29, Westmont, CA
58. Deon Kay, 18, Washington, D.C.
59. Steven D. Smith, 33, Syracuse, NY
60. Major Carvel Baldwin, 61, San Antonio, TX
61. Steve Gilbert, 33, Delray Beach, FL
62. Jonathan Darsaw, 28, Moscow, TN
63. Robert Coleman, 88, West Sacramento, CA
64. Darrell Wayne Zemault Sr., 55, San Antonio, TX
65. Charles Eric Moses Jr., 33, Brunswick, GA
66. Dearian Bell, 28, Atlanta, GA

67. Patches Vojon Holmes Jr., 26, Bellefontaine Neighbors, MO
68. Kurt Andras Reinhold, 42, San Clemente, CA
69. Willie Shropshire Jr., 57, Waggaman, LA
70. DeMarco Riley, 27, Decatur, GA
71. Jonathan Price, 31, Wolfe City, TX
72. Stanley Cochran, 29, Philadelphia, PA
73. Tyran Dent, 24, Queens, NY
74. Anthony Jones, 24, Bethel Springs, TN
75. Kevin Carr, 23, Los Angeles, CA
76. Dana Mitchell Young Jr., 47, Los Angeles, CA
77. Fred Williams III, 25, Los Angeles, CA
78. Akbar Muhammad Eaddy, 27, Rock Island, IL
79. Dominique Mulkey, 26, Tampa, FL
80. Marcellis Stinnette, 19, Waukegan, IL
81. Rodney Arnez Barnes, 48, Elmwood Place, OH
82. Gregory Jackson, 45, Moss Point, MS
83. Mark Matthew Bender, 35, San Bernardino, CA
84. Ennice "Lil Rocc" Ross Jr., 26, Kansas City, MO
85. Jakerion Shmond Jackson, 19, Sylvester, GA
86. Walter Wallace Jr., 27, Philadelphia, PA
87. Maurice Parker, 34, Las Vegas, NV
88. Kevin Peterson Jr., 21, Vancouver, WA
89. Name withheld by police, 42, Detroit, MI
90. Justin Reed, 34, Jacksonville, FL
91. Michael Wright, Sacramento, CA
92. Reginald Alexander Jr., 25, Dallas, TX
93. Frederick Cox Jr., 18, High Point, NC
94. Rodney Eubanks, 25, Baltimore, MD
95. Vusumuzi Kunene, 36, Lanham, MD
96. Brandon Milburn, 37, Oklahoma City, OK
97. Tracey Leon McKinney, Gulfport, MS
98. Angelo "AJ" Crooms, 16, Cocoa, FL
99. Sincere Peirce, 18, Cocoa, FL
100. Arthur Keith, 19, Cleveland, OH
101. Name withheld by police, Inglewood, CA
102. Shane K. Jones, 38, Dania Beach, FL

103. Shawn Lequin Braddy, 37, Laurel, MD
104. Jason Brice, 39, La Vergne, TN
105. Kenneth Jones, 35, Omaha, NE
106. Rodney Applewhite, 25, Los Lunas, NM
107. Terrell Smith, 17, Atlanta, GA
108. Rondell Goppy, 41, Queens, NY
109. Ellis Frye Jr., 62, Culpeper, VA
110. Cory Donell Truxillo, Houma, LA
111. Mickee McArthur, 28, Ferry Pass, FL
112. Udofia Ekom-Abasi, Phoenix, AZ
113. James David Hawley, 47, Pineville, LA
114. Kevin Fox, 28, Detroit, MI
115. Dominique Harris, 20, St. Petersburg, FL
116. Maurice Jackson, 42, Phoenix, AZ
117. Andre K. Sterling, 35, Bronx, NY
118. Casey Christopher Goodson Jr., 23, Columbus, OH
119. Kwamaine O'Neal, 47, Toledo, OH
120. Mark Brewer, 28, St. Louis, MO
121. Donald Edwin Saunders, 37, Dayton, OH
122. Thomas Reeder III, 44, Flint, MI
123. Joseph R. Crawford, 23, Fort Atkinson, WI
124. Joshua Feast, 22, La Marque, TX
125. Charles E. Jones, 36, Houston, TX
126. Bennie Edwards, 60, Oklahoma City, OK
127. Jeremy Daniels, 29, Concord Mills, NC
128. Johnny Bolton, 49, Smyrna, GA
129. Larry Taylor, 39, Mobile, AL
130. Andre Maurice Hill, 47, Columbus, OH
131. Isaac Frazier, 31, Houston, TX
132. Sheikh Mustafa Davis, 20, Midway, GA
133. Shamar Ogman, 30, Hartford, CT
134. Marquavious Rashod Parks, 26, Davisboro, GA
135. Larry Hamm, 47, Denver, CO
136. Helen Jones, 47, Phoenix, AZ
137. Jason Cooper, 28, Charleston, SC
138. Jaquan Haynes, 18, Atlanta, GA

139. Shyheed Robert Boyd, 21, Highland, CA
140. Dolal Idd, 23, Minneapolis, MN
141. Carl Dorsey III, 39, Newark, NJ
142. La Garion Smith, 27, Homestead, FL
143. Tre-Kedrian Tyquan White, 20, Richburg, SC
144. Vincent Belmonte, 18, Cleveland, OH
145. Shawn McCoy, Spokane, WA
146. Robert "Lil Rob" Howard, 30, Memphis, TN
147. Jason Nightengale, 32, Evanston, IL
148. Matthew Oxendine, 46, Pembroke, NC
149. Patrick Warren Sr., 52, Killeen, TX
150. Lymond Maurice Moses, 30, Wilmington, DE
151. Kershawn Geiger, 24, Carmichael, CA
152. Reginald Johnson, 48, Biloxi, MS
153. Zonterious Johnson, 24, Lawton, OK
154. Christopher Harris, 27, Toledo, OH
155. Eusi Malik Kater Jr., 21, Titusville, AL
156. Tyree Kajawn Rogers, 38, Wichita Falls, TX
157. Randy Miller, Los Angeles, CA
158. Roger D. Hipskind, 37, Wabash, IN
159. Karl Walker, 29, Dixon, CA
160. Marvon Payton Jr., 27, Las Vegas, NV
161. Jenoah Donald, 30, Hazel Dell, WA
162. Dontae Green, 34, Baltimore, MD
163. Treyh Webster, 18, Mobile, AL
164. Christopher Hagans, 36, Stratford, CT
165. Andrew Hogan, 25, Trotwood, OH
166. Dustin Demaurean Powell, 34, Lakeview, TX
167. Gregory Taylor, 45, Seattle, WA
168. Jordan Walton, 21, Austin, TX
169. Brandon Wimberly, Coral Gables, FL
170. Daverion Kinard, 29, Fontana, CA
171. Arnell States, 39, Cedar Rapids, IA
172. Benjamin Tyson, 35, Baltimore, MD
173. Donald Francis Hairston, 44, Culpeper, VA
174. Chandra Moore, 55, Detroit, MI

175. Andrew Teague, 43, Columbus, OH
176. Howayne Gale, 35, Lakeland, FL
177. Tyshon Jones, 29, Rochester, NY
178. Tyrell Wilson, 32, Danville, CA
179. Nika Nicole Holbert, 31, Nashville, TN
180. Christopher Ruffin, 28, Palm Bay, FL
181. Daryl Lenard Jordan, 50, Miami, FL
182. Kevin L. Duncan, 38, Bellefontaine, OH
183. Frankie Jennings, 32, Charlotte, NC
184. Travon Chadwell, 18, Chicago, IL
185. Malcolm D. Johnson, 31, Kansas City, MO
186. Donovan W. Lynch, 25, Virginia Beach, VA
187. Matthew Blaylock, 38, Los Angeles, CA
188. Michael Leon Hughes, 32, Jacksonville, FL
189. Willie Roy Allen, 57, Lithonia, GA
190. DeShawn Latiwon Tatum, 25, Rock Island, IL
191. Noah R. Green, 25, Washington, D.C.
192. Diwone Wallace, 24, Alorton, IL
193. Gabriel Casso, 21, Bronx, NY
194. Desmon Montez Ray, 28, Birmingham, AL
195. Dominique Williams, 32, Takoma Park, MD
196. James Lionel Johnson, 38, Takoma Park, MD
197. James Alexander, 24, Philadelphia, PA
198. Raheem Reeder, Tallahassee, FL
199. DeShund Tanner, 31, Georgetown, KY
200. Faustin Guetigo, 27, Rockford, IL
201. Daunte Wright, 20, Brooklyn Center, MN
202. Miles Jackson, 27, Westerville, OH
203. Mathew Zadok Williams, 35, Decatur, GA
204. Anthony Thompson Jr., 17, Knoxville, TN
205. Pier Alexander Shelton, 28, Bremen, GA
206. Lindani Myeni, 29, Honolulu, HI
207. Innes Lee Jr., 25, Cleveland, OH
208. Roderick Inge, 29, Tuscaloosa, AL
209. Larry Jenkins, 52, Winter Haven, FL
210. Name withheld by police, 31, Fort Worth, TX

211. Dequan Cortez Glenn, 24, Douglasville, GA
212. Doward Sylleen Baker, 39, Dothan, AL
213. Ma'Khia Bryant, 16, Columbus, OH
214. Andrew Brown, 42, Elizabeth City, NC
215. Tory Casey, 41, Rosenberg, TX
216. Michael Lee McClure, 26, Billings, MT
217. Marvin Veiga, 32, Nashville, TN
218. Hanad Abidaziz, 25, Kansas City, MO
219. Terrance Maurice Parker, 36, Washington, D.C.
220. Eric Derrell Smith, 30, Biloxi, MS
221. La'Mello Parker, three months, Biloxi, MS
222. Latoya Denis James, 37, Woodbine, GA
223. Ashton Pinkee, 27, Mesquite, TX
224. Adonis Traughber, 54, Clarksville, TN
225. Kalon Horton, 29, Leicester, MA
226. Lance Lowe, 30, Stockton, CA
227. Tyrone Penny, 21, Decatur, GA
228. Darion M. Lafayette, 24, Champaign, IL
229. Kortnee Lashon Warren, 23, Albany, GA

Research by Zola Salena-Hawkins - Websites:

https://www.dictionary.com/browse/ghetto

https://www.cbsnews.com/pictures/black-people-killed-by-

police-in-the-u-s-in-2020/

https://interactive.aljazeera.com/aje/2020/know-their-names/index.html

https://www.newsweek.com/full-list-229-black-people-killed-police-since-george-floyds-murder-1594477

https://en.wikipedia.org/wiki/List_of_unarmed_African_Americans_killed_by_law_enforcement_officers_in_the_United_States

I dedicate the Ghetto Sketches, 2021 to my Father, Mother, Sister, Daughters, and Queen Zola Salena-Hawkins, and to all the members of my Family, both living and dead, with deepest love and respect. . .

Love the Future, always,

Aşe,
Odie Hawkins

FOREWORD

[Note: Dr. Margaret Burroughs - Gone Home – Sunday, November 21, 2010. This Foreward was included in the Second Edition of *Ghetto Sketches* – published in January 2002.]

The DuSable Museum
of African American History, Inc.

As an art teacher at DuSable High School, Chicago, Illinois, I can say that I feel privileged and fortunate to have had so many talented students in my classes. Odie Hawkins is one of many hundred who have fulfilled the dreams I had for them, by virtue of hard work and perserverance.

In my art class I found Odie writing a "nasty" little story for a friend who had given him a fifty-cent commission for the job. As a seasoned teacher, it was quite obvious that he wasn't doing the work assigned to the class, he was doing something else. I plucked the sheets of paper from his surprised fingers and read it. He was embarrassed and I was pleasantly surprised.

Whatever the short story was about, I can't recall now, it was liberally laced with profanity. But beyond that, it was interesting and showed a certain kind of style. Years later, he told me how surprised he was about my reaction. Instead of punishing him in any way, I recommended a writing workshop that a friend of mine was leading at the community center on 51st and South Parkway (Martin Luther King Drive now.)

He was a teenager meeting with adults and, I think, after a few sessions, their sophistication overwhelmed him. But he continued writing and often showed me his work. Several English teachers will always have a checkmark next to their names because they accused this young writer of plagiarizing. He was not plagiarizing; he was exploring his own creative hemispheres. I gave him a ream of paper for the summer school vacation and told him to "write, write, write." He wrote his first novel that summer, an extravagantly structured work about "The Peps", a popular dance hall on 47th Street near St. Lawrence Avenue.

The Peps" that he wrote about was dance music, an atmosphere brimming with fire and teenage hormones.

He came to me two weeks after the semester started, looking miserable, to tell me that this then girlfriend had stolen the novel and weas accusing him of having a relationship with another girl, based on her misreading of his manuscript. So as far as I know she may still have the manuscript. Perhaps it is true that youth is wasted on the young.

Odie graduated from DuSable in 1956, pretended to go to Wilson Junior College for most of a year, and continued loading up the material for a writing life. Always visiting or writing me, I like that, the fact that he has always made an effort to stay in touch.

He moved to Los Angeles in 1966 and became active in the Watts Writer's Workshop. Within a year or so, he was seriously involved in the Hollywood business, writing manuscripts, television scripts. Always returning, periodically, to Chicago to visit his family and to update me on his activities.

A fellow traveler, like myself, we had a brief reunion in Ghana, in 1994, where he lived in the early 1990s and I was once again leading a tour group.

I would like to say that I've read each of his published books from cover to cover, but I've been too busy to do that. I have read the "Ghetto Sketches" from cover to cover several times, because the book is that compelling. I made it a part of my curriculum at Kennedy-King, and I've used it in writing classes in Cook County Jail.

Odie has dug deeply into the cultural nuances of our lives in his "Ghetto Sketches". We are taken into the lives of the people who've produced the language and the groove, if you will, of this special environment.

Yes, the action in the work happens in the ghetto in Chicago, but the characters are not superficially stereotypical, and the situations are universal, situations that all of us must cope with, at some point in our lives. How to handle the stress of this technological life? What to do about relationships between men and women, men and men, women and women, the young and the old?

He doesn't spend much time belaboring the obvious problems that exist because of institutional racism, he gives us credit for having the intelligence to know that racial ghettos wouldn't exist if racism was dead.

In a few instances, where the price of things and services are mentioned (Sweet Peter Deeder's Hoes, for example) we are made aware that the first issue of the book took place years ago, but the circumstances of the lives of the people in "Ghetto Sketches", reflecting the lives of millions of Americans today, is right on the money.

Odie Hawkins has borne honest witness for us and I feel pleased and gratified to think that I played a role in this work, a piece I am sure will be considred a classic.

Dr. Margaret Burroughs
"Ol' Teach"

The Dusable Museum of African-American History
740 East 56th Place
Chicago, Illinois 60637
Phone: (773) 947-0600
http://www.dusablemuseum.org/

Saturday Night

CHAPTER I
SATURDAY NIGHT

Saturday night…any Saturday… the main stem sizzles and crackles with the flicker of neon lights, the popping of stale fish grease, the mad aroma of bar-be-cued ribs, steamin' chit'lins, boiled greens, candied yams, ham hocks 'n thangs and the horny sounds of people in love with the night.

The stem swirls in a straight line down 47th Street, heading for Buttermilk Bottom, the Fillmore District, Crenshaw, or the dusty, crusty surface of Gwinnett Street in deepest Georgia…or to any other place in the New World where the Brother has had to take his chances.

A ramshackle, three-story, rim-shot building, stuffed full of people. . .a ramshackled rim-shot neighborhood, stuffed . . .overlapped with people, uncollected garbage, reeking with swift running Black Earth, Saturday night smells. . .on any Saturday afternoon, in any city in this country, in any of its Black ghettos.

The people sweltering through the early dog days of late spring... not warm enough to stay outside all the time, but too warm to stay inside the cracker box walls...and summer has not yet released its asphalt haze.

Congestion is what it might be called...human congestion... bodies stacked floor upon floor, children swathed in piss-stenched blankets, nibbled at by wandering rats, people stretched out layer by layer, a bittersweet cake, overpowering to the taste.

A noise, under the circumstances, can be very disturbing, pushed through thin walls, or beaten out on drums being played in the alley.

Jim Daniels twists and tosses around on his narrow, sweat-soaked bed, his arms folded across his broad chest, twitching and reacting to every heavy, accented beat of the congas. Finally, unable to stand the monotonous thump bop bop thump of the mediocre drumming, he springs out of bed, dashes through the kitchen of his apartment, ignoring the strange looks given him by his wife and children, and steps barefoot out onto the rotted planks of his second-floor porch.

"Heyyyy! Why don't y'all go somewheres else and beat them goddamned drums and stuff?! I'm tryin' to get some sleep!" The Saturday afternoon group of Willie Bobos and Chano Pozos, Armando Perazas, clop to a ruffled stop. One of the men in the alley looks up at Jim with wine-soaked disgust splashed across his face. "Awww shit, mannn! What kinda nigger are you? Don't you know it's Saturday?"

Jim Daniels, past the point of sympathizing with weekenders... "Awright now... I done asked you dudes nicely... stop beatin' them drums down there. I ain't gon' ask you no more! Why you hav t' gang up down there, behind my goddamned porch every Saturday, anyway?"

The dudes in the alley, pausing to pass the wine and the joint around, look up at Jim contemptuously. One of them, a coffee-can cowbell player, sings out, to no one in particular but as a matter of defiance, "Fuck him, man! Go 'head and play! That's one o' them habitual bitches! Don't nobody never complain about us playin' down here but him!"

The exchange automatically attracts the attention of people living in the building. They lean over the rickety banisters, smiling behind their hands, or actively agitating the situation.

"O wow! What's that you said to Big Jim?"

"You heard me! I didn't stutter. I said. . . fuck him!" He ain't got no right to come out here and tell us to stop playin'. We don't try t' tell him what to do!"

"What's that you say? Say it again!"

"You heard me, motherfucker! I said fuck you! And that's what I mean!"

The other dudes, sitting around on milk crates, loaded, continue passing the Ripple around, sniggling at the exchange between their champion and Jim. Jim hurries into his crib, face creased with an angry frown.

"What's wrong, Jim?" What's happenin" out there?" Lena Daniels asks him.

Jim ignores her question and rushes to his clothes closet, pulls a hat box from the shelf, takes out a .38 special and rushes back through the kitchen, murder obviously on his mind.

"Jim! Jim! Whatchu gon' do with that gun?! Jim?" Lena Daniels rushes after her husband, out onto the porch, and jolts his arm enough to prevent the shots fired into the alley from doing more than harmlessly ricochet.

"Git offa me, Lena! I told you motherfuckers! I'm tryin' t' get some sleep!"

The drummers and drinkers look up, surprised to see the figure above firing bullets at them. There is a shocked pause before anyone can get himself together to say anything,

"Hey mann! You outta yo' mind or somethin'?"

The men scramble for cover, pulling their champion...drums and wine bottle with them. "Man! I told y'all that nigger was nuts!"

"You better shut up fool! 'N haul ass 'less you want t' get a cap busted in it!"

Lena pulls Jim, calmed a bit after firing his piece, back into the house. "C'mon baby... you know that ain't no way t'do . . . ain't na'un one o' them fools worth doin' no time for." Jim is gently led from the porch, appeased but still scowling, eyes rimmed with dark bags from loss of sleep.

XXX XXX XXX

Sweet Peter Deeder's Ride – Fool's Gold

Saturday afternoon on the street, Sweet Peter Deeder, notorious body peddler, ghetto entrepreneur, lounges casually against the front fender of his burgundy-colored hog, smoking a cigarette, adjusting and readjusting his large, white-rimmed burgundy brim, pinkie ring catching lights and sparkling like stars as he listens, above the noise of rumbling El trains, street noises, and the music coming from "Li'l Mo's Record Shoppe, to the brother everyone calls Rappin' Rudy . . . rappin', as usual, on the opposite corner.

Rappin' Rudy has been called, amongst other things, a spellbinder! His tradition is the Nigerian-Muslim village lawyer-Southern jackleg preacher-at-the-Sunday-dinner-table-Martin Luther King Jr., Malcolm X-tradition... with liberal side orders of old Stokely, Rev. J. Jackson, Cannonball Adderley, Minister Cleaver, A.C. Powell (God Rest his Soul!) and whoever else might be considered charismatic at this day or any other time, all stroked into the corner pocket, straight back.

"I'm tellin' y'all! All you brothers 'n sisters! Yeah! Even the ones with them television antennas stickin' out they eyeballs! And all that programmed jive on they minds! Even if you don't wake up today… you gonna have to wake up tomorrow! Which, I guess, is sooner than later! And when you do! When you do! When you really do finally get it righteously together! I mean, like after you find out why yo' neck bones 'n hamburger meat cost three cents more than they should, and why yo' greens got worms on 'em, and why it is you can get some credit by markin' an X on the dotted line, and why it's so much easier to buy heroin and cocaine than pablum… I mean, after you get hip to all these treacherous games bein' run on you each and every day, when you really try to bring your head to an understandin' of all that… then you'll really be into a lil' somethin'… and that ain't even a big piece of it!! Can you dig where I'm comin' from? I mean, in earnest, can you?"

Several of the young dudes standing around digging Rudy's rap respond positively. "Right on brother! You ain't said shit wrong!"

"Really!"

Brother Rudy, feeling deeply for the pulse of his audience, slouches down into one of his more hypnotic stances… "I mean, like, dig this! Is it really gon' be possible, one o' these days, in this land of the bullshit and home of the pigs…"

"Go 'head!"

"Yeah. . . that's right, they is pigs! Do you really think it's gon' be possible, for our young sisters and brothers to walk down the street or go to school or whatever, one day, and not be under-educated, mis-evaluated, messed over, ripped off and tripped up? Just 'cause they Black! I say yeah! Yeah! . . . it's gon' be possible . . . it'll come . . . when Black people come to theyselves and stop askin' Whitey to educate and evaluate who we is, or who we think we are . . . when Black people come to theyselves . . . and be fo' real about what's important! Am I right about what I'm sayin'?"

A young brother standing near Rudy slaps his outstretched palm affirmatively. "I don't care what you say, Rudy . . . I still think we gon' have t' kill up a whole bunch o' these honkies… in the long run."

"Yeahhhh . . . yeah Son Lee . . . I hate to say it, but I think you might be right."

A couple of observers, checking the scene out from a second-floor window, make comments on the happenings. "Thelma, is them niggers still down there talkin' all that wild 'n woolly bullshit?"

"Yeah honey . . . they down there, running' they mouths, as usual. I'd like to get me a shotgun sometimes 'n blow 'me all away. Looka' that one there, Hattie! Over on the edge o' the crowd, wid his hair all twisted up into pigtails!"

"Hmmmmf! Don't you know what that mean?"

"Oh . . . is it 'sposed to mean somethin'? Other than the fact he ain't combed his damned hair?"

"That's 'sposed to mean they revolutionary 'n whatnot!"

"Revolutionary my ass! All they do is sit out there 'n talk, the minute the weather gets warm . . . Hattie, you got any more beer in the box?"

Rappin' Rudy, off on his trip, continues dealing with the shit as he sees it. "Hey . . . looka'here...ain't no doubt about it! I mean, what the brother here says may have to happen! I mean, offin' somebody might be necessary too...but...now dig it! Let's go to some other places! Can you make yourself believe, here. . . deep down in the twentieth century, in this . . . uh huh . . .mighty fortress of De-mock-racy, where they always runnin' off somewheres to 'help' somebody . . . some other country . . . Vietnam ain't been the only place! ... Can you believe that we damned near have to burn half the damned joint down before they'll throw us a few more bones? Can you believe that?"

"Tell it like it is, Rudy!"

Rudy stares, hypnotically, at a middle-aged man staring at him from the top of the porch steps. "Don't look at me like I'm crazy! Am I right 'bout what I'm sayin?"

The man, content to enjoy the newly arrived sunshine, is forced to make some acknowledgement of Rudy's rap. "Uh. . . right on!"

Rudy, smiling maliciously, continues, "Awright! Dig it! Here we are! In this fantastic country! Got a button for every reason you can think of . . . got a cure for damned near everything but the common cold and addiction, and if it wasn't for the fact that so many niggers was addicted and had colds, then you could bet your bottom dollar that 'they' would have a cure for drug addiction and the common cold. Maybe they're savin' all those goodies 'til they get all the White folks off the Earth . . . maybe off to the moon somewheres . . ."

"Hahhah hahhah . . . Rudy! Rudy baby! Lighten up!"

"Dig it! I ain't jivin' . . . do you realize we got so much food here that people can't even eat it all? 'They' have to put it in big old warehouses 'n stuff to let it rot! All of y'all that's workin' for yo' daily bread, remember that when you punch that clock on Monday mornin'!"

"What's he sayin' now, Thelma?"

"Same-o same-o . . . Damn, Hattie! Why don't you get a new refrigerator, this beer's warm as piss!"

"All I need is some new refrigerator money, honey . . . if you'd gon' 'n drank it 'stead o' listenin' to them fools it might still be cold."

XXX XXX XXX

Meanwhile, Rappin' Rudy, an audience in his hip pocket, with things to get off his chest, carries on. "Yeahhhh . . . here we are . . . damned near starvin' to death, or beatin' each other t' death, tryin' to git over. But it ain't just us. . . po' ass Black people! It's them browns, reds 'n yellers. . . and a whole lot o' them po' ass crackers too! Quiet as it's kept. The ones who used to think they was better off than we was 'cause they was White. But now . . .now... a helluva lot of 'em are finally wakin' up to the facts. And they realize, like us, after they take they heads outta them funny books 'n stop listenin' to all that White council racist bullshit, that the Game is bein' run on all of us by You Know Who!"

"What's the point, brother? What's the point?!"

"What's the point? I'll tell you what the point is, young blood . . . the point is this . . . we got to get our shit together and stop bein' niggers! Instead of acceptin' all the surface-type jazz we've always gone for, we've got to go behind the scenes for a change, to really find out what makes things work . . . we got to stop bein' niggers... for him, anyway. If we gon' t' be anybody's niggers...let's be our own niggers for a change."

Son Lee backs Rudy's last statement up with a quiet, serious, "I can dig it."

One of the men in the group whispers loudly into Rudy's ear, "Hey man, I just spotted Lodeen down the street."

Rudy steps quickly from his place of prominence and stars in the direction pointed out to him.

"Where you off to, bro'?"

Rudy turns to face the question with a mischievous smile. "Got to take care my own business for a change . . . I catch y'all later."

The small group reluctantly dissolves, the cohesiveness broken by the loss of its leader.

"What're they doing now, Thelma?"

"Well . . . the one that's always runnin' his damned mouth is walkin' off toward that lil' ol' fast gal from up the street. Hattie Mae, when you gon' get yourself a new pair of glasses, honey?"

Hattie Evans, picking up her brew for a short sip . . . "Just as soon as I get me some new glasses money."

XXX XXX XXX

Idella, Sweet Peter Deeder's #2 mud kicker, eases up to confront the love of her life. Sweet Peter D. cocks his lid ace-deuce, sticks his face three inches from Idella's and, after a quick count of his wages, begins to nibble on her buns, fiercely.

"Bitch! How many times am I gon' have to whip your jive, stinkin' ass before you stop tryin' to be nickel slick?"

Idella, eyes downcast, trying, somehow, to mollify her man. "I ain't tryin' to..."

"Shut up! Don't gimme that bullshit! Where's the rest of my money?"

"I...I...I got it, Daddy! I got it..."

"Awright then goddamnit! Where is it? You keep me waitin' here five minutes longer than I'm supposed to, knowin' motherfuckin' well I got things t' do... and then you come up with some lame ass...! Bitch! Stand up straight when I talk to you! Get your ass off my ride! You got a helluva lot o' nerve! Comin' up to me, money funnier than Chris Rock and then...then got nerve enough to be wantin' to lean all over my hog! Idella, I swear to God! I wonder to myself sometimes if I shouldn't just go 'head and bust a cap in your ass and be done with it, once and for all."

"Peter, Peter baby...I got the rest! I got the rest, baby...I was just savin' it 'cause I wanted to buy you some cufflinks I saw down at Mickums."

"Damn all that! Git it out! Now!"

From another window, on the opposite side of the street, above the point where Rudy was rappin' the apartment jointly rented by Slick Rina Dorsey and Taco MacNeal...Slick Rina calls to her roommate to come and check out the scene.

"Taco! Taco! Commere! Dig this! Idella look like she done come up short again."

The two women lean comfortably over the windowsill. Taco comments, between giggles..."Teee heee! Teee heee! Sho' is a shame the way that rotten sonofabitch treats them po' girls, ain't it?"

"Really! I just couldn't see no nigger takin' all my hard-earned coins...I wouldn't give a damn how pretty he is."

Taco and Rina exchange affirmative skin, and strain their ears to try to catch the conversation going down between Sweet Peter D. and Idella.

"Peter...can I set in the car and get the rest out? I got it...uh...I got it down...uh..."

"Goddamnit Idella! I'm gon' stick my foot in your ass in the next five seconds if you don't pull my money from wherever you got it!"

The women staring down on the scene are outraged ... "Girrrlll....will you look at that? He's got that po' child diggin' down up under her dress with all those people walkin' 'round down there."

"Love and drugs, Miss Lady. Love 'n drugs."

Sweet Peter D. disdainfully accepts the tight wad of bills offered to him from Idella's trembling hand.

"That's all I got, Daddy. That's really all of it! Like I told you I was just savin' this to get you somethin' nice."

Sweet Peter D. stands gritting his teeth, almost on the verge of tears with the pain, the anger he feels at Idella's betrayal. "Idella…I want you to listen to me close now, real close, 'cause what I'm about to say to you might mean your life. I want you to get out of my sight and start turnin' tricks faster than a Lorelei! And when I see you tonight at 12:00 p.m. exactly, right in this very same spot!…I want my money to be right or else you gon' have a terrible hurtin' put on you…Do you understand me, Idella?"

"Yes, Daddy…"

"Git on then! I don't know why I fuck with you triflin' Scorpio bitches anyway!"

Sweet Peter D., a member of a rapidly vanishing species, leans gracefully against his hog as he watches Idella slink away and finally, as she waves back to him from the end of the block, he slides into his hog, fuming.

Taco and Rina, fast ladies in their own right, continue analyzing the dripping drama down the streets.

"She really is a fool, ain't no way I'd be peddlin' my body for *no*-body…umh umh…"

"You notice how much Idella done aged in the last year?"

"Shit! You'd be lookin' old as sin too, if you was floppin' up and down bein' plugged by twenty or thirty tricks a night."

"Yeahhhhh…I guess you got a point, that fast life *will* put lines in your face.

"You damned right it will."

As Sweet Peter D. sits in his car, chain-smoking and dwelling on life's injustices, especially to members of his own profession, one of the neighborhood junkies, formerly known as George Washington Jefferson, but now simply as Bam, eases up to the car…nodding.

"Hey…what it is, bro' Sweets?"

Sweet Peter D. answers with a curt, "What's happenin', Bam?"

A car flashes through the street behind Bam, but in his state of awareness, he doesn't notice how closely it came to wiping a piece of his ass off on the right fender.

"Uh…uh…nothin' too much. Uh dig…me 'n Baby June just got hold of some pretty nice suits...knowin' how you like to style 'n go on…"

"Check with me later…after I get through takin' care business…"

"Yeahhh…yeah…right on!…bro' Sweets. Uh…where you gon' be later on?"

"Where I am every Saturday night…"

"Awwwright…that's cool…we'll check…you…"

Another car slices through the narrow street behind Bam, ruffling his coattail a bit, as he curls down into a fetal nod.

"You better straighten up, man! One o' these fools gon' rip through here and knock you on your ass if you keep noddin' in the street, like that 'n shit."

Bam scratches casually but intensively in his crack and then his crotch, as he junkie-shuffles away. "Uh…uh…yeah…yeahhhh… right on, bro' Sweets. We'll check you out later on."

The four gossiping ladies in the windows on both sides of the street maintain a steady, chatter-ridden interest in the whole business, passing out moral judgments as they observe.

"Hattie! Hattie! Look at that! Lawd in heaven! If it ain't one thing it's another…if it ain't the prostitutes 'n hustlers, it's the dope fiends! Boy almost got hit by a car and he didn't even notice it, fulla that dope."

"You must be talkin' 'bout Bam 'n Baby June."

"Uh huh…don't see nobody down there but Bam now…and you know, I thought at one time that they was gonna wind up bein' two of the nicest boys on the block."

Hattie Evans shrugs her shoulders, takes another sip of her brew and remarks philosophically… "Well, honey…you know how it is, can't never tell what that egg is gon' hatch into."

Taco and Rina's attentions are drawn to more romantic points of view. Each of them, trying to conceal it from the other, looks with slightly envious eyes at Sweet Peter D.'s #1 lady, LuLu, as she boldly opens the car door and slides inside.

"Did you see that?"

"You damned skippy I saw it! I ain't never seen LuLu go through the kind of shit Idella has to go through."

LuLu, in the hog, silently removes a roll of bills from her bra, passes it over to Sweet Peter D. behind the wheel. She studies his face closely as he intently counts the bills.

After ruffling through the small pile twice, he turns to LuLu with a frown on his forehead. "That it, LuLu?"

"That's it, Daddy...two hundred even. I got a live one goin' in an hour, down at the Stevens...might net us half a grand.

"Sounds good. But be careful downtown. You know how them honkies can be."

"I'm always on my toes, you know that. What's the trouble, Daddy? You look disturbed about somethin'."

"Ain't nothin' wrong! What makes you think something's wrong?"

"Awwww, nothin'...nothin', Daddy...I just saw a lil' frown on your face, that's all. Just thought somethin' was botherin' you, that's all."

LuLu leans closer to reach for Sweet Peter's cigarette. "Let me have a drag?"

"Nawwww...ain't nothin' botherin' me that I can't handle. Heyyyy, I thought you gave up smoking?"

"Yeahhh, you right. I did give it up. Here...I wish I could get you to stop smokin'...you know it's bad on your lungs.

"Don't worry 'bout Daddy, Sweetness, he can handle it."

"I know you can handle it, Daddy...I know you can handle it."

The two of them, pimp and 'ho, sit staring at each other for a long moment, with something that might be considered, in the square world, a look of affection. Sweet Peter D. runs his manicured fingers from LuLu's knee to her shapely, round, brown thigh... slowly, with feeling.

"Daddy...you better stop feelin' Momma's kneecaps like that if you want me to make this date."

Sweet Peter, with a mischievous smile on his face, asks, "What time is your date?"

"'Bout an hour."

He withdraws his hand, coldly, completely, and his face hardens into the mask most often seen by the general public.

"You better start steppin'...don't make no sense bein' late."

Sweet Peter leans a smooth-shaven cheek over to LuLu...she kisses it briefly, passionately...slides out of the car and closes the door softly behind her.

Lulu?...he calls to her out on the sidewalk.

"Yeah, Daddy..."

"I'll pick you up here at 12:30."

"What about your game?"

"I think I'm gon' cut it loose early tonight."

LuLu flexes her hip at a dude passing on the sidewalk, a potential customer, and turns back, immediately, to the cryptic conversation with her man.

"I'll be here, Daddy...I'll be here...did you say somethin' 'bout havin' a taste?"

"Uh...yeah...here."

LuLu leans quickly back into the car to take a small, glassine-wrapped packed of heroin.

"What kinda shape you in now, LuLu?"

"Everythang's cool...I'll save this for later on."

Sweet Peter D., his tight, cold, pimp-con smile drawing down the corners of his mouth, tells LuLu, "Go 'head with your bad ass, Miss Star...do your thang. Don't forget...12:30 right here. If you need me for anything before then you know where you can reach me.

LuLu lays a brief, electric wink on her man, and struts up the street, filling in the cadence of her own rhythm, smiling at the warm looks her quivering buttocks attract.

XXX XXX XXX

Saturday night...any Saturday...the main stem sizzles and crackles with the flicker of neon lights, the popping of stale fish grease, the mad aroma of bar-be-cued ribs (hic'kry smoked), steamin' chitlins, boiled greens, candied yams, bean pies, Lou'siana batter-fried shrimps, ham hocks 'n thangs and the horny sounds of people in love with the night. It carries its Sweet Peters swirling off onto fast tracks where they spend their lives twisting, turning and dancing on pinheads larger than their lives will ever be.

The stem swirls in a straight line down 47th Street, heading for Buttermilk Bottom, the Fillmore District, Crenshaw, or the dusty, crusty surface of Gwinnett Street in deepest Georgia...or to any other place in the New World where the Brother has had to take his chances...no matter whether the chance has been for a Fulani queen in glorious red, or for a change in fortune that may rest on the roll of a pair of loaded dice.

The gambling joint, in a basement. A large, round, green felt covered table dominates the room. The stench of men past and present, mingled with defective plumbing, dominates the atmosphere.

A single bulb hanging at the end of a single black cord and the light gleaming through the green visor around the bulb gives everything and everybody in the room a dead, shadowy look.

Cigarette and cigar smoke curls into the air above the table, creating a haze above the seven men standing around the table, mumbling bets, snatching, grasping and gambling.

The gambling goes on in a serious, dedicated fashion...and everybody knows why they're there...and they do not be jivin'... The action is Sweet Peter D.'s...but he is cool about it. A look, a motion, puts drama into the air, charges the atmosphere, suggests to the stickman that he should change the bones, or whatever.

The action of the table suddenly stops its flow as one of the men, veins bubbling in his temples, shouts across the table, "Nigger! If you don't lay that money back down, you gon' have all two hundred 'n fifteen pounds o' me in yo' motherfuckin' chest!! And I ain't just bullshittin' neither!"

He is answered with equal heat. "Is that right? Well, I don't see no goddamned fences 'tween us. The only thing keepin' yo' two hundred 'n fifteen pounds outta my chest is your good sense and the ass-kickin' you apt to receive if you keep on fuckin' with me. I know yo' momma didn't raise no fools!"

A couple of the other dudes, irritated by the interruption, voice their displeasure in no uncertain terms.

"C'mon, mannn! Y'all take that shit somewhere else! I'm losin'…

"Yeah, why don't y'all settle that shit some other time!"

"Fuck all you motherfuckers! That's the second time tonight J.D. done made an ass bet!"

Sweet Peter coolly measures the situation and slips in obliquely. "Let it pass, Mule Poppa…I'll make it good…git on with the game."

The sudden roaring levels out, quiets back down to the normal mumble! Grumble! Bet! Bet! Grumble! Mumble!… goes on for a few long minutes, hundreds of hard-earned dollars being exchanged, won…lost.

"I done had enough of this shit outta you, J.D. You think you one o' them slick ass motherfuckers!" The man called Mule Poppa whips around the curve of the table, snatching and hitting at J.D.

Sweet Peter D., obviously caught up with the idea of a little diversion, yells out, "Don't stop 'em! Don't stop 'em! Let them niggers gon' 'n fight! They been tryin' t' get a piece of each other's ass since last week! Go 'head! Let 'em have it out!"

The gamblers snatch their money from the green felt table and give the combatants room to duke in. And, naturally, being gamblers, pick favorites.

"Gon' kick that jive motherfucker's ass, Mule Poppa! He a hard-losing, chickenshit son of a bitch anyhow! Starts cryin' every time he drops a bet! Yeahhh! Gon' kick his ass!"

"Awww…what the fuck you talking' 'bout?!" Don't let that cocksucker git the best o' you, J.D.?"

Mule Poppa and J.D., two big strong working dudes, wrestle and pull each other around, each trying desperately to pull an arm free to jab at the other one, or to gain enough leverage to sling the other's ass to the ground. The scene is almost that of a human cockfight, the men lacking spurs, but trying to use their fists in the way that fighting cocks use their spurs, as the gamblers, in the shadowed fringes, make bets on the outcome.

"I got ten that say Mule Poppa gon' slam J.D. on his ass!"

"Make that twenty and you got yourself a bet!"

"Awright then goddamnit! Twenty says he'll do it, now put your money where your mouth is."

"Bet!"

The two men give their twenties to a third party, a neutral just standing in place, calmly watching the contest.

The noise being made inside drowns out the loud "Ouch!" made by Detective Jones as he bumps his shin against a solid object in the unfamiliar darkness outside the backdoor of the gambling joint.

"Watch your step, Jonesy!" his partner whispers to him. "These niggers may have booby traps set up out here.

Jonesy smiles in spite of the ache in his shin, thinking to himself…just like Murph, to make a joke, no matter what the circumstances.

They ease up to the door…

"What's the racket?"

"I'll be damned if I know. Sounds like somebody fighting… damnit! My shin bone throbs something awful!"

"You okay, Jonesy?"

"I'll live…"

"Hey…somebody is fighting in there."

"Go on! Knock! It'll be kicks to see the look on these monkeys' faces when we walk in."

Detective Murphy, jaws clenched tightly, authoritatively, thumps on the door with the butt of his pistol.

Sweet Peter cocks his ear to the sound. "Shhhhh! Grab them fools! Be cool! Sounds like…"

"Hey! What the hell y'all doin'?" Me 'n Raymond got a bet down on…"

"Shut up, Gene!"

Mule Poppa and J.D. are pried apart, each of them mildly grateful for the interruption, but reluctant to show it for machismo's sake. Each of them, held up, arms pinned, glare at each other, ribs caving in from the struggle, wind coming back in gasps.

Murphy thumps again. "Awright in there! Open up!"

Sweet Peter Deeder, playing the high post position, gives wordless, efficient instructions with finger, eye and head motions. A checkered tablecloth is pulled from underneath the table and quickly spread over the green felt.

Murphy and Jonesy, irritated beyond reason now, both thump on the door. "Open up in there, goddamnit!"

The well-oiled movements of the men inside snatch four folding chairs from a dark corner, arrange them quickly around the table. Four of the men sit at a table, a deck of cards pops from a breast pocket and one of the men begins to deal a whist hand, while the others lounge about casually… The whole situation, practiced to lardlike slickness, takes no more than a minute.

"Open this goddamned door! Or we'll break it down!"

Sweet Peter, standing near the door, throws a sly wink on the group and calls out in a soft voice…"Uh…who is it?"

Murphy and Jones turn to each other in the dark… "Well, I'll be! Jonesy…did you hear…?" Murphy turns back to the door with a vengeance! "Open up damn you! This is the police!"

Sweet Peter calmly unbolts a trio of locks and stands aside innocently, as the two detectives rush in, pistols out, looking red-faced, angry and insane. Both Jones and Murphy, dressed right wing style in their monotone three-buttoned suits, snap-brimmed hats and dull-hued ties, look at the colorfully assembled group of Black men with disgust and hate.

"Awright! Everybody up! Who's runnin' the game here?" Jonesy asks, waving his pistol from one head to the other.

Sweet Peter D. casually lights a cigarette, studying the two detectives. Gene, the whist dealer, looks around with big, innocent brown eyes and mumbles…"We playin' whist…uh…Officer. Don't need anybody to run that…you know? Hahhahhahhhah…just a good partner!"

The other dudes, digging Gene's subtle humor, share the spirit and feeling of him signifyin' with the pigs.

Jones, not quite certain of where the sarcasm is coming from, but feeling his way through the context..."Goddamnit! Don't be makin jokes with me, fella! We know you guys shoot crap in this hole every Saturday night. Now what we wanna know is who the hell's runnin' the damned store?"

Once again, Gene, trying to pull a little more humor over the white man's eyes by slyly using his language, responds for the group. "Ain't nobody shootin' nothin' here, Mr. Officer. You can see that with your own eyes."

Murphy, already highly pissed, rushes over to Gene the Joker and shoves him over the back of the chair. Gene springs from the floor, anxious to be in Murphy's chest. Murphy levels his piece at Gene's head and warns him in a cold, metallic voice, "Make one wrong move, tough guy, and I'll blow you away."

Sweet Peter D., standing a bit off to the side, checking out the tension in things, slides in smoothly, evenly. "Wasn't no need to do that, Officer. Like he said, all we doin' is just playin' some funny cards."

Murphy and Jones glance at the speaker, waving their pistols around like banana leaves, seeming to be aware, for the first time, that they are in a dank, dingy basement in the ghetto. It shows a bit in the overly harsh quality of Jones' voice as he yells, "Awright you monkeys! Line up three paces from that wall! Everybody! Move it! Lean into it! Three paces away! Lean into it on your fingertips! Spread your legs! You guys know how to do it! Whaddaya say, Murph! I've had enough. We can stick a disturbance of the peace on 'em, if nothing else."

Mingled with the disgusted, angry sounds of the men slamming their cards down on the table are the small, clacking noises of knives and other weapons being surreptitiously dropped under the table.

"Move it! Goddamnit!"

"Awww shit!"

"Ain't this a bitch?"

"Ain't you dudes got nothin' better t' do than go 'round hasslin' folks?"

"Be cool, Mule Poppa…be cool. Everythang gon' be all right."

Murphy with a special thing going for Gene, shoves him roughly. "Get your black ass next to that wall before I give you a mouthful o' pistol butt!"

The men grumble and reluctantly spread themselves along the wall, prodded by the Law. Jones hands his piece over to Murphy and begins moving efficiently down the row of men, frisking. He pauses at J.D., checks the bruises on his face and the rip in his shirt.

"What happened to you, buddy boy? Looks like we got here just in time…hah! hah! hah!…how 'bout that, Murph? We got here just in time."

"Pretty good, Jonesy. Pretty good."

Jonesy pulls a straight razor out of an anonymous pocket. "You boys really play for keeps, huh?"

The face at the wall comes back sharply with a sarcastic… "Right on!"

While Jones is two people away, searching bodies, Sweet Peter Deeder leans away from the wall and boldly faces the two detectives.

Murphy, a pistol in each hand, blinks several times, as though he were seeing something unreal happen, and then takes careful aim with his right hand. "Hey you! You! You heard the man! Face that wall! Lean into it and keep your legs spread."

Jones looks up from his ankle and calf rubbing to watch Sweet Peter D.'s action with the same incredible look on his face…moves quickly back from the line of men, snatches his pistol from Murphy and takes aim also. "Okay you! You got five seconds to git it back!"

Sweet Peter Deeder looks from one flushed red face to the other, seeming to measure the amount of hostility in each one…coolly… calmly… "Uh…Officer"…he directs himself to Jones…"Uh… Officer, I wonder if I could speak to you privately for a minute?"

Murphy thunders back at him…"Hell no! Now lean into that wall and shut your fuckin' trap!"

Once again, Sweet Peter addresses himself to Jones. "It might be more important than you think, Officer.

Something about the insinuating tone of Sweet Peter's voice grabs Jonesy up. "Okay you! Com' on over here 'n make it snappy! I'd like to have the bunch o' you bastards booked by twelve tonight. Okay, what is it? Spit it out!"

Sweet Peter strolls slowly, casually, over to a far, shadowy corner. "Can we step over here, Officer?"

Jones, showing off his fearlessness, trails Sweet Peter with his pistol held aggressively. "You the runnin' this show?"

"Maybe."

Murphy, from the side of his mouth, con-style..."Careful with that guy, Jonesy!"

"Don't worry, Murph...I got it, I'm covered. I wish he would make a wrong move.

Jones stands facing Sweet Peter Deeder in the shaded corner, his eye running hatefully up a burgundy tailored vision in two-toned, baby alligator Staceys. "Awright, 'Soul Brother,' whaddaya want? A separate deal from the rest of these monkeys or what?"

Sweet Peter looks slightly above Jones' head, as though he were staring at a distant picture, and replies in a low, flat voice... "Nawww, nawww, I don't want nothin' like that, Officer. I just want you and your partner to put your pieces away and split."

White Policeman-in-the-Colony Jones glares into the smooth dark face as though he can't quite decide which way he'd like to kill him...his face turns brick red and then stark grey with anger.

Sweet Peter, sensing the danger, goes on quickly, urgently... "Now dig it! I didn't really wanna get off into all this, but you've forced my hand, so now I'm gon' have to run the whole scene down to you 'cause evidently you new in the picture, at least this is my first time seein' you."

Jones raises his pistol butt at Sweet Peter's head. "I ought to..."

Sweet Peter cuts in sharply, to save his head. "Wait now! Hold on! Lemme finish! I'm payin' your Captain, that's right, your good Captain Rainey...sixteen hundred skins a month, plus bonuses... to have this lil' game every Saturday and...uh...some other lil' thangs...and I think he'd be highly pissed if Alderman Harley had to jump in his ass about you makin' an 'unauthorized' raid on our joint."

Sweet Peter finishes his statement, and it almost seems as though steam is rising between the two men. Jones is so put out he can only puff his jaws out before exploding between clenched teeth. "Are you…? Are you…!? Are you tryin' to tell me what to do? You?!"

"Uh…naw"…Sweet Peter purrs. "Nawww, I ain't tryin' to tell you what *to do*…I'm tryin' to tell you what not to do."

"What's your name, fella?"

Sweet Peter glances up and down the row of men leaning, casually now, on the wall, exchanges a wink with J.D., flicks an imaginary speck of dust from his razor-sharp creased pants and, with as much understatement as he can muster, replies… "They calls me Sweet Peter D."

Jones looking around uncomfortably to Murphy, his face still blotched from his hate-flush, calls out… "Murph! You hear that? I got a live one over here, calls himself Sweet Pickles! Or some such shit! Listen to me, Sweet Pickles…get this straight! When I want advice from the likes of you, I'll ask for it! Now move your ass back over to that wall! We'll have the wagon out in a few minutes, and you can give your 'special' little story to the desk sergeant."

Sweet Peter strolls nonchalantly back to his position, a slight smile breaking down each corner of his mouth.

Jones scuttles over to Murphy, pulls him a short distance from the men at the wall and begins to whisper into his ear, furiously, "Murph…this Black bastard says he's got Rainey in his hip pocket!"

Murphy shrugs, never taking his eyes from the men at the wall, and mumbles, "Mmmm yeahhh…yeahhh…I know."

"What the hell are you talkin' about, you know what?"

Murphy turns briefly to glance with a blank expression at his partner. "I know about Rainey's deal. I thought you did too."

Jones stares at Murphy with a classic idiot's droop of the mouth. "Are you off your nut? Do you think I would've suggested we raid this fuckin' joint if I'd known that Rainey had a piece of the action? Whaddaya take me for, a goddamned fool? I got four kids to feed!"

"Hell, Jonesy…I thought you knew."

The men lined up along the wall snicker softly at the exchange. Gene the Joker, having recovered his sense of humor sings out, in an ultra polite voice, "Officer Sir, are we gon' have to lean up 'gainst this goddamned wall all night?"

Jones stares hatefully at the back of Gene's head. "Shut your trap," he screams at him and turns back to Murphy.

"I thought everybody knew. I just thought you wanted to shake the Black bastards up a bit."

"Awww…well, you know how it is…you hear rumors, but I didn't really think Rainey was on the take."

Murphy shrugs his shoulders affirmatively. The two men stand, looking at each other for a long minute…understanding what has to be done.

Jones bursts out, the words almost strangling him, "Awright you bums! Turn around! We didn't catch you with the goods tonight, but…if we ever do catch anything fishy goin' on in here, we're gonna bust the bunch o' ya. Got that?"

The men, smirking at what has gone down, mumble agreement.

"Uhn huh."

"Right on!"

"Oh yes, Officer Sir."

Jones walks over slowly to Sweet Peter, glares hatefully into his face for a moment, and then, suddenly, rams the barrel of his pistol into his stomach.

The men respond to Jones' act with a show of hostility. "Sho' is rotten of you t' do somethin' like that, man!"

"Wow? That's what I call havin' a bad temper!"

Murphy and Jones stand watching Peter sink down into a nearby chair, holding his belly and groaning. The men begin to edge up on Jones and Murphy…"Okay you guys! Take one more step and somebody's gonna get hurt!"

Sweet Peter cautions the men…"Be cool y'all…let these crazy motherfuckers outta here…be cool!"

Murphy waves his pistol in Sweet Peter's direction momentarily and then turns to his partner… "Com' on Jonesy, let's get outta this rathole, the stink is making me sick." They move slowly toward the door, paying close attention to all the bloodshot eyes and balled-up fists. Murphy shouts to them at the door… "Remember what we said, if we catch a tiddlywinks game here, we're gonna bust the whole bunch of ya."

"I'll bet!"….Mule Poppa mumbles.

Murphy slams the door as hard as possible.

"You awright, Pete?"

"Yeah…yeah…I'm all right. Goofy-ass motherfucker put a helluva cramp in my belly."

"I think the little one just got transferred into the district…must be tryin' to put his bluff in."

"Either that, or he don't know what's happenin'."

"Why'd he shove his piece in your belly, Sweets?"

Sweet Peter Deeder stretches himself into an erect position in the chair, massages his stomach a bit…"Awww man, who knows? You know how these motherfuckers hate niggers. And Lawd knows I'm a supernigger. Take that fuckin' cloth off the table and let's get on with the game." He checks his watch and stands up quickly, groaning a little from the hurt… "Smitty, take the house for me, I got to go take care some business."

The men remove the cloth and reassemble around the table, the smoke haze gathering strength above their heads after a few minutes of intense concentration.

"I got my eye on you, J.D."

"Get yo' motherfuckin' bet down, nigger! And stop flappin' yo' jaws at me…I'd like to leave here tonight with your socks in my hip pocket."

"Whose dice, is it? Why don't y'all stop talkin' that shit and play! Damn! Motherfuckers worse than kids!"

XXX XXX XXX

Sweet Peter Deeder stands underneath a streetlamp, on his corner, leaning against his ride, smoking a cigarette, and riffling through Idella's dues deep in his pocket as he spools little honeyed bits of game into her hot little ear. From somewhere, like a liquid breeze, the sound of an Eastern wind instrument slithers through the warm night air.'

"Is the money right, Daddy?"

"It's right…now, but it was supposed to have been right this afternoon," he tells her, the tone of his voice warm and lush. "You know how much I hate havin' to bruise my knuckles and shit. Now you know that Idella…I just can't understand why you come to me the way you do, sometimes. I mean, like…your shit gets so far outta pocket, sometimes. All it does is force Daddy to keep that pressure on…and you know yourself, deep down, that strong as you is there really is no need for me to constantly stay in your ass about us getttin' our thang together."

Idella's eyes wander in circles around Sweet Peter…as though he were encased in a shaft of light, or as if a halo gleamed from his frame.

"I'm gon' do better, Daddy…you'll see…and then you won't have no reason to be salty at me. What time is LuLu coming in?"

"She'll be here in exactly fifteen minutes."

The sound of the slurring music pauses…and then starts again at a lower register…a sort of Eric Dolphy-Yusef Lateefish…sound… in an Arabic mode.

Bam and Baby June shuffle past…already a half-hour away from pain,…trying with all their dope fiend cunning to head *Jones* off at the pass.

Bam eases up to Sweet Peter's side, scratching and sniffling. "Hey…looka here bro' Sweetman…how 'bout them garments you said you wanted?"

"Yeahhhhhh," Baby June adds, picking delicately at the tip of his nose. "Yeahhhhh…we even got somethin' that would really look…" …he pauses to nod for a few sacred seconds, and then, picking up his thought again… "Yeahhh…sho' would be outta sight. Out of sight! On Miss Sister Woman here."

Sweet Peter waves them away with an impatient, "Check with me later on, I ain't got all my shit taken care of yet."

"Yeahhhhh…okay…cool, Sweets. We'll check you out later on…"

"Yeahhhh…cool. That be mella'…we'll check you out later on."

Bam and Baby June shuffle away, their faces twisted into unprintable expressions, lips cooked white, sniffling and scratching.

XXX XXX XXX

Home in the Hood

From an apartment building down the street, a couple of party-goers weave unsteadily down the stairs to the streets. The hostess leans out of her second-floor window, echoes of Roberta, Aretha, Mother Popcorn and B.B. drifting out over her shoulder. "You better hold his hand, Lucille! Else he might stumble out there 'n get hit by one of them cars...hahhah!hah!"

Lucille Smith, her arm firmly hooked into the crook of her husband's arm, looks up with a giddy, amused expression. "Don' chew worry 'bout a thang, child! My old man can take care of him and me…been doin' it for years. Ain't that right, baby?"

Fergy Smith nods his head agreeably.

"Lucille…you gon' t' make it to church tomorrow?"

"Lawd willin' and I wake up in time. Stop by 'fore you go 'n holler at me."

"All right, I'll do that. Y'all take it easy now."

"G'night! Had a real good time...see you in the a.m."

Lucille and Fergy Smith, heads smoky but held high, stroll past Sweet Peter Deeder...pause on the steps of their apartment building, listening to the keening, wailing sound of the Eastern-sounding instrument...quivering and throbbing with intensity now.

Lucille Smith holds her head in mock tragedy... "Oh m'Gawd! Don't tell me that fool is up blowin' on that thang-a-majig again!"

"Well,...it ain't no louder than the noise we just came from."

"It's a damn sight stranger, I know that!"

They weave upstairs to their apartment, giggling and feeling happy about being in the same uncoordinated state together.

Lubertha Franklin and Kwendi Jones stroll up the other side of the street, Kwendi checks Sweet Peter on his corner, disgust written all over his face.

LuLu steps up the street, moving fast, fast, fast. A few people lounge about the front stoops of the block, seeking the air of the street and the drama in it.

Sweet Peter D., as though timing a horserace or some other sporting event, stands looking at the second hand on his watch. His expression is deadpan as he tells LuLu... "Didn't think you were gonna make it for a minute."

"You know me, Sweets...I always make it."

"How'd it go?"

LuLu gives a brief, malicious, cutting look at Idella before answering, "I did twice as good as I thought I was gon' do." Sweet Peter, catching the look, rubs a pinch of salt into the wound. "Beautiful! Beautiful, star! My woman don't do nothin' but take care business. Dig...I've got to run on back over to the joint and check on thangs. You two run on to the crib. LuLu ...run some water for me, will ya, baby? Stick some o' that skin awful soft stuff in it."

"That oil, you mean?"

"That's right, the oil. Idella...see if you can't do somethin' right the first time, for a change. Lay out my ice water suit and my triple tone suede boots. If everything is lookin' awright, we might be able to get out here and party time a lil' bit with the rest o' these niggers."

"Oh yeahhh! Yeahhh! I could really dig that! They got a new group at *The Apartment* and people say they ain't doin' nothin' *but* playin' music, music and mo' music!

"Just be cool now! I told you, I got to go back and check on my action first…if it's flowin' smooth then we'll get out there… shouldn't take me too long to find out."

The trio splits. LuLu and Idella in one direction, Sweet Peter D., in another. The street, except for an occasional straggler, a castoff from someplace, or something, is empty.

XXX XXX XXX

"Psssst! Psssst! Awright June! Let it down, ain't nobody out here now. Be careful! Don't break it!"

Baby June, bracing himself from inside a first-floor apartment, lowers a portable T.V. down on the end of a length of clothesline.

"June…whatchu gon' tell your mother when she wake up tomorra 'n find her T.V. missin'?"

Baby June jumps out the window after lowering the T.V. into Bam's hands…lands lightly, athletically, beside him. "What the fuck you mean? What am I gon' tell 'er? I'm gon' tell 'er somebody stole the motherfucker."

"Uh huh…I can dig it. We wouldn't even be needin' t' be doin' this if you'd a lissened to me."

"Fuck all that! How was I supposed to know that the motherfucker was sellin' us face powder? Second time we'd ever copped from him! You didn't know yourself 'til you started tryin' to fix,…come on…help me carry this damn thing!"

"I told you…I told you…remember? I said…June…dig…" The two junkies ease off into the shadows of the alley…on their way to oblivion, the weight of the portable T.V. straining the strength of their tracked-up arms.

XXX XXX XXX

And thus mote it be...

And if the Sunday Services have not dealt with it all, or haven't had time yet...if a soulful problem remains, one that goes beyond the recognized boundaries, remains aloof from the sweet songs and glib prayers to Jesus the Christ, or dries up in a stifled puddle on the cracked sidewalks...then there is someone else, something else that can be brought to bear.

Dark powders, ground-up roots, scented herbs and flickering candles that burn seven days, blessed by holy mouths filled with sacred green snuff, can be sought out. The powders, roots, herbs and candles can be found in dark spaces that leak ancient rites filled with African blood....

Small, cramped huts stacked in piles, one on top of the other. Huts that are made of stone and steel now...but still carry a dark message sent from ancestors whose bones have found, in the New World, old bodies in which to live.

A timid, staccato, tapping on the back door of apartment #307... Miss Rabbit, glasses down on her nose tip, half dozing, half reading her Bible, looks up apprehensively at the sound of the tapping.

Miss Rabbit edges toward the door on tiptoe, every muscle in her squat frame tense..."Who is it?" she asks in a cautious voice.

"It's me, Miss Rabbit…me, Lena Daniels."

Miss Rabbit cocks her head, straining to determine if the voice is the person it says it is. "Who that you say?"

"Me, Miss Rabbit…me, Lena Daniels."

Miss Rabbit opens the door quickly and shoos Lena inside. "Honey what in the world you doin'? Traipsin' 'round out in the middle of the night? Don't you know Haints is loose out there? T' say nothin' o' them dope fiends 'n whatnot."

Lena stands in front of the door, her arms crossed under her ample bosom, looking around nervously.

"You right, Miss Rabbit…but I just had t' see you… I just had to…"

Miss Rabbit, one eyebrow raised perceptively, motions toward her worn sofa.

"Well…come on over here 'n sit down…sho' must be impotant for you t' be runnin' round in the alley this time o' night. What's wrong? One o' the chillun sick?"

Lena squirms around restlessly on the sofa, coming to the rest on the edge. "O…uh…no…they'all right…uh…it's…uh…"

Miss Rabbit reaches over to pat her hand reassuringly. "Awright now, honey…jest calm 'n tell Miss Rabbit what the problem is."

Lena turns her head away from Miss Rabbit's gaze, stares at a worn-down broom standing in a far corner. "Well…I don't rightfully know how t' come out 'n tell you…" Miss Rabbit pulls a pack of cigarettes from apron pocket, lights up and waits…and waits.

"Well…you see, Miss Rabbit," Lena finally continues, "…it's like this…uh huh…you know me 'n Jim been married goin' on nine years."

"I 'member when y'all first came up here."

"You remember that? We'd just got married and decided to move from Biloxi 'cause Jim thought…"

"Uh huh…yeah…I remember all that, go 'head 'bout the other thing."

Lena's eyes circle the room and drop down to her hands tightly folded in her lap.

"Oh...well...what I was gon' say was...well...we ain't never really had too many problems, me and Jim...I mean, it's been kinda hard at times, like when Jim lost his job but...well, here lately, he done started stayin' out late...gamblin' his money off 'n I don't know what all. And whenever I ask him about what he's doin'...he won't say nothin', either that, or he wants t' fight me."

Miss Rabbit looks into Lena's face with a faint smile tugging at her mouth. "You think he's got another woman out there somewhere? Is that it, honey?"

Lena nods sadly and looks back over into the corner, tears clouding her eyes. "I was thinkin'...I was thinkin'...uh...maybe you could help me, Miss Rabbit. We got five kids and I really love Jim, Miss Rabbit, I really do."

Miss Rabbit stares compassionately at Lena for a full minute, blowing smoke rings, and then suddenly she waddles away into the other room, returns minutes later with a small, brown paper bag.

"Now you lissen t' me close, Lena Mae! Do everything just like say and you won't have no mo' worries with Jim...leastways, not this year anyhow. Jim at home now?"

"No'm ...he slept awhile this afternoon, after he chased Chiyo 'n nim away from out back...."

"I heard all that commotion...but I didn't wanna get my head blowed off by accident..."

"Well,...after he chased them away...he slept for a bit, got up 'round 'bout 6:30 and I ain't seen or heard from 'im since then."

"Hmmmmmm...well, here's whatchu do. When you git the chance, first thang you do is put two pinches o' this in his coffee... first chance you git."

Lena reaches hesitantly for the little brown bag, a group of tension lines wrinkling her forehead.

"What is it, Miss Rabbit?"

"Stop askin' foolish questions, gal! You want Jim t' stop foolin' 'round in the streets, don'tchu?"

Lena dabs at a would-be tear in the corner or her eye, and answers, in a small voice..."Uhn huh."

"Awright then…after you done put two pinches o' this powder in his coffee…or in his food, either one…don't do nothin' else for one whole day, and then…Lena Mae! You lissenin t' me!?"

"Yes'um…I'm lisstenin'. I'm just scared! If Jim found out 'bout this he'd beat me t' death!"

"Honey, Jim ain't no different from the rest of 'em. If you do just like I say do…you'a have him strollin' 'round behind you on his eyebrows by the end o' the week. Now jest lissen! The day you done put the two pinches on 'im…don't use more than two pinches 'cause it's mighty powerful!! In exactly one day, he's gon' come home from work feelin' kinda bad, might have a bad headache and his stomach'll be hurtin' him some."

Lena dabs a bit harder at the recurring tears in the corner of her eyes. "Miss Rabbit...Jim don't never have no headaches or stomachaches. He ain't never been sick in all the time we been married."

Miss Rabbit makes an impatient gesture of despair with her hands, mouth, and eyebrows. "Lena Daniels! I swear fo' God! Now I'm tellin' you! If you make it hard for me, I'm gonna put you outta here and you'a lose that worthless bastard you married to."

Lena Daniels cringes at the sound of the word describing her husband, but answers hurriedly. "I'm sorry, Miss Rabbit, I'm sorry. It's just that I been so nervous and upset here lately."

Miss Rabbit strokes her on the arm, soothingly. "I know...I know you have, honey. Now then...when he comes home feelin' bad, he'a most likely wanna lay down. Now then...whilst he's layin' down sleepin', tryin' t' git rid of his headache, take these three bones and toss 'em under the bed and sprankle three mo' pinches o' this powder lightly 'round the bed. Jest lightly, mind you! If you sprankle too much in one place it's apt to make him go blind in his left eye for two days."

Lena Daniels squeezes the little brown bag firmly in her fist. "I sure do want t' thank you, Miss Rabbit. I...uh...I'll give you a lil' somethin' at the end o' the week. Jim messed up his check two weeks ago and we been havin' it kinda hard... Not only that, Suki-boy stuck a nail in his foot and we had to..."

Miss Rabbit subdues, brushes away the rest of the explanation with a brisk waving of her hands. "Gon' girl! Gon! Git outta here 'n do what I told you to. Brang me one o' them peach cobblers you make so good...after you done brung your man back to his senses."

"Thanks a heap, Miss Rabbit. I'm gonna do just exactly what you said for me to do."

"Hmf! You better...else you ain't gon' have nobody to hep you 'n them young 'uns. Now gon'...git!"

Lena opens the back door and stands there for a moment, looking down at the dark alley in front of her and then turns back, shyly, to Miss Rabbit.

"'Night, Miss Rabbit."

"'Night Lena...you be careful now."

Lena starts slowly down the steps, a firm line to her chin. "I will...'bless you, Miss Rabbit."

Miss Rabbit closes her back door, settles the latch and burglar chains back into place and walks slowly back over to her sofa...her worn house slippers making a soft clap-slop sound as she goes.

She picks up her Bible from the sofa, looks at it for a moment as though searching for something, and then gracefully kneels down on one knee and then the other.

"Dear God...I pray to you tonight...I pray to you for Lena Daniels.

A blond, blue-eyes, long-haired picture of Jesus Christ, a cross glowing on his chest, stares benevolently over Miss Rabbit's head... as she prays.

CHAPTER II

HE MAKETH ME...

On the main stem, every tenth man is apt to be some kind of prophet. Why not? Religions come and go but men stay the same, urgent to find answers for questions they've never asked, impatient to know a God they can understand and deal with. And the preachin' man is one who has figured that much out, has delved into a few of the reasons why people wound want to return to places they have never been.

The nearest storefront may smack the perceptive person's face with a fervor that is almost holy, the earthy cries bouncing form inside the glass-crusted walls and out onto the Sunday morning streets like ricocheting bricks. Thunderclaps spill from Black men in mohair robes with golden throats...thrills of an un-Godly nature grip the captive crowd, jerk and twist their bodies into ecstatic shapes, pull their beliefs in front of a life that they will never know on planet Earth.

They stand around in dark-suited groups after their transportation to Heaven has been arranged for, shaking hands with their hearts, and praying for the next Revival Meetin'. Amen!

Mrs. Diane Holt, almost Easter Sunday sharp, stands on the front steps of her apartment pulling on her white Sunday-go-to-meetin' gloves and calling up to her second-floor window. "Nathan! Nathan!..."

Nathan peeks cautiously out of the window, knotting a tie awkwardly around his neck. "Yeah! What is it?!"

"I'm gonna run up the street here 'n see if Lucille 'n Fergy are goin' with us. You be ready when I come back, hear?"

Nathan Holt, turtle-like, draws his head back into the window frame without saying a word, still finger-wrestling with the knot in his tie.

The woman everyone on the block calls Big Momma leans out of her first-floor apartment window, old-fashioned hairnet on, bottom lip filled with a morning dip.

"Dian...y'all goin' to church today...after all that partyin' you did last night?

Diane Holt, successfully masking a quick, irritated frown, turns to Big Momma in her window.

"Oh...uh...hi Big Momma...how you this morning'? Yeah, got t' make it. Hope we didn't make too much noise last night. We was celebratin' Nathan's birthday."

"Nawwww...didn't bother me none..." she leans back into her apartment to spit in a large tomato can... "Naww, didn't bother me a bit. I just don't see how y'all managed to survive 'til today... hahahahaha."

Diane Holt eases down two full steps, nursing her impatience out of respect.

"Uh...Big Momma...?"

Big Momma's eyes wander casually up and down the street, takin in everything for its real worth. "I oughta be goin' t' church myself, but m' knees been hurting me so bad... I thought you was goin' to that other church, over on 42nd Street, the one with the long name...?"

Mrs. Holt eases down another step before answering, "St. Anastasia's First African Presbyterian?"

"Ummm huh...that's the one."

"Well...I couldn't get Nathan or the boys to go over there with me...so I had t' start back t' Tilly's. Big Momma...I'll talk t' you later...I gotta go pick up Lucille and Fergy."

"Awright daughter...I'a see you later on."

Diane Holt walks briskly up the street to the Smith's building, kicking out viciously at a piece of newspaper that wraps itself around her ankle on the way. "Damnit!" she mumbles aloud to herself.... "When are they gonna pick up the trash again?" She stands in front of the Smith building and calls through cupped hands.

"Lucilllllllle! Lucilllllllle! Lucilllllllle!"

Lucille Smith finally sticks her head, swathed in a tattered black bandana, out of the window, hangover showing in every emotion.

"You all goin't' church with me n' Nathan?"

Mrs. Smith, dark circles under her eyes, holds her head in one hand and slowly nods negatively from side-to-side.

Diane Holt flashes an understanding smile up at her and starts away, terrier quick. "Awright...I'll give ya ring later on."

Lucille Smith waves lackadaisically at Diane Holt's back.

Nathan Holt, better known as Big Nat, stands awkwardly on the front stoop, hands folded protectively in front of him, listening to Big Momma's stream of words, looking uncomfortable in an outdated suit, so outdated that it is almost Now again, and a pair of canary yellow pointed toe shoes.

"Where're the boys, Nathan?"

"I looked in the bedroom and Byron was gone already to play basketball, and Perry started tellin' me somethin' 'bout not wantin' to go to church 'cause it wasn't in the...uh... best interest of Black Cul-ture Nationalism...or somethin' like that, he said."

He and Big Momma exchange indulgent shrugs.

Diane, standing at the foot of the front steps with hands braced on her hips, exclaims... "Lawwwd! This family's gon' be the death o' me yet! Well...COM' on, let's go! We near 'bout late for afternoon services already...in a lil' while we'll be late for evenin' services. I don't know what I'm gon' do with Perry sometimes...Black cul-tural nationalism, my buns! He just got in early this mornin' and didn't wanna get up."

They walk through the Sunday morning streets, delicately weaving past stumbling winos and puddles of Saturday night puke.

"Well...I'll say this...'bout the church thing... seems t' me a man should have a chance t' make up his own mind 'bout whether or not he should wanna go or not. My Daddy didn't force me to go."

"But Nathan," she tells him, tugging slightly at his arm to make him walk faster, "He ain't a man yet!"

Big Nat, slowing down slightly in response to his wife's tuggin... "He's eighteen, he's got a job...he's a man."

XXX XXX XXX

No Justice without Jesus

Rev. A. T. Tilly, Pastor and Founder
SECOND SUNRISE BAPTIST CHURCH
10:00 A.M. Sunday School
11:00 A.M. B.Y.P.U. Meeting
12:00 a.m. Sunday Sermon:

"JESUS IS THE LIGHT OF THE WORLD"

The church service blares out onto the street over a scratchy loudspeaker system. Bam and Baby June straggle past the church... loaded. They stand, nodding, on the corner. Bam absent-mindedly strokes an expensive sports coat draped across his left arm, hiding, from wrist to forearm, wristwatches of all kinds.

Little Black girls with shiny faces, carefully braided hair, patent leather shoes, slightly greased, and rustling taffeta dresses...little boys in Tom Thum suits and bow ties. Church members greeting each other...middle-aged sisters in flowered hats fanning themselves with Jesus Christ and Digby Jackson's Mortuary.

A choir of six, *Mahalia Jacksons* dressed in black with gold trim on their robes, and five *Ray Charles'* file solemnly into the choir sections from doors behind the altar, followed by a prissy, pompous, little pouter pigeon of a middle-aged Black lady. She looks over the choir members severely, pushes her rhinestone-crusted glasses up on her nose, holds up her hands for quiet, makes the motions for a few preliminary hmmmmmmms and then the first song.

Black, "sanctified" ...snuff dippers, numbers'-players, down home, soulful, funky...deep song.

Rev. Tilly eases from his chair off to the side of the altar at the conclusion of the song, steps sedately to the pulpit with his hands clasped behind his back. He stands, looking out onto the gleaming faces, his expression serious, his small barrel-shaped body held straight as a rod. Several sinners squirm slightly when approached by his direct gaze. A few of the Sisterhood of the Usherette Board in the front pew begin to fan themselves a little faster.

"I wants to say, first off," he begins in a full, round, gravelly bass voice, "I wants to say... that I'm mighty glad...mightily glad t' see so many fine sisters 'n brothers in the House of the Lawd this Sunday. Say Amen t' that!!"

The church, still quivering from the beautiful vocal vibrations of minutes before, erupts with a shock wave of spiritual comments.

"Amen Rev'n!"

"Yes Lawd!"

"Awright then!"

XXX XXX XXX

Bam and Baby June nod off briefly, looking like slow-motion puppets as they droop, ignoring the sermon spilling out onto the street.

Bam alerts himself to deal with a potential customer. "Heyyy... looka'here, good brother!" he calls out to a young dude duffing past, lifting his sports coat to expose the wristwatches. "Can you dig one? For ten cents? How 'bout it, bro'? Gimme eight bones 'n put it on! Twenty-carat gin-u-wine Swiss!"

The young blood throws a brief, disdainful glance in Bam's direction and keeps on steppin'. Baby June eases up out of his nod to mumble after the young dud... "You jivvvvve...ass..."

XXX XXX XXX

Rev. Tilly gazes around at the congregation once again...enjoying the feeling of being in the pulpit, surrounded by an audience with religious feelings.

I'm glad to see y'all heah 'cause I wants t' share the power of Almighty Jesus with you, heah...this Sunday!"

"Speak!"

"Tell us 'bout it then!"

"Umm huhn!"

Rev. Tilly pulls a white handkerchief from inside his robe and dabs at the corners of his mouth.

"I...I...I want t' talk t' ya today 'bout Jesus!"

"Preach to us Rev'n!"

"Go 'head! Say whatchu got t' say!"

Rev Tilly dabs his handkerchief to his chin and forehead, as though anointing himself, as he slowly builds fire and crushes ice in his throat.

XXX XXX XXX

"Come on, Baby June...les' go over here...and...sit down...I'm tired as a...mother...fuck...er.."

Baby June bends down to scratch his ankle, almost tilts himself over and straightens up as though nothing had happened.

"Bam...you know...how them...people is...'bout...folks sittin' on they...front...steps...'specially on Sunday."

"Fuck them! Com' on!"

XXX XXX XXX

"**Yes Gawd!**" Rev. Tilly growls out suddenly, scaring two little sisters in the third pew. "I wants to talk 'bout your Son t'day! Jeeesus! Jeeesus!" he calls out in a sudden frenzy of religious emotion. "I say Jeeesus is the light o' the world!"

"Whatchu say!"

"Amen!"

XXX XXX XXX

"Heyyy...looka here, good brother...lemme have one o' them good cigarettes you smokin'."

A man passing Bam and Baby June played out on the steps walks over and shakes a cigarette out of his pack for Bam.

"Mucho thanks, good brother."

Bam goes off into a deep nod as the good brother strolls on. Before he can touch match to cigarette, he burns his fingertips, is jolted out of his nod, strikes another match and finally gets his cigarette lit before he goes off into another nod. Baby June gently removes the cigarette from his partner's dope-stiffened fingers, takes a drag and goes off into the same number.

Big Momma leans, breast heavy, out of her window far down the street, taking in the sight of the two men in their stupor, and slowly, sadly shakes her head as she scoops another thumbful of Garrett into her bottom lip.

XXX XXX XXX

Rev. Tilly, a crescendo of words spilling out suddenly, explosively..."I'm tellin' y'all! I'm tellin' y'all! Uh...uh...I'm tellin' y'all you got to put Jeeesus Christ in yo' life if you wanna be saved! You cain't be saved by L.S.D., mary-juana or none o' that trash! You gotta put Jesus the Son of Gawd in yo' life to be saved...!"

He pauses, stands off to the side of the pulpit, and in confidential tones, a rumbling undercurrent, say, "You know...I hear people runnin' 'round talkin' 'bout how much money they need, or what kinda car they need, or what kinda clothes, or how much this or that or one thang or the other they need...I say...ya ain't got nothin' 'less ya got Jeeeesus!"

"Yessuh!"

"That's right!"

"Amen, Rev'n!"

XXX XXX XXX

The sudden, explosive noise from the church works its way into Bam's semi-consciousness. He casually farts and turns to Baby June, whose nod has released him for a moment.

"Hey June...what did you tell yo' Momma 'bout her TV set?

Baby June, scratching his crotch and leaning over the spit, slurs out..."What the fuck did I tell you I was gon' tell 'er? Somebody stole it, shit!"

Bam, taken up briefly by a fierce dream, a mini-nod, paws gently at his crotch. "Uhhhhh...shat she say?"

"She didn't say shit. She just said she was gon' ask Father Love t' pray for me."

"Mmmmmm...yeahhhh...I can dig it. That sho' musta been a cold shot for her t' find her T.V. gone..."

XXX XXX XXX

Rev. Tilly, still bouncing his cadences from high to low, from fast to slow...eases back behind the pulpit and grips both edges.

"You know...lots o' folks 'shamed to admit they got Jesus Christ in they lives. Lots o' folks 'shamed to admit they ain't got Him in they lives!" And here he pauses dramatically, seeming almost to stare hypnotically into each of the faces looking up at him. "Well...I'm tellin' y'all, all o' y'all! he rumbles, "with no shame whatsoever...I *got* Jesus Christ in my life!"

The choir cued into the proper response for his outburst, is plunged off into "*He's Got the Whole World in His Hands*" by Mrs. Anna Lee Boggs, Choir Director.

XXX XXX XXX

Bam eases himself into a more comfortable position on the steps, unconsciously tapping his foot, off time, to the solid rhythm of the Black church music.

Idella strolls up the street, matching, somehow, in the same way as Bam's foot taps, the rhythmic pattern coming from the Second Sunrise Baptist Church.

"Idella!" Bam calls out to her..."Hey! Looka here Miss Sister...I know you wanna get somethin' nice for that man in yo' life? Can you dig one of these...?"

Idella walks over cautiously, eyeing the armful of wristwatches with childish fascination.

"How much you want for...?"

Bam, scratching frantically, methodically, at a sudden itch on the side of his face, interrupts her obvious question.

"Gimme twenny cents 'n take your choice..."

Idella, a crinkled frown between her eyes, as though she had heard wrong... "How much?"

Baby June, sliding away from a deep nod..."Awww man...gon' give the sister one o' those pieces for a dime."

Bam, checking his partner quickly... "Yeah! Here!" He pulls a watch off his wrist... "Here! Take this one! Gimme a dime! And git on!"

Idella accepts the watch hesitantly, holds it up to her ear like a child listening to a talking toy.

XXX XXX XXX

Rev. Tilly catches the last line of "*He's Got the Whole World in His Hands*"...and shouts off into second, "**Yesss Lawd!** I'm gonna preach a lil' bit now! I'm gonna preach a lil' bit now!"

He grabs the Bible from his pulpit and holds it up..."I'm gonna preach outta this Book! The Good Book! I wants to preach to you about a man, just like us, you 'n me! Who had some troubles...but he also had Him in his life...!"

The fans rock back and forth faster in the first pew..."Awright Rev'n! We hear ya!"

Rev. Tilly bends over as though a huge cramp was bubbling from his shoe tops and then explodes..."There was a man in the Land of UZ! I...I...sayyy! There was a man in the Land of UZ! I sayyyy t' you! There was a man in the Land of UZ...and that man's name was Job!"

XXX XXX XXX

Idella holds the watch out to Bam, her lips pouted..."This watch don't run, Bam. I can't hear nothin'!"

"Wind the motherfucker up, baby. Wind it up!"

Idella carefully screws the little knob around and holds it back up to her ear skeptically. Bam and Baby June look at her hopefully.

"Mmmm...yeah...yeahhh...it's runnin' now..."

Bam settles back on the steps and crosses his legs with a confident air.

"Goddamned right it's runnin'...that's a god watch."

"This man Job feared Gawd 'n hated the Devil! And...uh...uh... unto Job was born seven sons and three daughters! Job had...Job had everythang a man could want!"

Idella goes down into her cleavage and spools two five-dollar bills from a small roll.

"I catch y'all later...I got to git on...Sweets sent me out for some cigarettes."

"Yeahhhhh, Miss Sister Lady...Awright, later on!"

"Tell bro' Sweets we still got a few pants suits left. Got three or fo' just yo' size. Can you dig it?"

"Right on! I'll tell 'im."

Bam and Baby June, satisfied to have achieved the-next-bag-money, sprawl back gently on the steps as Rev. Tilly takes his sermon into fourth.

XXX XXX XXX

"He had...! I saayyy! He had seven thousand sheep, three thousand camels, five hundred yoke o' oxen, five hundred she-asses...and...aha! Lawd Almighty knows that's a lotta asses! And unto Job was born seven sons 'n three daughters! Had everythang in the world he wanted! And up there! Up there he had Gawd!"

The small church bubbles with the poetic rhythms, the bull-like bellows and the whispered slurs that spill from Rev. Tilly's throat.

"Now Job," he whispers to the congregation...his voice taking on a confidential tone..."I say..." and then bursts up to full volume..."Jooooobbb was a good man in ever' way!" He lays his Bible down and paces back and forth in the pulpit. "I say Job was a good man in ever' way! But the Lawd had to put Job to a test! The Lawd did put Job to a test! The Lawd let the Devil into Job's life! To test him! The Lawd let the Devil put boils all ovah Job's body... When Job said...'Man is born of a woman, he has but a few days and they will be full of trouble...man comes forth to this earth like a flower and is cut down'...when he said that...he knew just what he was talkin' 'bout!"

"Speak the word, Rev'n!"

"Awright then!"

A contrapuntal thing begins to happen in the church, emotions bouncing from the back of the church to the pulpit, from one side of the aisle to the other side.

Diana Holt gently nudges Nathan from a would-be nap.

XXX XXX XXX

Lady Mayflower, Mr. Maybaby, Soul Queen...or as he is very often called, Maybaby...steps out onto his front porch, arms folded across his would-be bosom, leans his fleshy buttocks daintily against the banister-support and surveys the scene, feeling the rollers in his hair from time-to-time. He waits for Bam and Baby June to escape a nod before trying to talk with either one of them.

"What on earth are y'all doin' out here on my front steps, Bam? You 'n Baby June...takin' in the afternoon breezes?"

Bam looks back over his shoulder with a mischievous glint in his eye. "Ooooo...hey Maybaby...whas happenin'...?"

"Yeahhhhh...whasssss happenin', Mr. Maygirl?"

Mayflower tightens a couple of loose rollers in his hair, crosses his thighs seductively, and squirms around on the railing for a more comfortable spot.

"Ain't nothin' shakin' but the leaves on the trees 'n they wouldn't be shakin' if it wasn't for the breeze."

Bam winks on the q.t. to Baby June.

"Uhn huh...right on, Momma. Right on!"

"Yeahhhh...uh ha hah! I can dig it."

Mayflower smiles patronizingly at Bam and Baby June as they nod away, cocks his ear to catch Rev. Tilly's sermon.

XXX XXX XXX

"Now Job had friends! Just like most of us...who tried to sway him from the Lawd, tried to talk him into forsakin' the Lawd when he started havin' troubles...hah hah...just like most of our friends do. When the Lawd let the Devil take away Job's camels, his oxen, and his family 'n all...Job's 'friends' tried to make Job break Faith with the Lawd! But Job said NO! He kept the Faith! Yes, Gawd Almighty!"

Rev. Tilly stops suddenly, the veins in his throat constricted by emotion, and whirls around... "Yes, Gawd Almighty!"

XXX XXX XXX

Bam looks up to see Mayflower swish back into his apartment. "Where you goin', Maygirl?"

"Here comes that dreadful little John 15X man again! I'll see y'all later, honey. I have no time to listen to anybody tell me not to put ham hocks in my collard greens 'n such shit as that."

Mayflower slams his front door as Bam and Baby June return to their world.

XXX XXX XXX

"Now finally," Rev. Tilly continues, dabbing at the tiny beads of sweat on his nose, "because the Lawd rewards Good 'n punishes Evil...finally. After the Lawd had saw that Job was his man, his main man...He blessed Job and gave him more in the End than he'd had in the Beginnin'! 'Stead o' him havin' seven thousand sheep, the Lawd blessed him with fo'teen thousand...'stead o' three thousand camels, He blessed him with six thousand, 'stead o' him havin' five hundred yoke o' oxen, He blessed 'im with a thousand! And 'stead o' him havin' five hundred she-asses, like befo' the Devil was put into his life, He blessed 'im with a thousand! And after all this, Job lived one hundred 'n forty years and saw his sons grow up, yes Lawd! And his grandsons! And his great-grandsons! And his great-great-grandsons! And I'm tellin' all o' y'all! If Job hadn't had the Lawd in his life, none of that would've happened!"

The choir bursts spontaneously into a hummed version of "*The Lord's Prayer*"...as the church glows and shimmers with dancing eyes and exalted feelings.

XXX XXX XXX

Jihad

John 15X, dope addiction, past tense, crime, time...saved by the Nation of Islam, strides briskly down the street selling copies of Muhammad Speaks to the citizens of the neighborhood.

"Looka here, brother... have you got the Messenger's word? I know you can dig where Minister Farrakhan is comin' from! All you got to do is read up on what's in here! He matches a potential customer stride for stride, for a few steps, 'til he receives a positive or negative response.

"I already got one," a man tells him and hurries on.

"Thank you, brother"...he calls softly after the man, and spying a young lady a few yards away, approaches her.

XXX XXX XXX

"Thank ya Jesus!"

"Yes! Thank ya sweet Jesus!"

"And now, now sister 'n brothers..." Rev. Tilly goes on, dabbing at the back of his neck, his eyes blazing with a message, "Deacon Percy will lead us in a short prayer. Sister Fant will direct the usherettes in the collection of o' offerin's whilst we bow our heads in prayer. Deacon Percy, will you begin please?"

XXX XXX XXX

"Good afternoon, Sister...may I interest you in a copy of Muhammad Speaks? Minister Farrakhan is tellin' it like it is."

Lubertha Franklin buys a paper, turns a dazzling smile on John 15X and keeps on stepping. John pauses to straighten his papers out and, as he does so, spots Bam and Baby June on the steps...nodding.

XXX XXX XXX

Deacon Percy stands and bows his head, the sharp planes in his thin face gleaming with oil. He begins his prayer in a high, wailing voice.

"Oh Deah Lawd...we thank ya for bein' heah t'day...t' share in the gracious power of yo' glory, amen! To know that you have given the breath to our bodies for another day, given us the Almighty News from Heaven, Lawd Be Praised! Let us know, thank ya' Jesus! That You is the Power, Hallow would be Thy Name, Thy Kingdom *is* t' come, and we knows, deah Lawd, that Thy Will *will* be done down heah as well as up there! Amen!"

XXX XXX XXX

John 15X dances up to Bam and Baby June on the balls of his feet, a concerned expression wrinkling his face.

"As Salaam Alaikum, brothers. How 'bout a paper for you two brothers?"

Bam and Baby June, somewhat surprised to see the figure in front of them attempt to sell them somethin, for a change, peek out from behind their drug stats and nod heavily, slowly...negatively.

XXX XXX XXX

Deacon Percy finishes his prayer and resettles himself in his chair on the altar-stage. Rev. Tilly quickly eases over to whisper in his ear.

"Uh...uh...Deacon, would you lead us in another short prayer? The offerin's have not...uh...been completely made yet."

Deacon Percy, without a change of expression, stands again... "Sisters 'n Brothers... will y'all jine me once again in praise o' the Lawd?"

XXX XXX XXX

"I guarantee you two brothers would be off into a more beautiful thang than you got now, if you got off into the Nation, if you read the Word and understood."

Both Bam and Baby June, looking slightly annoyed, the monkey tightening his grip on their backs, sit up to take full notice of the dude trying to sell them the Muslim newspaper.

"Sayyy mannn...ain't yo' name Johnny? Johnny One Shot? You look like a dude I did a year and a day with...back in '98."

John 15X places both feet together and sticks his chin out aggressively, a small pile of papers under one arm, a newspaper, ready to be sold, in the other hand.

"That's right, brother...I'm the same dude. They used to call me Johnny One Shot before I was given the true knowledge, All Praise to Allah...of my lost self in the Nation!"

XXX XXX XXX

"Deah Lawd...who art in Heaven...we know that the glow'rie of yo' Almighty Bein' is flashin' all over us here today! Thank ya Lawd! Right heah in the Second Sunrise Baptist Church..." Deacon Percy pauses to pull a snow-white handkerchief from his breast pocket, to dab at the corner of his mouth ... "And we thank thee O Lawd...for..."

Rev. Tilly spreads his arms out, looking for all the world like a huge bird, with the folds of his robe spread...slices into Deacon Percy's prayer with a small, annoyed frown on his forehead as he checks out the Deacon's handkerchief technique.

"Deacon...that was wonderful! Really wonderful and inspirin'! Sister Burns and Sister Fant will now count the shekels that have been gathered in the name of the Lawd...

XXX XXX XXX

Baby June, checking John 15X out a little more closely, becoming even more annoyed, scratching a nonexistent bug on his arm..."Uh... why'd they call you One Shot, man?"

Bam lets out a quick, dry series of sounds meant to sound like laughter and answers for John 15X. "Uh...as I remember...this cat was layin' honkies out right and left, so they started callin' 'im Johnny One Shot. Am I right 'bout that, Bro' John?"

XXX XXX XXX

Miss Anna Lee Boggs, in a burst of creativity, hums the opening bars to the Lord's Prayer, realizes that it has been done already, and just as quickly snaps her arms into a cut off gesture. Several members of the choir snicker, pleased to see her make a mistake.

XXX XXX XXX

"Well...I was lettin' the devils know that I was not to be trifled with. But I needed more, a lot more than a good right hand to solve my real problem, and that was me. I had the very same problem you two brothers have, the devil was forcin' the same poison into my system to, 'til I got off into the Nation."

"Ummm...yeahhhh, yeahhhh mannnn," Bam mumbles, rubbing his nose feverishly... "I know a bunch o' brothers who converted in the joint."

"Yeahhh," Baby June adds, "I knew a couple or three dudes who got off into it myself."

Sweet Peter D. walks up the street briskly, an irritated frown on his forehead. John 15X turns from his conversation with Bam and Baby June to hold a paper out to Sweet Peter D. "As Salaam Alaikum brother...would you like a paper today...Minister Farrakhan..." Sweet Peter D. interrupts John 15X as he digs down into his pocket absent-mindedly... "Bam...June...you all seen Idella?" His eyes continue searching up and down the street as he pays for the paper, ignoring the vendor of it.

"Nawww, man...I ain't seen 'er, you June?"

"Naw...not lately."

"I'm gon' break that bitch's neck when I find her! She can't even go to the grocery store without fuckin' up!"

John 15X shakes his head sadly, watching Sweet Peter Deeder stomp away angrily with an edition of Muhammad Speaks under his armpit.

XXX XXX XXX

"Now then...let us hear from Sister Burns. Sister Burns, will you give us an accountin' of the Lawd's benedictions?" Sister Burns, her front gold tooth gleaming, beams up from the collection table in front of Rev. Tilly's pulpit... "Yes Rev'urn...we have collected...in the Lawd's name, exactly sixty-three dollars and eighty-six cents."

Rev. Tilly, trying to iron out the irritated frown on his forehead, nods graciously to Sister Burns. "Thank ya, Sister Burns. And thank y'all for this contribution to the upkeep of His House...say Amen t' me, Sisters 'n Brothers!"

XXX XXX XXX

"Bam...if you remember me from back there, I mean, really remember me and the bag I was in, I was pretty far gone, right?"

John 15X lays his palm out for Bam to smack it in agreement... Bam does, weakly.

"I had a pretty good chance of becomin' a star welterweight 'till that monkey climbed up on my back."

John shrewdly measures his message to give Bam a chance to slide in from the side with something, some kind of indication that he is diggin where John is coming from.

"Yeahhhh...yeahhhhhh...I hear ya...bro'...I hear ya."

John props his foot on the steps, rests his newspapers on his knee and leans, confidentially, closer to Bam and Baby June.

"Mannnn...I can remember some things...dig it! I was married to a beautiful little sister named Catherine; why she married me, I'll never know. But anyway, I fell short on my hustle one night, Jones was on me, so I came home and stole the baby's milk money to get down with, and didn't feel a thing! I would've sold the baby, if anybody had wanted to buy it. You know what I'm talkin' 'bout? Committin' any kind of little old funny, off brand type crime in order to make sure I had a wake-up shot."

Bam throws a quick, hostile look in John 15X's direction, too aware of where he's comin' from.

"Yeahhhhh...yeah...that monkey don't be jivin' when he get a grip on yo' back."

XXX XXX XXX

"And now...sisters 'n brothers...while the choir gives us a soft ren-dition of '*Swing Low, Sweet Chariot*'...now that we have praised the Lawd! Sang and shouted His praises! Amen! Felt His Spirit in our souls...I'm gonna ask all those who have not previously done so...to take that step...that biiigggg step...in Jeeesus' Name! I want ya t' step forth 'n declare yourself for Jesus Christ! Step lively, and fear not 'cause if you are for Jesus, Jesus is for you!"

The choir begins to sing, very softly, "*Swing Low, Sweet Chariot*"...forming a quiet blanket of spiritual sound behind John 15X's spiel on the street.

XXX XXX XXX

"For ten, long, dirty, rotten years...I was a stomped-down dope fiend! A junkie! That is, 'til Minister Farrakhan found me and took me into the Nation."

John 15X looks from one drooping face to another, beseeching the two men to give up the devils holding them motionless.

"Come on in, brothers! Become a brother in the Nation of Islam and you'll be free...you'll be free because you'll find out the truth about yourselves and the game these blue-eyed devils been runnin' on you all your life...you'll know."

Baby June, an irritated, disgusted expression pulling the corners of his mouth down, interrupts John 15X... "Yeahhhh...I dig the program, man. Like I said, you know? I knew some cats who converted and they sho' 'nuff righteous got they shit together... you know..."

XXX XXX XXX

"We thank thee O Lawd...we thank thee for this day...and for all the days you lets us have...without yo' devine guidance 'n leadership, we would be nothin' but lil' old fools runnin' 'round this big old ball...tryin' to find a hole to climb down into when our time has run out. We thank thee for givin' our lives some kind o' meanin' and purpose. Say Amen to me!"

Mumbles, grumbles, hallelujahs and fervent Amen's resound throughout the church! Before the conclusion of the last rumble, the choir begins to softly hummmmmmm through...*Glory, Glory...*

XXX XXX XXX

Bam hunches Baby June in the ribs and they both come fully alive for the first time since they've sat on the steps.

"Aww shit! Here come them crazy, young radical ass motherfuckers!"

"We better split, June! Kwendi put the word out that he was gon' kick my ass 'bout his lil' brother next time he saw me."

"Uh...dig Bro' John...we gon' have t' talk about gettin' off into the Nation some other time."

John 15X, checking out the situation closely, realizing that there is the possibility of an emotional situation to be played on, suggests urgently, "Why don't you brothers come with me!? I'm parked right 'round the corner. I can come back and sell these papers later on. I'm tellin' you, brothers...once you get to the mosque and talk with Minister Shabazz, and find out where it's really at..."

Bam and Baby June, stirred by danger from their dope lethargy, by the young radicals calling to them from the other end of the block... "Heyyy Bammm! Junnnee! Wait a minute! I wanna see you! Both o' y'all! Wait a minute."

Bam and Baby June ease off of the steps, sliding immediately into a Hong Kong coolie trot..."See ya later Bro' John! We got to git on!"

John 15X takes a few involuntary steps with them and then pauses, trying to readjust the newspapers that are fumbling from his grasp... "As Salaam Alaikum, brothers!"

Bam and Baby June ease around the corner, maintaining a speed that would please Dr. Meriwether and keep Kipchoge Keino happy.

John 15X, watching them escape, mumbles again, sadly... "As Salaam Alaikum, brothers!"

XXX XXX XXX

Rev. Tilly stands in the doorway of the Sunrise Baptist Church, shaking hands with members of his departing congregation.

"Good to see you and your Missus, Brother Holt...mighty glad you made that step for Jesus...welcome to the congregation." Nathan Holt stands, looking down awkwardly at his shoes, squirms one hand around in his pants pocket... "Uhhh...well..." Diane bursts in diplomatically... "Thank you, Rev'urn...thank you...wonderful sermon, really inspirin'...we'll see you next Sunday."

Rev. Tilly lays a knowing little smile on them and turns to the next couple as she pulls Nathan away by the elbow.

They stroll down the street, arm in arm, Diane Holt whispering fiercely up at her husband's ear... "Nathan Holt! I'm really surprised at you! I almost fell off my seat when I looked up and...whatever in the world made you walk down the aisle and declare yourself for Jesus? I'll never know! You know good 'n well you ain't 'bout ready to even start goin' t' church regular...let alone declare yourself for Christ!" Nathan Holt, holding his head high and muffling a wide grin, responds quietly... "Ahemm...I don't know honey. I guess the Devil made me do it."

Mrs. Holt flicks a quick look of mock disgust up at him and then bursts into girlish giggles.

"Nathan...I swear fo' Gawd...you ain't got a bitta sense!"

And the beat goes on

CHAPTER III
SHINE IT ON!

The fire never goes out on the stem...in the 'hood. The grimy little faces and sloganed t-shirts, children of the dust, carry a self-flaring spark, a torch that is always being lit again and again by men who remember.

Men who remember people, places and things that they have never actually known...but remain no less real because they are passed on to the young.

The men who remember seat themselves on high places up and down the stem...spin around on effervescent barstools, perch on the edges of mini-park benches, or simply sit tall and proud on milk crates in the center of muggy, tribal nights...whispering dangerous stories in hoarse, wine-soaked voices about who shot John. Or telling, in their own ways, what yesteryear has to do with today.

The little black faces pressed against the opaque white windows surrounding them listen...they don't really care what the others say... all they want is a little bread, of one variety or another, some kind of love and a few dreamy fairy tales they can relate to.

Sherman, Willie Burkes, BoBo, Billy Woods and Chico Daddy, junior members of the Afro-Lords, lounge around on the front steps of Miss Rabbit's tenement apartment building, puffing on cigarettes, surreptitiously passing a bottle of cheap wine around as they deal with the passing scene and try to forget that tomorrow is Monday...meaning school.

Mayflower strolls by...his head held high, the muscles in his slender face twitching as he tries to ignore the 'Lords.

"Whatchu up to, Mr. Lady?"

Mayflower stops instantly and turns, hands on hips, to her questioner.

"I'm mindin' my own business, Billy Woods...junior! And leavin' yours alone!"

The gang members, enjoying any kind of scene, try to agitate the drama.

"Tell 'im 'bout it, Mr. Sweetthang!"

Mayflower flashes angry eyes at Billy Woods, gives the whole group a careful, well-cultivated look of disdain and prances off like a brood mare...knees high...past the Great Lawd Buddha and his woman Josie, hassling as they stroll up the street. Josie, her words slurred slightly...talks loudly into Buddha's ear.

"Now listen Buddha! If I've told you once, I've told you a hundred times! I'm not gonna keep on goin' through all these changes with you!"

Mayflower nods pleasantly at the couple, a slight smile of amusement dimpling his jaws. "Hi Buddha...hi Josie!"

Buddha turns from Josie jerking her mouth off in his ear with a grim look. "Oh...hey May...what's to it?"

Josie, taking a quick shot at Mayflower... "Hello Mayflower! Turns back to her number with Buddha. "Awright, now you just tell me! Just tell me what makes you think you too good to work? Just tell me 'cause I sho' as hell wants t' know!"

The Great Lawd Buddha, a deep-clefted series of frowns wrinkling his brow, on top of the grim expression covering the rest of his face, speaks to Josie from between clenched teeth. "Josie! Goddamnit! I *am* workin'! I'm doin' my thing! Why should I waste my time on some jiveass job when it prevents me from doin' my very own thing, huh? Answer that, if you can!"

"Bullshit! You just lazy, that's all. You don't wanna work!"

The Great Lawd Buddha, Benin-Mao-masked face, touches delicately at his polka dotted orlon ascot, pulls his ivory-bone holder out of his breast pocket, gently screws a Russian cigarette into the end of it, and stands back from Josie, better known behind their backs as Miss Heatwave.

"Josie..look! You go on upstairs! We'll talk about all this later on.

Josie, her hands on her hips, pouting her bottom lip out aggressively, stands looking at Buddha as though he were a turd.

"Why can't we talk about it now?"

Buddha leans in close to Josie, blows a stream of smoke slowly into her face... "'Cause now ain't the time! I said...we'll talk about it later...now why don't you go on upstairs and cool off? I'll be up in a little while.

Josie squinches up her eyes hatefully at Buddha, stifles the urge to say something nasty and turns, with every eye on every lush curve, to clack-click up the stairs.

The Great Lawd Buddha, shaking his head from side-to-side in a disgusted fashion, looks from one young face to the other.

"Women! Hmf! Can't do with 'em, can't do without 'em...what was it Nietzschee once said?... '*When you go to women, carry the whip*!' What are you young bloods doin' out here this late? Plannin' some kinda offbeat crime, or something?"

BoBo, giggling foolishly at the attention being paid them by one of their favorite people, answers for the group.

"Tee hee tee heeee...naw Buddha, nothing like that, we just coolin' it...drinkin' Ripple, that's all. You want a taste?"

Buddha nods no, in a reserved sort of way, wrinkling his mouth up at the sight of the proffered bottle. "Not for me, sport. I can dig it for you, but it would mess my stomach up for days. What kind of wine is that anyway?"

"Ripplino."

The Great Lawd Buddha, his mouth unwrinkled into a slight smile, stands authoritatively and announces to the group. "That isn't wine my friends. Chateau d'quem is a wine. Pommard '39 is a wine...that shit you all are drinking is just a bunch of chemicals them people stirred 'round in a vat and shot some carbonation into. Why don't you cats put your coins together and get some good wine?"

The Afro-Lords look blankly into each other's faces and then... as a chorus, react. "What coins?"

"Shiii-it! We had to struggle to get this."

"Fo' real!"

Buddha, the slight smile widening a bit, looks down benevolently on the group. "You lil' po' ass motherfuckers! Here!" He pulls a ten-dollar bill from his watch pocket and holds it out to the group. "Who's gonna be the runner?"

All eyes point to Sherman, who reaches out proudly from the steps and skips away like a gazelle.

Buddha, watching him pull away... "He looks kinda young...will they sell him...?"

"One of those winos'll cop for him, for fifty cents."

The Great Lawd slowly settles grandly on the steps, sighing a little as his bottom touches the chill of the stone, makes an elaborate ritual out of tapping the roach of one Russian cigarette out of his ivory-bones holder to replace it with another...has it lit immediately by a member of his attentive audience and takes a few, long, leisurely drags.

"Any of you cats ever been t' China?"

Chico Daddy, his head cocked to one side like the Victrola dog, asks a one-word question, "China?"

Billy Woods, moving down a couple steps to be nearer... "Where? China?"

Willie Burkes, his eyes dancing from the last pull on the previous corner, slops in... "Nawwww...ain't nobody here ever been nowhere...not really. You been t' China, Buddha?"

Buddha, suavely pushing twin streams of smoke through his nostrils, nods affirmatively, casually.

"Uhnnn huhnnn...where I got my name. They took one look at me and decided my name should be Buddha, after...the...uh...deity, you know. Naturally y'all stuck that Great Lawd part onto it. Who went to cop the vino?"

"Sherman."

"Here he come..."

Sherman, barely breathing hard, sprints back up the street clutching a brown paper bag with three bottles of wine in it... Willie Burkes, BoBo and Chico Daddy each snatch a bottle, uncap it and start passing it around in the loose circle they have eased around Buddha.

"Where's my change?"...Buddha asks, noting the cheap brand name going around. "I thought you were gonna get some good wine?"

Sherman, handing the change over reluctantly... "Uh...well.. there's five of us, and one bottle of good wine wouldn't go too far anyway."

"What's good wine?" BoBo asks, bringing his bottle up to one side of his mouth. "I mean, what do you call good wine, Buddha?"

"Hah!! One good sign is that it costs at least three dollars 'n somethin' a bottle...or maybe it has a good name...for example... Cordon Rue de Splap...or Boojoilee...."

The bottles go 'round and 'round as Buddha pedantically whips off a series of French-like names.

BoBo, winking at Chico Daddy... "Uh...what was you startin' to say 'bout China, Buddha?"

"China? What about China? I missed that runnin' to git the pluck."

"Buddha was startin' to tell us that that's where he got his name...that right, Buddha?"

"That's right."

"What...I mean, why'd you go to China?"

"Miss'ssippi," Buddha deadpans, nutrolls on them, as the Afro-Lords crack up around him. After the last sniggle, he continues.

"Actually, it was just a little bit more complicated than that. But to keep it simple, even though Miss'ssippi is the very best reason I can think of...let's just say I got on a boat one day and wound up in China."

The second-floor window socks open and Josie leans out, mouth curling up viciously... "Chester! You goin' stay down there all goddamned night?!"

Buddha, not raising his voice, but lowering it to a bull-like rumble... "I'll be down here 'til I get ready to come upstairs!"

Josie cocks a long, hard, mean look at him and then abruptly slams the window back down.

Buddha, turning back to the group, shakes his head grandly, sadly... "Lawdddd...ain't women hard to deal with?"

"Really."

"Yeah...you can say that again!"

"When did you leave outta China, Buddha?"

"Oh...uh...ahemmm...well...that's a little bit less complicated than the way I got in. Actually...in a manner of speaking, I was forced out. What happened was I was living' in this palace 'n shit... doin' it to the lady of the house, a young grass-widow-princess... and the next thing I knew, them crazy-ass Chinamen had started to revolutionize 'n whatnot, so I beat the princess out of ten pounds of pure jade and split to Europe."

"Europe? Why Europe?"

Buddha takes a long, reflective look at his interrogator... "Wellll...I'll tell you somethin'...I'd gotten on a boat, going anywhere, and wound up in China, and when the shit hit the fan in China, I figured...what the hell! I been overseas for awhile, why not stay over, why not go to Europe? I was hip to the East, you dig? Why not check out the West? One thing I was damned certain about...I sho' as hell wasn't gon' back to Miss'ssippi!"

Sherman pauses in the middle of a swig of juice and sputters it on the people around him, laughing. "Hahhah hahhahhahhah!"

"Shit! Watch it, man!"

"Sooo...Europe it was," Buddha coolly continues, ignoring everything else but the past vision.

"What was it like?"

"Oooohhh...well...you young dudes have to keep in mind that the Europe I knew may not be the Europe of today, or the Europe some of you all will know when you get there."

"What was it like for you, Buddha?"

"Clean outta sight! Somethin' else! Like I said, I'd managed to get my black ass out of China with this jade 'n all, thinkin' I was home free...but the first thing I know, I'd been rooked out of my jade by some slick talkin' Armenian cats runnin' the most sophisticated Murphy I'd ever encountered and, instead of landing in Europe richer than Carnation cream, I wound up in Marseilles on pure ass, hat in hand, stumblin' 'round lookin' for a way to get down."

"Where's Mar'say?" Chico Daddy asks, shyly.

"It's...uh...it's a port city in France, lil' brothers...a port city. And I'm gon' tell you right now, if you ever want to go there, don't try it on a Greek freighter...like I did. We must've sailed halfway 'round the goddamned world, stoppin' here and there, unloadin' shit here and droppin' shit there, before we finally made it to France. If I hadn't been a young man, like you all, I probably would've died from eatin' all that wormy bread 'n shit! That's mainly why my stomach is all fucked up today, I think. I was sailin'...incidentally, on one of those freighters owned by that old dude who's married to...uh...what's 'er name?"

"You mean...uh...?"

"Yeah! Yeah! That's the one. Anyway...by the time we got to Marseilles, I'd already decided to cut the freighter loose. If I'd stayed on the bitch too much longer...I'd either have starved to death, caught a red-hot case of the bubonic plague, or been nibbled up by the rats, hard t' say which. Believe me, it was a truly wretched experience." Buddha pauses to replace his cigarette. The Afro-Lords pause in their movements with the bottles.

"Anyway, I jumped ship five hours after we docked, and started lookin' 'round for a way to get down. Awright...I'm in the city of Marseilles...fantastic booyea base...and, after two or three days of hustlin', scufflin', doin' a lil' this 'n a lil' that, I managed to catch a fantabulouss Malay bitch named Daisy and a place to hang my hat. The next thing I looked around for was a way to make some grand theft dough. Well...I didn't have to look too far...some Algerian cats...they're somethin' like the Mafia over there, them and the Corsicans, got in touch with me to act as a go-between. My job was to get together with sailors comin' in from the Orient and make deals for the heavy drugs they were smugglin' in for the the Algerians. It was, of course, full of all kinds of pitfalls 'n whatnot but I stuck for about two months...'til one day I got greedy and..."

"What kind of bread was you into, Buddha?"

The Great Lawd Buddha taps ash from the end of his cigarette before going on. "Oooo...somethin' like, sometimes eight bills a week. That's where the problem existed, you see? I just couldn't see myself makin' peanuts, runnin' the risk of gettin' busted and spending fifty long years in the Bass-tille, while those motherfuckers at the top were steady rakin' in anywheres from fifty to a hundred thousand grand a week. I mean, that's how lucrative the enterprise was. So... first chance I got, I palmed a half-pound of uncut heroin, fresh from the laboratory, by way of Turkey, and split, along with my women. By this time, I had collected myself a regular lil' harem. I had Daisy, the Malay broad... a big blonde Alsatian bitch named Yvette and a lil' jet black diamond of a sister from Senegal that I called Mademoiselle Diop...she was so black that her gums were black, and talk about being fine! Didn't nobody have to tell me Black was Beautiful when I copped her...I could see it with my own eyes!"

Billy Woods, his eyes brightening, asks in a slow, awestruck voice. "Uh...Buddha...how much dope did you say you cut out with?"

"Half a pound...give or take a few grams."

"Oh wow! A whole half pound o' smack!"

"That's right, lil' bro' ... one half pound of pure heroin.

Without warning, the second-floor window socks open again and Josie leans far out over the ledge.

"Chessster! Goddamnit! Are you gon' bring yo' jive ass up here or not? I'm not gonna be yellin' out this window all night long!"

"Woman! I told you! I'll be up there when I get up there!"

Josie, mumbling a stream of dished up motherfuckers out, slams the window down again, rattling the pane.

"See there! That goes to substantiate a theory I've had for years... don't ever get yourself involved with one woman, lil' brothers. Get three or four but never one. There really is safety in numbers."

"Yeah...I can dig where you comin' from."

"Uh...about that dope. How much was it worth? You know, a whole half a pound?"

Buddha, his lip corners pulled down in a haughty fashion... "'Bout a half million...just the way it was, uncut, you dig?"

"O wowwww!"

"Gawwwwdamn!"

"Anyway...I split with my ladies. Had t' cut Yvette and Mademoiselle Diop loose, excess baggage...no pun intended, ha ha...and believe me, that was one of the hardest things I've ever had to do. I held onto Daisy 'cause she had some relatives in Paris that I could deal my shit off to. Paree! Paree! S'il voo play! Magnifique! Ravissan'...hey! Gimme some of that rotgut pluck!"

Two bottles, three-quarters empty, are thrust out to him, gallantly.

Buddha snatches the nearest one, takes a long swallow... "Ugggghhh! I don't see how you all can drink this shit, terrible as it tastes." He takes another long, professional wino gulp and continues his story, breathlessly...

"Now dig it! Here I am, in Paris, a queen of a city! In one hand I got half a suitcase full of monies and in the other hand I got half a pound of uncut hoss, and one of the planet's hippest bitches trailin' me like a lovestruck puppy dog... I'm really in a bag, you dig...? I got to do several things at once. One of the first things I got to do is get rid of all these narcotics because ain't no way I can get it 'cross the border. The next thing I got to do is get *me* 'cross the border 'cause them Algerian cats don't be jivin' and I know they gonna be on my ass like white on rice, soon as they discover that I have confiscated and cut out with all this dope I have."

Buddha pauses for a long pull on the wine bottle, absent-mindedly sticks another cigarette into his ivory holder... "Within a week's time, Daisy had put me into her cousin's brother, or her uncle's nephew or somebody, and I had managed to deal off my drugs for two hundred and fifty million old francs.

"How much would that be in real money?" Willie Burkes and Billy Woods chorus together.

Buddha casually adjusts the polka dot ascot around his throat before answering. "Ooooo...'bout half a million dollars.

The Afro-Lords lean back on their elbows, astounded by the figure, eyes glazed and shiny from the wine.

"I started to hold out for a million, but I thought, you dig...what the hells the difference, really, between a half million dollars and a whole million, 'specially since I was flirtin' with instant Death (no replay) every day I was in France, what with the Algerians, sniffin' 'round for my rectal opening...so, I settled for half a million and got on the first thing smokin', goin' to Germany."

Sherman, intently following the story, pops in as the question is slowly being formed on Chico Daddy's lips.

"What happened to the May-lay broad, Buddha?"

"I...uh...well, I stuck ten grand to her, for services rendered, gave her one last, hard, supersonic fuckin', and sent her down the road. Had to...it would've been too easy for us to get racked up together. Can you see it? A little slant-eyed nigger and a high yaller Mongolian bitch. Can you dig where I'm comin' from?"

"Uhhhhnn huh."

"Sure hated to part with that chick too...she was really a righteous lady. I think she went back to Indochina, what they call Vietnam now, or what's left of it, after we split." Buddha pauses for a long swig, looks far off into his memory...daydreaming, remembering for a few seconds... "Hmf! Uh...where was I?"

"On the way to Germany!"

"Yeahhh...Germany, Dutch land uber alles...ha!"...he says, and sticks his chin out aggressively. "I didn't really dig Germany all that much. There was a helluva lot goin' on there' round about this time. Maybe some of your mothers 'n fathers remember the German thing about then. The Nazis were comin' into power, and they were givin' the Jews pure idee hell...and everybody else they didn't dig! I mean, you would've had to actually be on the scene to believe the trips they were takin' the Jews on! It was a lot like what niggers in this country been goin' through, from Day One...with a few slight differences.

"I had a lil' taste of what was happenin', in Munich, when a mob of young dudes, 'bout you all's age...Hitler Youth, they called 'em, chased me down a street throwin' lumps o' coal at my head. It didn't take too much more of that kind of treatment for me to decide that I wanted to be somewhere else...so I schemed and bribed everybody in sight and got on.

"Dig it now, lil' brothers! Dig it! I didn't really know what was happenin' in the States, havin' been away so long...but Europe was in an uproar! The Hitler thang was goin' on strong and I didn't want any part of that...but I didn't want to go back to those Nazis in Miss'ssippi either."

"Right on, bro' Buddha! Right on!"

"Soooo...with all my money 'n pretty clothes, I decided to make a Scandinavian scene."

BoBo, Sherman and Chico Daddy exchange puzzled looks and nudge Billy Woods.

"The who scene?"

"Denmark, champ, Copenhagen to be exact...it was the spring of the year and everything was happenin'...I could see, when I got there, why people called it the Italy of the North. I can remember walkin' through Tivoli Gardens, a big old amusement park they got over there, tippin' my lid to every fox in the place and damned near gettin' ripped off every time I flashed my smile on somebody.

"It was a real groove. But I still felt kinda shaky, 'cause I knew the Algerians wouldn't be givin' up if they had the slightest chance of rippin' me off...and they were the kind of cats who would pinch your nuts off and stuff 'em in your jibbs...before you were tortured to death."

Several pairs of knees subconsciously draw themselves together slightly.

"O wowwww...sound like a cold-blooded bunch o' dudes!"

Buddha, spilling the corner down his throat, from the side of his mouth, pro-wino-style... "Right on, young blood...right on... but they didn't keep me awake at night, I mean, not really. I had everything I wanted, livin' like Viennese pimp in a swank hotel downtown, spendin' money like it was goin' outta style and doin' whatever I felt like doin'...and, to top it off...within a month I had copped an I-talian Countess who had more bread than I did."

"Mannn! Them chicks stayed on your case, didn't they?"

"You better believe it! Not only that, the broad had old, old money too. You know what I mean? Or so I thought. When I first cut into the broad, at a party on the fifteenth floor in my hotel, I couldn't believe she was into too much. But...there was somethin' about her...some kind of...flavor. The bitch had class! That's what it was...class! That old style class that can't be bought with money. She wasn't outrageously beautiful or anything, she was just fine as a motherfucker! Like an antique chair or somethin'! In addition to that, if that wasn't enough, she had so many names 'n titles stuck to 'er ass that it took the cat who introduced us, a Lawd or somethin' himself, five minutes to rumble through 'em. I could never remember all those names...so, right from the beginning, I wound up calling the bitch Suzy."

The Afro-Lords snicker, give each other fives all around, half drunk on cheap wine.

Bam and Baby June trot past...like slim dark wolves, looking back over their shoulders apprehensively.

"Wonder what them fools done stole this time?"

"Or on they way to steal."

"Ain't no tellin', man...ain't no tellin'."

Chico Daddy shushes the group... "Go 'head, Buddha! Go 'head...what happened then?"

Buddha, his hand a little less steady now, places his empty bottle in a corner of the steps, pulls another cigarette out of a flat box and lights it without using his holder.

"Within a month after me and the Countess hooked up...funny how I caught her. One minute we were in a room full of people, discussing international bullshit in six or seven languages, next minute we was off in the study or the library, or somewheres... standin' behind some heavy drapes and I had shot about three yards o' tongue off into her jibbs and wobbled four fingers of my left hand up into that royal pussy. Just...ahemmm! One of those love at first sight things, I guess. Anyway..." he pauses to take a long drag on his cigarette..."just to make a long story short...we got off into it. Believe me, lil' brothers...it was heavy, heavy drippin' drama.

"I bought me and the Countess matchin' Ferraris to buzz around in... I knew if push came to shove, we could fall back on her dough...and we were takin' holidays in Greece, and swimmin' around Capri 'n shit...you know, livin' that jet set life to the absolute jibbs.

"I found out then how easily dough can slip through your fingers... I checked my accounts one day and discovered I was down to a couple hundred grand...but it didn't really matter 'cause I knew the Countess had bread...so we kept on partyin'. Every now 'n then I'd have a slight chill slither up 'n down my spinal column, thinkin' 'bout the Algerians...but, what the fuck!

"I was livin' high off the hog, so it didn't really matter. Nothin' mattered but that sweet life. The Countess used to call it 'La Dol-che Vi-da!' I think I can give that so-called "Sweet Life," and the Countess, credit for takin' me off into heavy drugs."

"We didn't know you was a hype, Buddha?"

"Well...I'm not now...but I was one, for damned near five years. I had gotten onto a fast track with Suzy and one night, probably for lack of anything else to do, we stuck some hypodermic needles off into our veins and the next thing I knew, both of us were hooked.

"I'd hate like hell to try and guess how much of that 'H' I'd sold in gay Paree finally wound up in my own veins...talk about poetic justice!

"I tried to kick, a whole bunch o' times, in fancy Swiss sanitariums 'n whatnot...you know, where rich White folks go when they want to try and get their heads straightened out. But nothin' worked...for one thing, the Countess was hooked and she didn't give a damn! She actually dug the whole trip!

"So...like the fucked-up weakling I was, every time she shot up, I shot up too. By this time my money was startin' to get funny, I was hooked and to beat it all, I found out the Countess was a fuckin' phony!

"The bitch was a dago from Arkansaw or somewhere like that, and she'd been trippin' 'round Europe for years, runnin' one of the grooviest games ever known.

"And if that wasn't bad enough, me bein' addicted and her bein' a phony...I found myself in love with the 'ho! Innnn luvvvvvv! Lil' brothers! Can you dig where I'm comin' from?"

Buddha leans closely into Billy Woods' face, gesturing wildly... "In fuckin' love! We had a long way to go before we'd have to start worryin' about where the next fix was comin' from...you dig? I had enough dough to keep us from becomin' a Bam 'n June, for awhile anyway...but both of us were goin' down like the Titanic...and I couldn't cut the bitch loose 'cause I was in love with her!"

The second-floor window socks open again... Josie leans out, her hair in rollers, cold cream smeared on her face, drunk. "Awright! Awright!"...she screams down to Buddha... "You lyin' ass sonofabitch! You wanna stay down there tellin' lies to them lil' simple-assed punks the rest of the night, huh? That's all you wanna do! Sit 'round on your lard ass tellin' them gotdamned fictitious ass stories...!"

Josie clutches sheets of paper in each hand as she screams, the whole effect of her in the window both comical and tragic.

The Great Lawd Buddha half-raises himself from the steps, panic on his features.

"Josie! What the hell you call yourself doin'? Josie!"

"And gotdamnit! If you ain't tellin' 'em, you writin' 'em! Here! Why don'tchu read some o' this shit to 'em! Since they so innerested in yo' every gotdamned word!"

She flings handful upon handful of handwritten manuscript out of the window. "And while you're readin' that shit to 'em!" She follows the papers, drifting down in the heavy night air like square flying birds, with shirts, suits, shoes, hats and three or four slow fluttering polka dot ascots. "Maybe one of 'em will give you a place to sleep, 'cause you sho' as hell ain't gon' lay up here behind me no mo'! With yo' worthless jiveass!"

Buddha, standing straight up now, the panic look replaced by rage, shakes his fists at her.

"Josie! Goddamn you! I told you not to ever touch my stuff!"

Buddha sprints up the stairs... The Afro-Lords, suddenly shocked out of the story groove, make a half-drunken game out of scrambling for the loose sheets of paper, and deck themselves out in Buddha's clothes.

"What the hell is it?"

"Dig this! All the pages are numbered..."

"What the hell is it?"

"Mannn...I'm tellin' you the truth, you dudes ain't got a bit o' couth! It's a play, Chico Daddy...a play."

The gang members continue gathering pages and bring them under the light of the streetlamp.

"Here's the title page... The Great Lawd Buddha by Chester L. Simmons."

"I never knew Buddha's whole name."

"Let's get all the pages together."

The unmistakable sound of a pistol shot...and then five more, in slow succession, punches through the night.

The Afro-Lords, frozen in place by the first shot, stand looking sadly up to the second-floor window...Buddha's hats and suit coats hanging loosely on their slender shoulders.

The street, quiet up 'til now, except for rumbling El trains in the distance, and the million miscellaneous sounds of the ghetto hummmmm-thrummm-throbbbbb, is suddenly alive. The 'Lords scramble to get the rest of the sheets together. Neighbors peek cautiously out of their windows, and then, as if by spontaneous combustion, congregate in front of Buddha's building.

They buzz around, gossiping already, speculating, making predictions, and stare at the Afro-Lords in their haphazard Buddha garments as though they were freaks. The colony's law-keepers arrive within minutes, pistols drawn...five carloads full.

They make their way arrogantly through the group.

"Awright here! Everybody move aside! Clear the way here!"

They cautiously invade the building...come out minutes later with Buddha, handcuffed. The Afro-Lords wave sheets of paper at him as he is pushed toward a squad car.

"We got yo' play, Buddha!" Billy Woods shouts out to him... "We got yo' play!"

The police react as though a new style riot were on the verge of happening, with the boys waving sheets of paper at them. A sergeant backs toward his car, frightened but trying not to show it, shouts "Awright now! Clear the streets! Excitement's over! Move along now and we won't have any trouble!"

The people laugh at his fear and stroll away grumbling. The gang shuffles away into the hallway of the building next door...a few minutes later, two ambulance attendants arrive, bring Josie's body out, the cold horse-plaid blanket nursed carefully against her curves.

After the ambulance leaves, the gang wanders, in a daze, back over onto the steps. They sit there, silently putting Buddha's play together by the numbers, and passing it to Billy Woods, who reads each page aloud as it is passed to him.

"Is that it? That the last page?"

"That's all we got..."

Billy Woods nods his head sadly, from side to side, and announces to the group around him... "Ain't no endin' to it... it ain't got no endin'.

CHAPTER IV

MOTHER WIT

Her hands, gnarled at the joints by her only disease, the affliction imposed on her by being born Black too soon, carefully smooth out the ample space between her once blazing thighs, and there the baby is propped up...gurgling up into the only face he will ever know that will contain four hundred years of pain, suffering and pride.

And there on her lap she sings to him.

She sings of the two bookends that make the world, of the twenty fingers that carry the touch of sacred love to the first people...and cries as she sings...sad within the walled-up visions of her own hell... reaching out to suffer pain for the pains she knows her grandson will someday feel.

She cries, silently...inside...way past the baby on her lap. She seeks peace, crooning wise old love words into the young-old head flopped against her milkless breasts...her words are pecan dry, seasoned by a flavored live that has shaped the lines around her mouth, but left her Inner Places, the places from which her love, wisdom and advice come, as sweet and succulent as fresh-cut cane...

"Son, if I tell you a chicken dip snuff...look under his left wang."

XXX XXX XXX

Monday morning, smoke blue, ghetto gray... Big Momma sticks her head out of her first-floor window, carefully checks out the scene of last night's excitement and, minutes later, appears on the front porch with a cane-bottomed easy chair...prepared to spend the day recording the happenings for those off on the various plantations around town.

Bam and Baby June lope up the street looking like prowling wolves, nerves on obvious edge, scowling, light taste of a wake-up shot blowing up the strain in their faces.

Hy'do boys? Hi y'all this mownin'?" Big Momma sings out warmly. They both turn hostile looks up to the top of the steps.

"Mornin' Miss Washington!"

"Mornin'!"

She smiles sadly watching them walk to the end of the block. The mailman slowly trails them up the street, briar pipe jutting out of the side of his mouth, wandering through the nooks and crannies of the tenement buildings and, behind him hesitantly...like a proverbial babe in the woods,...a young mini-skirted, black rimmed eye-glass-wearing, ash blonde, blue-eyed, shoulder-strapped Social Worker, obviously trying to find an address.

"Who you lookin' for, honey?" Big Momma calls out to her with a touch of humor in her voice.

Cynthia Moore, nearsighted, looks around at ground level for the source of the voice, discovers it above her.

"Oh...hi there! I'm...uh...looking for Mr. Henry Mayflower. Do you know him?"

Big Momma, checking her out, left eyebrow raised skeptically, "Maybe. What you want wid 'im?"

Miss Cynthia Moore, brushing wisps of hair from the corner of her eye, "Oh...well...I'm a social worker and...uh...uh Mr. Mayflower applied for aid last week."

"You sho' you ain't from one of them collection agencies?" Big Momma asks her sharply.

"Who, me? Hahhah hah...gracious no! Not on your life!"

Big Momma double-checks her carefully, completely...coldly. "Go on down t' the end of the block, first house on the corner, first floor."

"Thank you...thank you very much," the social worker calls up to Big Momma and with coltish grace, the warm ghetto winds blowing past her bare white legs, trips down to the end of the block, knocks on Mr. Henry Mayflower's door.

Mayflower stands behind four inches of golden burglar chain... peers through the open space cautiously.

"Yessss...what can I do for you?"

"How do you do? My name is Cynthia Moore and I'm from the Department of Public Welfare...are you Mr. Mayflower?"

Mayflower, still reserving opinions... "Some folks call me that."

"You *are* Mr. Mayflower, are you not?"

"Yes honey...I am *the* Mr. Mayflower."

"And you applied for aid last Thursday at our office?"

Mayflower's reserve disappears immediately as he begins unchaining his door. "Oh yes! Yes indeedy! Come right on in, honey! Don't stand out there...come on in!"

Miss Moore, gently but firmly led in by pressure on her elbow, stands in the center of the front room, surreptitiously checking out Mayflower's garishly furnished apartment.

"I hate to go through a thing about names...but one must be careful. I spent an hour the other day interviewing the wrong lady... hah hahhah."

Mayflower, even though he is standing in place, measuring, calculating, gives the impression of movement anyway.

"Yesssss, I know *exactly* whatchu mean, honey. One really can't be too careful...ain't no tellin' just who one might be dealin' with..."

"Uh...yes. Well now, Mr. Mayflower, about your application for aid?"

Mayflower, having quickly taken the measure... "Cynthia? Is that what you said your first name was?"

"Yes"...warm, toothy smile... "That's right."

Mayflower, prancing over to pick up a pack of You've-Come-A-Long-Way-Baby cigarettes... "Why don't I call you Cynthia and you call me May? I don't reeeelly take all that Mr.. stuff too seriously. If you know what I mean?" And then poses his slender, girlish body in a brief, high fashion model stance. "Would you like a cup of coffee?" Mayflower asks, fluttering his eyelashes rhythmically. "I just reeeeelly can't start my day off without that second cup. As you can see I still got my leotards on...just finishin' up my exercises...just can't let oneself go, strong as competition is out there these days. You want yours black, cream 'n sugar or what?"

"I'll take mine...uh...black, thank you."

Mayflower, in one lithe move, starts for the small kitchen area at the back of his apartment. "Won't take but a sec, all I have to do is heat it up!"

"Uh...Mr. Mayflower, about your...uh...application?"

"Can't hear you, honey!" sings out to her... "Be back in just a sec!"

Miss Moore stands in the center of the room, drumming her nails furiously on the notebook clutched to her bosom.

Mayflower gracefully re-enters the room, a cup and saucer balanced in each hand, cigarette dangling from the corner of his mouth.

"Mr. Mayflower...about your application?"

"Oh yes...my application. Please call me May...sit down! Sit down! We can talk about it over our coffee."

Mayflower steers Miss Moore to a corner of his sofa, supplies her with coffee and delicately perches on a chair in front of her, legs wrapped from ankle to knee.

"Thank you...mmmmmm...that's really good coffee."

"I *makes* good coffee! My mother, bless her sweet soul, taught me how! She used to use eggshells, you know...to settle the grounds."

Mayflower pauses for a quick sip of coffee and suddenly stares at Miss Moore in a wild way. "Hon-neeey! Where on earth did you *evah* get that lovely purse? I knew there was somethin' on you that caught my eye when you first walked in the door."

"There's only one like it in the world," Miss Moore informs Mayflower proudly... "A little old lady made it for me in Sicily."

"Sicily, you say?"

"Yes! I was there last year, with my parents...Madrid, Lisbon, Florence, Rome...do you know Sicily, Mr....uh...May?

"Hmf! Naw honey...no more than what I read in the news. I am plannin' to go someday though."

"Are you really?"

"Uhm huh."

"Really beautiful place, actually. But very, very poor...I mean, you know, in comparison to America."

"Well, I can skip Sicily. I got e-nuff pov-er-ty right here. Lawd knows I don't need to be goin' no where else where they got po' folks!"

Miss Moore squirms slightly in her corner of the sofa... "hah hah hah...I can certainly understand that. Now then, about your application for aid...?"

"Cynthia...would you care for another cup? You're welcome to it."

"Oh no! No thank you! It's delicious, but I really must get some information and then go...uh...May. I have six other applicants to see before one o'clock."

XXX XXX XXX

Father Love, neighborhood clairvoyant, and self-styled Divine Character, turns the corner, majestically attired in the latest fashion...strolls grandly up the steps and into the apartment building across the street, heading for Sister Sadie, apartment #107.

XXX XXX XXX

Mayflower, taking a quick peek through his lacy curtains at Father Love, stifles a sarcastic laugh and turns back to Miss Moore.

"Just go 'head, ask away, honey! I got all the answers...'scuse me just a minute! I just don't know where my mind is sometimes! I left the coffee on the burner!" Mayflower flies to the kitchen, Miss Moore's words follow her out.

"What I have to find out is...?"

Mayflower returns, dabbing at his hands with a paper towel. "Yes...Cynthia honey...now what were you saying'? Coffee perked all over the stove...I'm gonna have to..."

Miss Moore, becoming slightly pissed... "What I was saying is...what I have to find out is whether or not you're eligible for aid."

"Hmf! Well...I don't know what you have t' be to be *eligible*, but I know one thang for damned certain...I ain't got nothin'!"

"Yes, yes...of course. Now then, you are single? Unmarried? Unemployed?"

Mayflower gracefully perches his buttocks on the edge of the chair, puffs glamourously on his cigarette.

"That's right...I am unmarried, but...tee hee hee...not single, leastways not all the time anyway. And I am unemployed...here's what went down..."

Miss Moore...scribbling frantically... "Just a minute May...just a minute! Have you applied for compensation?"

"Honey...I'm always applyin' for compensation. No...but seriously...I really can't apply because I wasn't covered while I was workin'."

"May I ask what your job was."

XXX XXX XXX

Father Love readjusts his handkerchief in the breast pocket of his French cut suit, flicks an imaginary speck of lint from his left sleeve, and knocks softly but authoritatively on Sister Sadie's door.

A wheezy, pain-slugged voice calls out dryly, "Who is it?"

Father Love, grasping both lapels with his manicured thumbs, answers... "It is I, Father Love."

The pain disappears from the voice within, and is replaced by something else...anxiety.

"Father Love? Did you say, Father Love?"

"Yesss Sister...Father Love," he replies, shuffling his gaunt shoulders around in the tailoring of his expensive clothes.

XXX XXX XXX

Mayflower rushes away to his bedroom...returns in seconds with an album of large, glossy photographs. "I was doin' a specialty routine over on Grove Street, at Nick's place. Ain't these beautiful shots? This pose here..."

XXX XXX XXX

Sister Sadie, a plump, moon-faced woman, moves quickly from a sofa where she has been reading a True True Confession magazine and sipping a can of brew. She whips the brew in the refrigerator right quick, pushes the magazine under the sofa, takes the burglar chain off, and, as a last, religious act, snatches her Bible from a nearby table...returning to her plumped down sofa at the end of all of her activity...slightly out of breath.

XXX XXX XXX

Miss Moore shuffles through the glossy photos, a detached, neutral look on her face... "Oh yes, yes these are lovely. Now you say you weren't covered...?"

"Not a damned thing! I was gettin' paid every night I worked... but...well...I wasn't covered by Social Security or nothin' like that."

Miss Moore, her detached look replaced by a frown, scribbles on ...and on.

XXX XXX XXX

"Please come in, Father Love...the door is open."

Father Love opens the door slowly, pauses in the half-opened door dramatically.

"How are you, Sister Sadie? My poor, dear Sister Sadie...we missed you terribly last evening, at our third, tri-annual grand fund-raising dinner."

"Well," Sister Sadie starts off, coughing delicately into her open palm, "coff! coff! You know, Father Love, it had to be somethin' real serious for me t' miss a service."

Father Love slowly closes the door and stands with his back to it, staring hypnotically at Sister Sadie's full form.

XXX XXX XXX

"Now May...could you please give me a figure, the approximate amount you were earning...during the time of your employment at Nick's place?

"It would be reeelly hard to say, Cynthia, honey...reeelly hard t' say, that damned Harvey was snatchin' that money outta my hand as fast as Nick laid it in there."

"Harvey?"

XXX XXX XXX

Finally satisfied that the full impact of his entrance has been achieved, Father Love struts across the small space separating them, peacock-like, bends stiffly to take both of Sister's rough, ashy hands in his own as he looks searchingly into her eyes.

"Is it...? Is it really serious, Sister Sadie? Are you in deep pain?"

XXX XXX XXX

"Yeahhhh honey...Mr. Harvey M. Lester...finest nigg...uh...one of the finest men around! You hear me!? One o' the finest!"

Miss Moore, a sympathetic smile on her mouth, "You say Mr. Lester took all of your money?"

"Ever' blessed cent, except for cigarette money," Mayflower answers with a little sighhhh at the end.

"Why didn't you report this to the authorities?"

Mayflower runs her eyes up and down Miss Moore's body as though studying some alien form of being.

"Baby, are you serious? Harvey Lester would've killed me, sure as I'm sittin' here! Without even so much as a change of expression."

Miss Moore purses her lips thoughtfully for a couple seconds, flips another form over in her notebook and scribbles on.

XXX XXX XXX

Sister Sadie scrunches herself up against the back of the sofa, inviting Father Love with a silent plea to sit on the edge. He ignores her move and drags a nearby chair over to sit on.

"Father, I'm so glad, thank the Lawd! That you could come to see me. I been feelin' so bad here lately. Somebody stole my lil' old tele-vision set...and...uh...I know how busy you are and..."

Father Love cuts in smoothly, obliquely...frowning his brow up a bit, the weariness of it all.

"Yes...yes...it's true. I am very busy in the service of our Father, Bless His Holy Name! But never too busy to comfort a member of my flock...never too busy.

Sister Sadie looks into Father Love's face shyly, trying to ignore the fact that they are holdin' hands.

XXX XXX XXX

"I see. Now then, let's go on. Do you have some source of income at this time?"

"Honey, I has nuthin' comin' in from nowheres! You hear me? Nuth-in!"

"Well...May, in my opinion, there seems to be a great possibility that our agency might be able to aid you. But first, it'll be necessary to contact Mr. Nick...what's his last name?"

Mayflower, casually cleaning his nails with a matchbook cover... "I never did know that fool's name...but the address is 333 E. Grove Street, just ask anybody where Nick's Jewel Box is."

XXX XXX XXX

Father Love pulls his left hand out of Sister Sadie's tight grasp and calmly places it on her well-rounded right breast.

"Now Sister...ahemm...Sister, I want you to say, after me, word for word, as you feel the Almighty Spirit of Our Father enter your heart and go through your body. I want you to say, and feel, yess... my dear sweet Sister Sadie...feel the Power!"

He massages her breast gently, erotically. "Say it Sister! Say to me...I feel the Power! I feel the Power! The Almighty Power of Our Father and He will make everything all right! *He* will make everything all right!"

Sister Sadie's eyes grow dreamy and her lips tremble a bit as she attempts to say the words.

XXX XXX XXX

"Well...thank you so much for the coffee, May. I'll be talking with you on Friday, or by next Monday at the latest. Here's my card. You may call me if you have any questions meanwhile...there are special provisions to aid single males...a lot of people don't know about them, but they're there."

Mayflower, from the corner of his mouth, softly..."hmff! Bet Harvey knows 'bout it."

Miss Moore gathers her belongings and reaches out to shake hands. "Well...once again, it's been enjoyable, coffee was delicious, I'll be talking with you."

Mayflower ignores her outstretched hand and plants a brush-kiss on her startled cheek. "Alrighty now, Cynthia...'bye now...you take care!"

XXX XXX XXX

Sister Sadie sucks in air passionately and chews lightly on her bottom lip.

"Ooooohhh Father...Father...I feel the Power, Father! I feel it! I feel the Power of Our Father and everything is goin' to be all right! Every thing...is...goin' to be all right!"

A delicate smile plays about the corners of Father Love's mouth as he plays with Sister Sadie's hardened nipple. "Now Sister...I want you to join me in silent prayer, in silent prayer to...to...reaffirm His Will be done."

Sister Sadie bows her head, peeping from under he eyelids at the soft, gentle hand kneading her breast... Father Love looks vaguely bored, stares at a crack in the wall above Sister Sadie's bowed head.

Dope – Bam and Baby June

As Miss Moore reaches the bottom step, waving at Mayflower blowing kisses through his lace curtains, Bam and Baby June turn the corner, spot her, exchange addicted-understanding looks...race toward Miss Moore on quiet junkie toes.

Bam pushes her roughly to one side while Baby June rips the purse from her arm...her glasses, notebook and form sheets splash all over the sidewalk. Miss Moore hits, dazed for a minute, on the sidewalk and then scrambles up to chase Bam and June.

"Help! Help!" She calls out to no one in particular. "Stop those men! They snatched my purse!"

Bam and Baby June reach the end of the block in a dead heat, cut up the alley. Miss Moore, sobbing, stumbles across the street to where Big Momma has coolly observed the whole scene go down.

Harry Matthews and Leo Terry smile cynically as they walk past Miss Moore...enter Mayflower's building and go up to the second floor.

Miss Moore jabs her finger angrily in the direction the purse-snatchers took. "They snatched my purse! They snatched my purse! Did you see them!? With all my credit cards and everything!"

Big Momma looks down at Miss Moore coldly, spits out a stream of snuff juice... "Yeahhhh...they been doin' that for quite awhile now...done probably bought some o' that ol' dope and shot it up by now."

"May I use your phone? Please?"

Big Momma quick scans both ends of the street, ignoring Miss Moore's question.

"May I use your phone, please?"

"Ain't got na'un."

"Oh my God! What am I going to do?"

Big Momma checks out her distracted behavior for a moment... "I'd say buy another purse...'bout the best thang I can tell you t' do."

"You don't understand! My beautiful Sicilian purse! What on earth will my mother say? She told me when I took this job...she told me..."

Miss Moore staggers down the street, leaving the block as quickly as possible, stockings torn, glasses cracked, hair messed up, muttering savagely to herself.

XXX XXX XXX

"I hate to leave you in your hour of trial 'n tribulation, but I must get on, Sister. You will be well enough to be at my side, along with the other sisters 'n brothers this comin' Sunday...won't you, Sister Sadie? I *do* need you to carry on the business of Our Father."

"I'm gon' certainly try to be there, Father Love. I feels positive, with the Lawd's blessin's 'n your prayers.

Slick Rina and Taco's P.O.V.

Taco McNeal and Slick Rina Dorsey, the talented tenants in the apartment above Mayflower, lean out of their window in time to see Miss Moore make a bedraggled disappearance. Taco, threading the wire ends of a pair of large, wheel-shaped earrings through her ears... "Looks like Bam 'n June done ripped off again!"

"Them two niggers would steal the sweetness out of a ginger cake."

"Dig who's talkin'!"

They exchange fives and remain in the window, checking out the mid-afternoon scene, wave down the block at Big Momma who returns their greetings politely, and continue gossiping about people, places and thangs.

XXX XXX XXX

Father Love bends over and suddenly lays a long, juicy kiss on Sister Sadie's full mouth...quickly retraces his steps to the door.

"Thank you, Father!" Sister Sadie beams at him, "Thank you for your blessin's!"

"I'm mighty happy to be able to pass along the blessin's of Our Father...wish I could help others to know the...ahem...blessed powers of Our Father...but...my work is always limited because of... wellllll, how can I put it, Sister? You know how expensive everything is these days."

Sister Sadie fumbles down into her ample cleavage, as Father Love makes a caterpillar movement back to the sofa's edge... "Father, I know it ain't much," she tells him, holding out a limp, crinkled-up bill, "but it's all I can give r'at now. Baby June just steals every cent I lay down...Lawd...I don't know what I'm gon' do with that boy.

Father Love plucks the bill from her hand with thumb and forefinger. "Thank you, Sister...thank you, the good Lawd bless 'n keep you for makin' this *small* donation in His Almighty Name." He pecks her swiftly on the cheek and jet-shuffles back to the door. He opens the door quickly, goes halfway out and leans back as though he has forgotten something.

"Remember Sister! Remember now, Father loves you!"

XXX XXX XXX

Outside her apartment, he looks disdainfully at the sweat-stained ten-dollar bill, pulls out a large, rubber band-bound roll of bills, adds the ten. And then, with a disgusted expression, spits into a brown bag of garbage leaning next to the Sister's door.

He walks quickly through the dim, burnt-bean and urine-stenched hallway, peering anxiously back over his shoulder.

He stands on the front steps for a brief moment or two, sucking in air and looking grand.

From across the street, Taco calls to him sarcastically... "Heyyy! Heyyy! Mr. Daddy Love!"

Father Love pretends not to hear, but finally, after Rina and Taco have shouted six or seven versions of his assumed name and title, he looks up at them hatefully.

"What's the happenin's, Father Lovely? How much you beat her out of this time?"

Father Love sniffs his aquiline nose up at them and camel struts down the stone slabbed steps.

"Awwwwww...so that's the way you gon' act, huh? Gon' try to front us off, huh?"

"Ain't that some shit! See that, Rina? That's the way it is, see how them jiveass niggers act when they get Cadillacs? Where you got yo' hog hidden this time, baby?"

Father Love pauses at the foot of the stairs and mouths a silent but fully articulated, "fuck you bitches!" up to them. The gesture infuriates the two women, who turn from polite sarcasm to pure venom.

"I wouldn't let you! You little fat assed cocksucker!"

"I wouldn't let you fuck it! But you sho' as hell could suck it! Just as soon as I pull this bloody rag out!"

Father Love, looking angry and embarrassed, hurriedly walks to the corner, running a gauntlet of insults.

"You better move faster than that! The Devil's on your track! Run creepy nigger! Run!"

"What did you do? Suddenly remember you had a Momma?"

"You really think he did? Lookin' like that?"

"Yeah honey...even faded bags o' turtle shit, like Fatherrrr Luvvvvv, had to have a Momma!"

"Maybe his Momma wasn't shit!"

"Right on!"

Big Momma watches and listens to the whole thing with a small frown on her brow...obviously displeased to hear young women using such language.

CHAPTER V

BO'GARDIN'

Urban Constipation

"Heyyyy!" Harry Mathews calls from within the apartment. "Why don't y'all close that window and quit fuckin' with that man? He's just tryin' to do his thang, just like the rest of us...and besides, you lettin' all this good smoke out!" The two women, seeing the logic of the suggestion, close the window, slurring out a stream of open-edged cuss words. The apartment is shadowy, sparsely furnished...a portable record player, two beat-up sofas, a couple of sprung loose easy chairs, a small coffee table, holding on its top a dime bag, a gram of neatly diced hash, one pack of Bambu papers... and 'round the table goes the pipe, to Fred Lee, Harry Mathews, Jake the Fake Willis and Leo Terry.

Slick Rina, crossing the smoke-heavy room to get to the record player... "That just gets to me sometimes, watchin' that lil' old jiveass punk rip those old sisters off like that."

"They say he's got two or three old wrinkled up rich white broads stickin' coin to him too."

"Where, Leo?

"I don't know where...somewhere...that's what they say."

Slick Rina, changing sides on the box... "Yeahhhh...yeahhhh... that's cool, that's cool. He oughta stick it to all the old wrinkled up White bitches he can reach, they can afford it."

She pauses and turns to the group with one hand planted aggressively on her hip. "You know somethin'? I wish some jinny ass nigger would even dare try to approach me with some of the bullshit...ha! Father Luvvvv! Ain't that some shit!?"

Harry Mathews, listening to Slick Rina and keeping an eye on the hash pipe at the same time, comes down on Fred Lee. "Goddamn Fred Lee! I been watchin' yo' greedy ass! Whatchu gon' do? Smoke all of it?"

"Be cool, man. You act like you ain't never had no (coff!) (coff!) hash (coff! coff!) before (coff! coff!) coff!)." He reluctantly passes the pipe on to Harry, wracked into a coughing spasm by the hash smoke.

Harry drags on the pipe... "I notice a funny thing about you (puff!) (puff!) Fred Lee...(coff!) no matter what goes around (puff! puff! puff! whewww! coff! coff!)...that's some pretty nice smoke. Yeahhh...no matter (coff! coff!) what's goin' around...you always seem to be (puff! puff!)...the mother (coff! coff!) who gets the lion's share. Why is that? (coff! coff! coff!)."

Jake the Fake, slyly observing the scene from an elbow-rest position on the sofa... "Shiiii-it! Both you niggers is hogs!" Leo Terry leans over to slap Jake's palm in agreement. "Right on, bruh! Right on!"

The pipe is refilled and passed...Lady Day, Miss Flack, Brother Hathaway and Coltrane, both Alice and John, are played, turned over and played again.

Taco, renowned for her delicate touch, rolls four joints and passes them around behind the pipe.

Eyeballs redden, lids weigh themselves down, the talk becomes contagious.

Harry, with a wind to those in the know, signifies with Leo. "Hey man...when's the last time you seen yo' runnin' buddy, Old Gimps?"

Leo, holding marijuana smoke in, "Mannn!" ...almost loses it answering the question, sucks it back down quickly, "Mannn! Don't talk to me about that lame-ass motherfucker! The last time me 'n that fool was together, he got me put in jail!"

"What happened, Leo?"

Leo takes a couple quick hits on the last half-inch of his joint, settles back....

"He stumbled up in my face one day, tellin' me he'd just put in a day pearl divin' at some restaurant on the Northside, and that the White boy who owned the place kept grand theft dough in a cracker box in the rear of the joint."

"See him?!" There go Fred Lee again, bo'gardin' the smokes!"

"Be quiet, Harry! Shit! Go 'head, Leo."

Leo looks indulgently at Fred Lee and continues. "Well... anyway. I was suspicious of the old bastard, you know? I mean, he's one o' them natural bone liars...just like somebody else we know. But I was goin' through one of those deep money slumps...luck was out to lunch...so I decided to go on and try to pull off a little sting with the old asshole. He'd made it sound so easy I couldn't resist. 'All you got to do', Leo, he says to me, 'is climb up over some shit in the back of the joint, rip off and walk on out the front door if you want to. You dig?' It was gon' be that clean. Awright...sounded mellow to me, so I runs on to the pad, puts my 'work clothes' on and goes over to Gimpy's place to get the complete lowdown on the thing before we 'sposed to get over there, by 12:00 p.m."

There is a sudden screeching noise from the street…the sound of someone's car brakes being suddenly applied. All heads turn quickly toward the sound but Rina's...she takes a hard hit on the joint and mumbles... "Kill 'im! He ain't no kin t' me!"

"You sho' is cold Rina," Jake tells her, with just a tinge of admiration in his tone.

"Gotta be, sweetthang...life is a cold-blooded game."

Leo catches the last half-inch of another joint making the round and goes on.

"Awright...me 'n Gimps sit around, him givin' me the full rundown on the setup, 'til...ooooo, 'bout 11:00 or so, drinkin' wine 'n smokin' some of the baddest weed I'd smoked in a long while. I really didn't know how bad the shit was 'til we got on the bus headin' north. Yeah Jake! The fuckin' bus! That's how cold it was! Hahahhah...I'm listenin' with all ears to this old motherfucker run this bullshit down on me, tellin' me 'bout how much pussy I'd be able to buy 'n shit, ...when all of a sudden I look up 'round us, and discover we the only niggers on the bus. When the motherfucker had said, out north...I just thought, you know, he meant out...North. I don't know where my head was, behind that jive wine and that bad gunny. We had got so far off in one of them snow-lily-white neighborhoods, I was scared that me might git busted for ridin' in the front of the bus. But...well, anyway, it's too late now, and besides I'm feelin' kinda White myself, what with all that pluck and weed in my system."

He pauses to take a grateful hit on the joint making the current round.

"We must've really been unnoticed...just about as unnoticed as Death strollin' downtown munchin' on a dry soda cracker! Gimpy, with his black ass, had on a white beaver skin hat, the brim turned down all around, and he's scuttlin' 'long like a fuckin' crab...got nerve, if you can b'lieve it! T' be tryin' to high step off that light green!"

The people in the room break into laughter, contagious, marijuana-hash laughter...sustained, rib-tickling laughter.

"Maaannnnn! I don't know who we thought we was! Gimpy was fucked-up lookin' with his hat 'n shit, but I was just as bad. I had on a new pair o' Staceys, yaller as canaries, and since I had my hair conked in them days, I had my 'do rag 'round my skull. And we was supposed to be goin' t do a job lookin'...uh...uh..."

"In-conspicuous!"

"Thank you, Professor Lee...yeahhh, that. But I don't think it was workin' out too damned swell. I didn't really notice at the time, but I guess every hunkie in the neighborhood must've called the po-lice soon as they saw us walkin' down the street."

Taco stares at Leo, frowning.

"You say you had a 'do rag on?"

"Yes m'am! I had my 'do rag on... I hadn't got Black and proud yet. Number one, I was too po' to be proud, and if someone had called me Black, I would've been insulted."

A knock on the door freezes everyone, stifles beginning laughter. They look at each other paranoidly. The two women drop the dope on the table down into their panties, the men stuff out the roaches and curl them into their inner palms. Quickly, Rina steps to the door, leans her ear against it for a moment before asking, "Yeah... who is it?"

After a long pause, tightening everybody in the room a bit more, a tired voice answers... "It's me, baby...me, Baby June." The group relaxes, and immediately slips back off into the groove.

Rina opens the door a full six inches worth. "Whatchu want, June?"

Baby June, his quick ferret eyes darting over her head, his nostrils sniffing hungrily at the dope fumes... "Uh ruh...dig Slick, me and Bro' Bam done copped a half box load of pants suit sets and...we... sniff...sniff...uh ruh...wanted to see if you or Taco wanted...?"

Fred Lee calls out from across the room..."Hey June! Why don't y'all come on back through in a couple hours from now? I'm 'spectin' some change to be laid on me in a lil' while, soon as my woman gets home. We might be able to do each other some good then."

"Yeah June," Rina adds, firmly, slowly closing the door. "Come on back in a couple hours."

"Yeah...awright Miss Lady," June says, a hurt look in his eyes. "I'll catch y'all later on!"

Rina re-bolts the door and steps away from it with a malicious smile on her face. "You really think he's got somethin' nice?"...she asks Fred Lee.

"Shiiii-it! You can't never tell 'bout Bam and June. I've bought some boss things from 'em, from time-to-time." He holds out his wrist, "Can you dig this gin-u-wine Swiss movement timepiece?"

"Yeah...if they say they got somethin', nine times outta ten, they got somethin'...either that, or they'll run right out and beat somebody for it."

Taco turns her back to the men, modestly...goes down into her panties to retrieve the hidden dope.

"Go 'head," she tells Leo, "go 'head 'n finish your story...I know y'all went through some changes."

Rina heads for the toilet with a mischievous smile on her face... "Hold on a minute! Lemme go clean this pack off." Taco cracks up, understanding immediately what the deal is. The men look at each other, puzzled for a minute before the full realization comes down. Fred Lee wrinkles his nostrils subconsciously.

"Awwwww goddamn, Rina! You mean t' tell me...!?"

The men sit looking vaguely disgusted, as Taco is taken by little giggle-spasms from time to time. Rina returns to the scene, straightening her skirt and wiping the glassine baggie off with a bit of toilet paper... "Didn't get *too* wet."

"You sho' is cold, baby," Jake smiles at her, in spite of the situation... "Sho' is cold."

Rina tosses the bag back on the table and tells him, "Don't worry 'bout it, it's still smokeable."

Taco begins to clean and roll a couple more joints, the atmosphere of the crib slips into a mellower groove, having been touched by a threat, a danger that really wasn't a danger at all. Hail Baby June!

"Awright Leo, what the fuck happened?"

"Like I said...we in this lily-White neighborhood. Done got

'round in the alley, to the rear of the place and I'm climbing up through the window...high as a motherfucker! Gimpy hadn't told me that the motherfuckin' window as almost two stories off the ground. Anyway, I climbs in, locates the cracker box right where he said it would be, skim a nice little taste off the top 'n then I pull Gimps up and we split the rest on the spot. Came to 'bout three bills apiece, 'scusin' my extra taste. Awright...we gettin' away clean! Dig it!? But nawww! Gimpy, with his crazy ass, got to stop and brew some coffee!"

The room suddenly suspends its motion, the joints pause in mid-toke, mouths are turned onto cynical angles and a chorus of disbelief sputters out from all present.

"Bullshit!"

"You got t' be jivin'!"

"Awww shiiii-it!"

"Uh hah hah!"

"Sho' is cold brother...sho' is cold!"

Leo gestures urgently, trying to convince everyone of the truth of the thing.

"I swear fo' God! If I'm lyin' I hope God'll strike me dead! Gimps had dug the cat who owned the place makin' this...uh... expresso shit, and he had had a couple cups, back in the kitchen, between trays...so I guess he figures now was a good time for him to have a cup out front. Or somethin'! I'll never know what was on the brother's mind! 'Cause Lawd knows I wasn't in the right frame o' mind my ownself!

"Anyway, you dig? I'm tellin' him...mannnn, pick up a couple bags o' the shit and take on home and make it! And he's tellin' me, I ain't got no expresso machine to do it with, and I'm tellin' him, nigger! You got three hundred motherfuckin' dollars - buy yourself one! And there we are, arguin' 'n carryin' on, both of us loaded back! And the next thing I knew, the damned joint is surrounded by fifty squad cars, three helicopters, eight Hollywood spotlights and half the motherfuckin' neighborhood! You would've thought they was comin' in after Dillinger or somebody. Well...hahhaaaa hahhhhh...anyway, to make a long story short, by the time the pigs came in on us, I had tried my goddamnest to beat Gimpy's ass to death! Po-lice thought it was really funny...two niggers fightin' over some bags of coffee on their way to the Black Maria. I ain't seen Gimps since then, and that was 'bout five years ago...and, quiet as it's kept, I don't wanna see him either."

Jake leans over to drop a palm onto Leo's outstretched hand... "Yeah...I can dig it, man! I can really dig it!"

"We've done all got caught up in them binds, brother. Believe me! I got busted on a hummer, somethin' like that, my first day in."

"'Scuse me, Taco," Fred Lee pops in politely. "Hey Rina, whatchu got to snack on, baby? I could really dig some sweets, 'round about now."

Harry, for the first time, reaffirms a feeling with Fred Lee... "Hey...that sho' is a good idea. I could dig somethin' sweet myself."

Rina goes into the small kitchen section, makes jelly sandwiches... weaves back into the main room with a plate full.

"How 'bout it? Can y'all dig some jelly bread sandwiches?"

The apartment, in one of those hip, dope, comatose stages by now, flutters with feelings, both honest and slick...full of implication.

"Watch Fred Lee!"...Harry Mathews calls out. "He 'a spoon out the whole jar, if you don't watch 'im!"

Fred Lee, snatching up a grape-jelly sandwich, "Fuck you in your nose, motherfucker!"

All of the people in the room munch on jelly slammed on bread, momentarily meditate as their jaws gently crunch air-filled white bread and too sweet jam...ruminating.

Taco, munching on her sandwich, looks over at Rina and starts giggling.

"Okay...Taco! Don't start that shit!"

"Lemme tell 'em about what happened to us yesterday?"

"Girl! Don'tchu mention that!"

"Awww Rina! Shit! Lemme tell 'em about it! It was funny as hell! Ha!ha!ha!ha! Me 'n Rina was in this supermarket buyin' somethin' for a change..."

Jake the Fake responds to the idea with mock humor, "I don't believe it! You all were actually buyin' somethin?'"

Taco puffs her nose into the air and announces, in a dry, cool voice, "Yes dearie...we were shopping. Just plain ordinary shoppin'. Well...we had stuck a few packs of baloney away in different places, but most of the stuff was in the cart... Anyway...how did you manage to wind up with...?"

"We made a bet, remember?"

"Oh yeahhhhh...we made a bet, me 'n Rina...that she couldn't get out of the store with a big item. Hah! hah! She puffs her chest out at me..."

"Y'all musta been loaded huh?"

Taco circles her natural with a quick defensive touch... "Ahhhem...yes, we were," puffs her bosom out full force. "You know somethin'? I bet I could walk outta here with anything I wanted, she says t' me. Betcha can't, I says to her, you know, like a challenge... but not really meanin' for it to be a challenge."

Rina, puffing quietly on a joint, smiles, and shines it on.

"Shit! she says, I could walk out of this fuckin' store with half a shelf fulla this jazz if I wanted to...go 'head, pick somethin'! Go 'head, pick somethin' fo' me, she says to me. So...teeee hahhh hahhhhhah! hah! huahhh! I picks one o' those Polish hams, you know, the five-pound ones in the can?"

"Oh wowwww!"

"Yeah baby...a five-pound canned Polish ham!"

"What was the bet?" Leo asks, toking up.

"What did we bet? A pack of cigarettes?" Rina asks, her eyes telling everyone she remembers what the bet was.

"A pack, hell! We bet a carton!"

Rina smacks Taco's outstretched palm in reaffirmation of the truth... "Right on! A carton, that's right, a carton!"

"This chick takes the ham, this five-pound canned ham, goes to the end of the aisle...ho hum ho hum...and wedges it up 'tween her legs and walks back past me just as cool as you please. I'm lookin' at her and thinkin'...if this bitch gets outta here with a ham between her legs...I'm gon' pay her double. I'm not jivin'... I felt a lil' bit shaky...but everything is cool...we stand in the checkout line, chit-chattin'...you dig? Just two lil' nilly dilly housewives doin' their weekly shoppin' ...gits up to the checkout girl...by this time I'm about to bust out laughin'...and the security guard strolls by and gives us the eye.

"We thought he was checkin' us out, at first."

"But nawww," Taco continues, "that wasn't it, the nigger was gittin' flirty...not only that, the checkout girl has to call one o' the managers over to ask the price of somethin' we had, and the next thing I know, with the manager on one side of us and this Uncle Tom guard on the other side, I hear a loud clunk. The man behind us looked down between Rina's legs and said somethin' like...Uh... hey lady...you dropped your ham!"

"The damned thing almost broke my ankle."

"Awww, but you played it off really beautiful. She bends over, oh so ladylike and says... Why thank you, sir...thank you very much. And placed it up on the counter with the rest of the stuff, like it had just been pushed off, or somethin'. And then we staggered out past the guard, laughin' our asses off!"

"I'm still waitin' for my carton 'o cigarettes."

"If I recall correctly...we had to pay for that damn ham...which makes it a complete different thang altogether, a helluva lot different from boostin'."

Fred Lee, his eyes darting from one face to another, opens his mouth on the con. "You all really somethin' else. I'm tellin' you the truth! Really somethin' else...uh...coff! coff!...we smoke all that hash?"

"Naw, we didn't smoke it all." Harry answers, on his way to the toilet. "We got some left, go 'head, fire it up. This'll be the last time I go in on anything with you, with yo' greedy ass."

"Fuck you in yo' armpit, motherfucker!" Fred Lee calls after him, in a half-serious manner.

A gentle tapping on the door cools everyone out. "Damn! I bet that's Bam and June and I ain't even been home to check my trap yet."

Rina whispers loudly on her way to the door... "Did you see the look on Baby June's face when I opened the door and he sniffed all that good hash smoke?"

"Hahhahhah...it wouldn't have done him any good anyway, not even if we had given him a hit! I don't think he and Bam can get high from smokin' anymore."

"Probably not...not behind Mr... Jones."

"Yeahhhh...who it is?"

"Me, baby."

Rina opens the door a pinch before realizing her mistake.

Two Black detectives in stylish dress blast through the door, followed by their superior, a White boy. Fred Lee, Taco, Leo and Jake the Fake, their states of mind immediately and intensely altered by the abrupt intrusion, scramble for the back door, to be confronted by more policemen. The group is rounded up in the living room.

"Jackson, you and Rogers go over this place with a fine tooth comb. They've probably got narcotics stashed all over the damned joint."

The two Black detectives go about their work with a will, throwing sofa pillows on the floor, pulling things apart.

"Uh...Officer, have you got a search warrant?" Jake asks the White boy.

"Move it, Jake!" he snarls at him. "We don't need one to get the goods on you!"

Harry nonchalantly strolls out of the john, buttoning his fly. Realizing what the deal is, he casually turns to re-enter the toilet as though it were the most natural thing in the world to do.

Officer Jackson pulls him back out by the neck. "One more t' go."

A few curious people stand around in front of the building, watching the group being led out with sullen, hostile faces. Big Momma stands up, both hands braced on her ropy waistline, to better check out the happenin's. Bam and Baby June, lurking amongst the faces in the small crowd, signal to the group being led away that they didn't bring the goods. Fred Lee holds his cuffed wrists up and shrugs in a disgusted manner.

Big Momma reseats herself as the squad cars roll past, whips her snuff from side to side in her bottom lip and spits out a hard, heavy stream of brown juice.

XXX XXX XXX

Evening time, streets crowded, folks returning from the plantations, back to the reservation, a Bantustan that is politely not called that, ghetto is more acceptable. Kids playing, unmindful of anything and everything but play. Rudy and a small group stand on a corner after having sold their strength again today...rappin'.

Bessie Mae Black, neither young nor old, a bit stocky in shape, dark-skinned and wearing a natural hairstyle that is more the result of hard work and sweat than design, trudges unsteadily up the street carrying a shopping bag in each hand. She pauses on the fringes of the small group of men gathered on the corner, resting her bags and casually listening to Rudy, Kwendi and the others.

"Okay, Kwendi...you say we got twenty two million Black people in the United States, huh? I say we got twice that many! Maybe three times that many, if you could count all the 1/15ths 'n whatnot we got runnin' 'round!"

A Chair, A Chain, an Epic...figure it out.

Kwendi Jones, shaking his head in a very irritated manner. "Probably so...more than likely, but all of 'em ain't committed to revolution! And what we got to have is Black folks who ain't afraid of revolution!"

"What revolution?! What goddamned revolution...?!" Niggers buyin' more Black is Beautiful hairspray and forgettin' they got minds! Niggers wearin' dashikis, really 'sposed to be called Danshikis!" And tryin' to figure out the next brother's political phi-losophy by how long his chin whiskers is! Niggers goin' to see jiveass movies made by Whitey that tell them how to act! That ain't no revolution! Malcolm told us what a revolution was! Naww, brother! Whatchu talkin' 'bout is on the outside, the face thing! You don't go into no revolution lettin' your enemy have a script of what you plannin' to do next!"

Kwendi cuts off Rudy's speechmaking abruptly. "Awright! Awright! You always talkin' theory, now get down to somethin' practical. You *do* agree to that, don't you?"

"You motherfuckin' right! By any and all means necessary! But first of all we gonna have to get rid of a lot of this superficial bullshit we got goin' on. I ain't sayin', don't be *us*, 'cause we probably the grooviest thing goin' on this cold, foul, jiveass country..."

Ojenkasi, his lips pursed in disgust, leans close to Rudy. "Brother, there you go again! Talkin' outta both sides of your mouth!"

"No Ojenkasi! Nooooo, I'm not! Lemme finish? I'm sayin' this, in order to change this shit, by any means necessary...what we gonna have to do is take care maximum business. And learn how to stop talkin' so gotdamned much! And payin' less attention to all these rituals we got goin' on. Do you know I stood up on the corner shakin' hands with a dude for five minutes the other day? We shook hands upside down, inside out, from the side to side and I don't know from where else, and that same dude would break into my crib and rip every damned thing off the first chance he got, or else he'd stab me in the back, if he thought he could get away with it."

"Mannn...damn all this ramblin', get to the point!"

"Hey brother"...Rudy's face develops serious lines, "I ain't ramblin', I know exactly what I'm talkin' about. I'm sayin' three things, I'm sayin' the war, the revolution has to take place, number one, in us...yeah, *us*! When we stop beatin' n killin' each other rappin' some jazz about brotherhood. Or sayin' Whitey made us do it. Number two, the revolution has got to be a battle between the Haves and the Have-nots...and I ain't talkin' 'bout His-story, or how the shit got that way. I'm talkin' 'bout how much stronger our thang would be if we pulled in all those Third World brothers 'n sisters, and as many of those po' ass crackers as possible, the ones who've gotten their heads straightened out."

"Get to the point, brother! And stop b.s.in' 'round!"

"I'm tryin' to! If you'd shut your goddamned mouth!"

"Who you tellin' t shut up?!"

"You, motherfucker! That's who!"

Kwendi and Rudy square off, baited by the agitating around them.

"That's the trouble with you niggers!" Bessie Mae Black yells out, above the hubbub... "That's the trouble! You always ready t' kick *each other* in the ass! Or else talk each other to death, but you ain't never willin' to lissen to each other."

Something in the strength and tone of Bessie's voice pulls heads her way, a couple people comment behind their hands about the slurred texture of her words.

"Bitch sounds like she's drunk t' me."

"Dig her!"

"I don't even know what the damned argument was all about... but if it's like the rest of that Black-Black-Black bullshit I hear passin' this corner every evenin'...I'd be willing to bet anybody that he could go his way, and he could go his way and both o' y'all would wind up in the same place! What difference do it make how each one o' y'all get there, or what you wearin', or any that, long as you Git! One damned thing is for damned certain! You sho' in hell ain't gon' git no place fightin' each other!"

"Right on sister!" bubbles from the throat of someone in the crowd.

"Speak t' 'em, Momma!"

Bessie, hefting her bags... "You so-called Black men gimme a pain in my ass. Whitey send y'all over the goddamned world fightin' for him, bring ya home and stick you back down in the ghetto, and all you can think of doin' is fightin' each other."

Bessie trudges slowly away from the group...muttering. "Black men! Hmf! I bet both o' you niggers got some lil old White chick off somewhere..."

Rudy, glancing around self-consciously, calls out to Bessie... "Who you make love to ain't got nothin' to do with our struggle."

Bessie stops and drops both bags to the pavement, turns to face Rudy with both eyes gleaming. "It ain't, huh?! Well...goddamnit! If that's the case then, why don't you fools stop woofin' at each other and git on out there 'n Struggle! I think y'all fulla shit! That's what I think!"

She picks her bags up and continues up the street, the weight of each bag forcing her into a wobbly, rolling walk.

The small group quietly melts away, leaving Kwendi Jones and Rappin' Rudy facing each other. They stand, looking sternly at each other for a minute, and then burst into spontaneous smiles.

Kwendi wipes a mock sweat from his forehead, tosses the imaginary droplets onto the ground. "Oh wowwwww! I feel like the sister just ripped a new hole in my buns!"

"Right on!" Rudy replies, and lays double slaps on Kwendi's palms to reaffirm it.

"Sister had some nice points."

"Yeah...she's on her job," Rudy replies, "but then, Bessie always has been outspoken. Even if it was outta pocket, she'd still say it."

"I can dig it. Looka here Rudy...I got to get on, gimme a ring later on, I got somethin' I want to lay on you."

"Okay...cool. How you and Lubertha doin'?"

"Couldn't be sweeter...just couldn't be."

They shake Afro-Power-Now and split...smiles.

XXX XXX XXX

Bessie Mae Black reaches the bottom step of the entrance to her tenement apartment building. Big Momma sits, in her day-long position, on the porch at the top of the cracked stone steps.

Other tenants of the building, trying to cop a stray breeze from anywhere, lounge about the steps sipping warmish brews and fanning themselves with folded newspapers.

Bessie exchanges casual nods with the people and weaves up to Big Momma.

Big Momma double-checks the bulk of the bags. "Goodness gracious, Bessie Mae! I bet you didn't leave them folks nothin'!"

Bessie leans over into Big Momma's face...she recoils slightly from the smell of alcohol on Bessie's breath.

"You right, Big Momma...almost. I walked 'way with 'bout much as I could steal...and drink!"

Big Momma folds her heavy arms across her mountainous breasts and chuckles. "Go 'head, Miss Bessie Mae Black! Go 'head wid yo' bad self, honey!"

Several people, lower down on the steps, look up to check out the ebullient happenings.

"They may not pay me a damned thing! But you can bet a fat man I ain't gon' starve because of it." Bessie grabs up her bags again, starts to struggle upstairs.

Big Momma grabs her arm as she goes by, holds on firmly. "Uh...what you got in those bags, daughter?" she asks her in a confidential voice.

They check each other out like major league conspirators. "You wanna see...you wanna see what I got?" Bessie sets the bags back down again and bends down into one.

"Number one, I got some chicken pot pies, you know how much Fred Lee likes chicken pot pies..."

"Bessie," Big Momma attempts to interrupt, "I got somethin' to..."

"Awwww shit! I just remembered, my refrigerator ain't workin'. Would you keep these in your box, Big Momma? You can have one. And here, I got a quart bottle of what looks like water but..." she leans close and whispers drunkenly into Big Momma's ear... "it ain't...it's some o' that fancy English gin."

"Daughter, I don't see how in the world you manage to walk out with all this stuff."

"They got so much stuff they don't even know it's gone. And right here...I have some...uh...Big Momma, you know what a P-A-T-E is?"

Big Momma pulls her spectacles out of her apron pocket, squints over the rims at the two cans... "P...A...T...E... hmmm...I'll be damned if I know! Oh...oh yes m'am! I do know what this stuff is. I 'member seein' it on the pantry shelf, in an old rich White woman's house I used to wash for, down home. It's some o' that cat food rich White folks puts on they crackers 'n whatnot, at parties 'n stuff. Daughter, you sho' these is cullud folks you workin' for?"

Bessie takes a quick sip of the gin, turns back to Big Momma with a grimace. "Might be hard t' tell what the lady of the house is...but the man is a sho' nuff Black man, if color has anything to do with it."

"Hmf! Well, I say! Cullud folks sho' is eatin' some strange stuff these days."

"Umm huh...and, down here, in the bottom o' this one, I got three silk shirts for Freddie..."

"Sit down here for a minute, daughter...that's what I been tryin' to talk to you 'bout since you walked up."

"Huh?"

Big Momma looks sadly up the street at a group of children playing tag, darting in and out of the street from between parked cars.

"Fred Lee's in jail, baby."

"In jail?! For what?!"

"Well"... Big Momma shrugs, "I don't rightfully know for what. But I saw the po-lice pullin' him, Leo, Jake Willis, Harry Mathews 'n nim out of...uh...Taco and Slick Rina's place this afternoon."

Tears slide down Bessie's cheeks... "I told that fool to stay 'way from them thugs! If I told 'im once, I must've told 'im a thousand times, stay 'way from them thug-ass niggers! They don't mean you no good! No good at all! All they do is steal, lie and cheat...but nawww he wouldn't listen to me...just wouldn't listen."

Big Momma pulls a small packet of Kleenex out of her pocket, silently hands it to Bessie, a deep, compassionate look on her face.

Bessie dabs at the tears, wipes her eyes. "Big Momma, would you keep this stuff for me? I guess I better run-on down t' the station t' see what I can do."

"Don't be too hard on 'im, daughter... Not bein' able to find a job and all, after comin' back from that Viet'nese war and everything... couldn't have done too much for the boy's morale. You go 'head and do whatchu can, I'll keep this stuff 'til you get back. Uh...you better let me have that firewater too, don't make no sense gettin' all fuzzy-minded 'n goin' down there t' talk to those people."

"Wait! Before you take that in...lemme have a lil' shot? I need somethin' for my nerves."

"Well...come on in the house, I'll give ya a glass."

The two women lug a shopping bag apiece into Big Momma's first floor apartment.

Mrs. Hattie Evans leans out of her second-floor window, scans the block quickly. "Any o' y'all seen Phyllissine?" she calls downstairs.

One of the women looks up to Mrs. Evans, points to the end of the block. "I saw her turn the corner, lil' while ago...with Chu-man."

The muscles in Mrs. Evans's jaw lump up as she turns from the window shaking her head. "I done told that girl...!"

On the third floor, directly across the street from Miss Rabbit's apartment - apartment #300... Lubertha Franklin, a well-developed, eighteen-year-old girl-sister-woman, with a beautifully shaped mushroom Afro, sits on the edge of her bed by the window in her cramped bedroom, looking down onto the street and writing on the uneven bottom surface of a straight-backed kitchen chair.

Lubertha's eyes swim up and down the street, take in the sight of lazy scraps of paper gently drifting along on the early evening breezes, the stacked piles of garbage at the curb on both side of the street, waiting...since week before last, to be picked up. People moving along in a slow stream, coming home to their section of the layered cake.

Old dudes sit across from each other, a checkerboard braced on their knees, making a move from time-to-time, oblivious to everything but their game.

Bam and June on the nod, on the prowl, on the nod, on the prowl, a vicious cycle.

Two White men in uniform, with badges on their chests, in a squad car, slowly wheel through the neighborhood...looking cold, mean, merciless, White. They ease past the Afro-Lords, sitting on the front steps of Lena Daniels' building, rappin'.

Lubertha's eyes mist over a bit, watching Bessie Mae Black stagger out of Big Momma's apartment and up the street. "What the hell is there to cry about?" she asks herself aloud, surprised to hear the sound of her voice above all the other sounds spilling into her open window.

Lubertha places her pencil carefully on the chair bottom beside her paper and starts to wipe the beginning tears from her eyes, but while her hands are there, she pauses to sniff at the odors coming from the food being cooked in her mother's kitchen...the sudden, rank smell of burnt beans from another open window in the building. The sudden shifting of a breeze brings her another smell and then another one...almost too many for her nostrils to deal with.

And then, subtly, as she removes her hands from her eyes, leaving them closed...noises swirl around in her ears...replacing the smells.

The music of every description forcing a framework for every other sound...the quick laughter, from somewhere a baby crying, the rumbling, screechy grind of a nearby elevated train, the impatient yelling of Mrs. Evans for her daughter Phyllissine...and from below her, on the second floor, the savage sound of two people fighting, the clear, furious sound of things being thrown, broken, the rotten curses screamed out. A large piece of something being thrown jars Lubertha's eyes open, the piece of whatever it is seeming so close that she involuntarily flinches back.

Her eyes open, instantly, draw themselves to the wall opposite her bed, to a hole sealed by the tin top of a can. The tin seal bulges, buckles as though pressure is being applied from the other side. Lubertha stares at the tin buckling, fascinated...but realizing exactly who and what is causing the round piece of tin nailed into the rotted wood to give way, more and more with each inner push.

She quietly curls her legs up under her and waits, her eyes slowly going from the open window, where the twilight casts shadows on her walls, to the hole. The tin seal falls away from the hole with a light metallic clatter and seconds later, a slender gray head pulls a large, quivering body through the hold.

Lubertha's breath comes in short, frightened bursts as she studies the rat's body, the gray hair missing from his back, singed away by some long ago accident, revealing gnarled pink skin.

The rat moves along the baseboard a few inches at a time, in swift, darting motions. He turns slowly to face Lubertha, his tail twitching against the wall, as though he had known she was there all the time but had decided not to pay her any attention unless absolutely necessary.

His brother slips out through the hole in one swift motion...a larger, healthier version. The two rats, making small, nervous movements, keep their bead eyes trained on Lubertha as they sniffle along an inch at a time.

Lubertha moves her eyes around, wildly, for something to throw at them. Only her shoes are in reach, but on the floor, and the thought of reaching down to where the rats' fangs are, almost turns her stomach. Finally, having cast around for whatever might be throwable, and finding nothing, she frantically slaps her hands together and makes a loud "shoose" noise.

The rats give her an insolent look and waddle back into their hole...the one with the hair missing turns to look out at her from the darkness of the hole, his small round eyes burning. Lubertha claps her hands again and the eyes disappear. She sits, tightened up, breathing hard, feels her heart and smiles at the thought of how scared she felt...jumps off of her bed vengefully and takes her shoe heel to hammer the covering back on the hole, returns to the bed slightly out of breath and leans back wistfully against the wall, casually looking at two silhouetted figures on Miss Rabbit's rooftop across the street, passing a slow-burning joint back and forth between them.

Mrs. Charlotte Franklin, a middle-aged version of her daughter, leans against the doorway to her daughter's room, arms folded, looking at her affectionately.

"Lubertha...why don't you turn on some light? You gonna be blind as a bat trying to read and write in the dark...or are you just sittin' up mooning about that young man? What's his name?

Lubertha turns from the open window to study her mother's face in the fading light.

"Whose name? she asks, bringing herself all the way back.

"Your young man...the one with funny name?"

"Oohh Kwendi. I wasn't thinking about him, I was thinking about a better mousetrap."

Mrs. Franklin wrinkles her brow, a familiar expression with her of parental indulgence. She steps into the room to glance at the sheets of paper on Lubertha's chair-desk.

"What're you writing?"

"A poem."

"A poem! My God! I thought you were writing a new Declaration of Independence or somethin'', long as you've been at it."

"Who knows? Might be someday...we could sure use a brand new one. You want to hear it?"

"Honey...I'd like to, but your Daddy'll be home in five minutes, hungry as a bear...and if I don't have it on the table, ...well, you know how he is! Uh...why don't you read it to me later?"

Mrs. Franklin bustles away to the kitchen as Lubertha stares, absent-mindedly, at the covered hole on the other side of the room. And then back out onto the darkening street.

CHAPTER VI

THE PINK LADY, HIMSELF

Trip lightly, sweetheart...and take pride in the idea that you are one of the few flowers allowed to grow, develop and blossom on the ghetto streets...trip lightly, sweetheart...trip lightly...

Fantasy in a Jug...

Tap tap! tap tap! ...tap! tap!

Mayflower cocks his ear cautiously toward his back door.

"Yesssss, who is it?"

"It's me, Miss Sweetthang...Bam."

Mayflower places a lid on the pot of greens he has been stirring, touches the finger curls at his ears, and swishes to the door, shortie p.j. top open to his navel. He opens the door halfway, poses seductively.

"Why are you all comin' to the back door? Must've stolen somethin'?"

"Uh...no m'am," Baby June answers, scratching the side of his face absently, "we just peddlin' magazines, t' try to git through college. Can you dig this?" He brings his other hand out from behind his back, Miss Moore's purse in it.

"Bayyy-beee!" he squeals, "you know goddamned well I can dig it! June...I know exactly where you got that from!"

"That's beside the point...gimme twenty for it."

Mayflower's exuberance dies quickly and is replaced by a shrewd, lady-shopper look.

"I ain't got that much money t' my name."

"Awww, come on now, sweetthang! This is us! You know damn well you got twenty bones! This thing is worth sixty or sevenny dollars at least."

"If not more!" Bam pops in, giving Mayflower a dirty look.

"I'm not sayin' it ain't worth that much..." Mayflower answers, dimpling a bit, "I'm just sayin' i ain't got that much."

"Tell ya what...give us fifteen bucks and you got yo'self an outta sight purse."

Mayflower flutters his hands up to his chest, flattens his palms across his chest and looks positively angelic.

"Baby June...I swear on my dear Momma's grave I ain't got but nine dollars! That's all the money I got in the world! Fo' real!"

"Awww sit! Mayflower!" Bam spits out in total disgust.

"I ain't jivin'! You know I lost my lil' old gig...that's why that chick was here in the first place, Harvey had told me what to do. Now you *know* if I had it..."

"Yeahhh! Yeahhh! Awright! Awright! Don't go into yo' motherfuckin' act! Give us the nine dollars and save that fucked-up story for somebody else."

"Wait right here...be right back!"

Mayflower closes the door quickly and sweeps breathlessly through her small kitchen, checks the pot simmering on the back burner, reaches up for a jar labeled "cookies," pulls a wad of bills out and carefully peels nine ones off the roll.

He turns back to the door, carefully composes his face and opens the door...a little less this time.

"Maybaby...you know you gettin' the best of this bargain... I guess you know that, don't you?"

"Yeahhh...you really are, Maygirl."

Mayflower delicately straps the purse onto her shoulder and counts the money out into Baby June's hand...murmuring seductively as he does so, with a quick wink to Bam, "Don't worry 'bout it. I may be able t' turn you all onto somethin' nice one day."

"Can we count on it?" Baby June asks, sarcastically, reaching inside to pinch Mayflower's left nipple.

"Yeah sweetthang...can we count on it?" Bam adds, reaching for the other one.

Mayflower playfully slaps their hands away and slowly closes the door.

"I swear t' God! Y'all just so vulgar sometimes! Really!" He stands against the door for a moment, smiling and admiring the purse, and then, remembering the greens, minces the few steps to the stove, swinging the Sicilian purse against his side.

XXX XXX XXX

Lubertha picks up her pencil, scribbles a couple words, erases one, sticks the pencil into her Afro and sits back with her chin propped on her fists.

Her contemplative mood is broken by the sound of the front door opening and being slammed shut, followed seconds later by a gruff baritone.

"Lubertha! you gon' stay in there scribblin' all night? Or are you gon' come in here and eat with us, like people.

"I'm comin', Daddy!" Lubertha calls back, with a tolerant smile on her face...scribbles a couple more final words, stacks her pages into a neat pile and, with obvious reluctance, strolls into the family dining room-kitchen.

Mr. Ed Franklin, robust, gruffy, top lip framed by a thick walrus shaped mustache, sits at the head of a small, round dinette set, wolfing down spaghetti, meatballs and round, medium sized pieces of hot water corn bread.

He pauses in his eating to glare up at Lubertha. "Well? You gonna sit down and eat or just stand there in a daze? Act like you been smokin' them funny cigarettes sometimes! Don't she, Charlotte? Better not ever let me catch you with o' them things in your mouth!"

Home, Your Sweet Home

Ed Franklin's comments occur between mouthfuls of food, washed down with grape Kool-Aid. He is completely humorless, and it shows in the bitter lines creasing the sides of his mouth. Lubertha sits. Mrs. Franklin pops up and down, flipping 'hoe cakes of corn bread over. Lubertha pours herself a half glass of Kool-Aid and nibbles on a piece of corn bread.

Mr. Franklin looks at her suspiciously. "That all you eatin'?" he asks her.

"I had a big lunch at work today, Daddy."

"That ain't no excuse." he tells her, spearing the last meatball on his plate. "When I was growin' up, we ate everything that was put in front of us, and was glad t' git it 'cause wasn't no tellin' when or where the next meal was comin' from...baaaaalch!"

"Guess Lubertha's tryin' to save her shape, Ed," Mrs. Franklin eases in obliquely, with a sly wink to Lubertha.

"Too skinny now...that's what's wrong with these young'uns these days...take everything for granted, wouldn't be trying to save her shape if wasn't no food on the table...keep it up and she ain't gon' have no body, let alone a shape...be lookin' like a sack o' bones in that lil' old short dress."

Lubertha rolls her eyes to the ceiling in a brief, helpless gesture as her father dries his mustache off and fishes in his shirt pocket for his cigarettes.

"Oh...Daddy...I just remembered; Mr. Smith told me yesterday to remind you that you all have a bowling date Friday."

"If he can get out of the house, you mean?"

Mrs. Franklin bustles about the kitchen, clearing dishes from the table, taking little cleaning swipes at the refrigerator, the kitchen sink, any place it seems might harbor a smudge or a stray crumb.

"Lubertha...you goin' out tonight?" Mrs. Franklin asks, swiping at a stray crumb in front of Lubertha.

"Uh...just down to the club for awhile."

Mr. Franklin, lighting his after-dinner cigarette, frowns through the haze of his first puff. "What's all this club stuff? That's all I been hearin' for the last month or so...club this, club that...what club?"

"Well...uh...we had a creative writing club in school and when we all graduated, some of us decided to organize a group of our own. You know, people who were really interested in writing. Old man Adams is letting us use his storefront 'til we find something better."

Mr. Franklin gives Lubertha an intensely skeptical look and seems to be on the verge of going off into a number when the doorbell rings.

Lubertha hurriedly gulps the last of her Kool-Aid and hurries away to answer the door. Ed Franklin sits at the table, frowning and smoking, as Mrs. Franklin wraps up leftovers in tinfoil.

A couple of minutes later Lubertha shyly leads Kwendi Jones in, little fingers interlocked.

"Momma...Daddy...this is Kwendi Jones."

Mrs. Franklin nods pleasantly, but in a deadly-serious-boy-i-got-my-eye-on-you fashion.

Ed Franklin, looking up suspiciously from Kwendi's sandals to his dashiki to his neatly trimmed Van Dyke, reaches out to shake his hand. Kwendi performs the Ritual on it...Ed Franklin looks displeased and puzzled.

Charlotte Franklin hides a quick smile behind her hand and asks Kwendi, "Would you care for a bit to eat...Kwanjo?"

"Kwendi! Momma."

Kwendi shoots Lubertha a small rap-on-the-knuckles-look.

"No thank you, Mrs. Franklin...I ate a little while ago."

Lubertha takes a glance at the crease in her father's forehead, turns to Kwendi. "What time does the workshop start tonight?"

"Eight o'clock."

"We'd better be goin' then...it wouldn't do for the man in charge to be late, would it? I've got a new poem, be ready in a minute."

Kwendi smiles uneasily at Mr. Franklin.

"Sit down," Mr. Franklin orders gruffly. "You know how these women are...and you know, with all that bush Lubertha has on her head these days, she's gonna have t' play with it awhile." Mrs. Franklin discreetly makes her disappearance, taking another quick, objective look at Kwendi.

The two men sit across from each other, awkwardly, Kwendi drumming his nails lightly on the tabletop. Mr. Franklin lights another cigarette, offers Kwendi one, he nods no.

"Kwendi? Kwendi..." What kinda name is that? That what your parents named you?"

Kwendi squirms slightly, looks directly into Ed Franklin's bushy eyebrows. "It's an African name, Mr. Franklin. No...my parents didn't give it to me."

"Well," Mr. Franklin leans across the table aggressively, twin dragon streams of smoke blowing from his nostrils, "how come you go 'round callin' yourself somethin' your mother 'n father didn't name you? I notice lots o' you young folks is doin' things like that... changin' your names 'n whatnot. Lubertha was talkin' 'bout..."

Kwendi interrupts smoothly. "Like...uh...maybe it's just that we feel that that's closer to where we're at."

"Whatcha mean?" Mr. Franklin asks, cigarette bristling from his mustache. "Whatcha mean? Where are you at? You in the U-nited States of America, young man. And it don't make sense to add any mo' confusion to what we already got, with different names 'n stuff."

Kwendi's jaw muscles twitch slightly as he folds his arms on the table. "Look at it this way, Mr. Franklin. I'm not talkin' about geographical location. I'm talkin' about where I feel my soul comes from...which is a far, far diff'rent place that the White Power structure here has ever wanted it to be."

Mr. Franklin sits back slowly in his chair, his temper obviously threatening to overwhelm him. "Hell! Sounds like to me..."

Lubertha, lurking just beyond the kitchen, sails in, her father's developing anger acting as a cue.

"Kwendi! I'm ready! We'd better go before we're late!"

Mr. Franklin grumbles incoherently into his mustache, as Kwendi shakes his hand again, straight-arrow style this time...and nods goodnight to Mrs. Franklin, who quietly materializes.

"I hope we can continue our conversation again some other time, Mr. Franklin. G'night, Mrs. Franklin."

"G'night Kwanji...y'all be careful now. Lubertha don't be out too late y'hear?"

"Don't worry, Momma... I'll be home right after club meeting." She pecks her father affectionately on the cheek. He nods grumpily, looking Black-Father-in-the-Ghetto-mean.

Lubertha and Kwendi split.

Ed Franklin goes to the refrigerator, pulls out a brew, pops the top and sits back down at his place at the table, looking moody.

"I don't too much like these smart aleck types that girl's runnin' 'round with these days...too quick to give ya a lotta lip!" he blurts out suddenly.

Mrs. Franklin wraps her arm around his neck. "She's eighteen, goin' on nineteen, Ed...ain't too much can be said about who her friends should be. Lubertha's a good girl. Kwanni doesn't seem like too bad a young man...lil' bit hairy 'bout the gills, but that's the way young folks seem t' be these days. I remember when nobody, but my granddaddy had as many chin whiskers as some of these youngsters got."

"Hmf! Smart alecks! That's what they are! Plain ol' English names ain't good 'nuff for 'em, they got to go to the African dictionary or somewheres to git a name..."

Mrs. Franklin breaks her embrace, begins running water into the sink to wash dishes...

"What it is baby. What it is."

XXX XXX XXX

In the apartment above Big Momma's, second floor front, Nathan Holt slouches in his favorite easy chair, slippered feet propped up on a worn ottoman, his features glazed by the glaring light of the portable television directly in front of him.

The soft, slurpy sound of Liberace playing Rachmaninoff's 2nd gradually begins to drown out the mellow tenor of the sports announcer on the television.

Nathan Holt looks over his shoulder in the direction of the sounds, an annoyed-as-hell expression pulling his bottom lip out.

"Diane! Diane! Why you have to turn that junk up so loud? Man can't even hear the baseball game!"

Diane Holt pops into the doorway leading into the front room, an Afro-dana wrapped stylishly about her well-straightened hair.

"Nathan Holt! It's a shame how uncouth you can be at times! This junk, as you call it, is the...the...uh...Tchaikowsky 5th. If you were to take your eyeballs and ears out of that idiot box for a hot minute and pay attention to..."

The announcer goes off into an excited "three balls, two strikes n the batter" thing...building to a climactic inning. Brother Holt suddenly stands up near his chair in a threatening way, although his eyes never leave the television set. "Diane! I'm tellin you, woman! Gon' back in there and turn that junk down! It's the last half of the ninth, bases loaded and Frank Mays is up t' bat. I called it junk and I mean junk!

Diane Holt moves back slightly, blown by the strength of her husband's voice, pouting. She turns away from him in a huff... mumbling to herself as she returns to the kitchen, "Uncouth...!" Nathan Holt remains standing, long muscular arms hanging loosely, his face lit by a pleased smile as the music from the other room goes down and the hometown announcer screams hysterically.

"Frank Mayyys! Frank Mayyys! Frank Mays has just poled a tremendous shot into the centerfield stands, sports fans! A reeeelly tremendous shot!! With a count of three and two, bases loaded and two down, he socked one outta the park! Weeellll...that wraps it up folks! Final score, six to three, Giants!"

Nathan remains glued, hypnotically, to the spot...watching and studiously listening to a banalized recitation of batting averages, comparisons between hitting fielders and fielding pitchers and all the other miscellaneous information dished out to the dyed-in-the-wool baseball fan, after The Game. Finally, satisfied that he has all the latest dope, Nathan steps to the set, flicks around the channels, finds nothing to hold his interest and flicks it off. As the television flickers off, the sound of clashing cymbals and crashing cannons comes up. Brother Holt sprawls back in his chair, his head thrown back, an amused expression on his face.

"Diane!" he calls out above the sounds.

A petulant voice answers him, "What do you want?"

"Bring me a brew, will ya honey?"

"Why don't you come in here and get it yourself? I'm busy cookin'! The boys'll be home in a few minutes."

Nathan booms back in a louder than necessary voice... *I would come in there, but it sounds like I'd git blowed away before I made it through the doorway! What the hell are you listenin' to!?"*

"What did you say?" she calls back.

"I said...*What the hell is that?"*

Diane Holt appears with a cold can of beer. "That's Tchaikowsky, baby...you like it?"

"Thanks...it's okay...I guess, if that's what you like."

She takes a quick sip of his brew and starts back into the kitchen.

"Baby?" he sings out to her in a smooth baritone, "ummm, what is that you cookin?"...Smells," winks at her seductively, "better than sin."

"Gumbo," she answers curtly. "It'll be done in a few minutes," and continues stepping.

He causes her to pause again.

"Uh...baby?"

"Yes Nathan...now what?"

"Baby...you mind turnin' that...uh...stuff down a lil' taste? I can really dig where it's comin' from, believe me...but it don't have to be that loud to let me know it."

Diane walks on scowling...but within the next minute, the sound slides down a few decibels. Nathan Holt sips his brew and picks up a nearby newspaper, turns to the sports page.

Byron Holt clunks up the steps, unlocks the door and walks in, between his father slouched down reading the paper and the television set.

Father Holt rustles the paper down and glares up fiercely at his number two son. "Goddamnit Byron! Don'chu speak to folks when you come in the house? Just like yo' Momma! So far off into them highbrow thangs you just forget about common courtesy!"

"Sorry Daddy, I thought you were readin'..."

"Yeah Momma, it's me," he answers, trying to evade his father's eyes.

"Com on in here...lemme give you a lil' taste o' this."

Byron turns quickly, gratefully, from his father's glare and lumbers into the kitchen. Mother Holt holds up a wooden spoon for him to taste from.

"Ummmm, that's outta sight, Momma. How much longer will it take?"

"'Bout another fifteen minutes."

The front door is jerked open by Perry Holt, son number one. He bounces over to stand in front of his father.

"Who won the game?" he asks him breathlessly.

Nathan Holt lowers the paper slowly, revealing a wide smile. "Hah! hah! hahhhh! You know the Eagles didn't! And there wasn't *but* two teams playin'.. Now I'll just leave it up to you to guess who won."

Perry digs down into his pocket with mock tragedy stamped on his face and slams two dollar bills into his father's outstretched hand.

"Thank you, old bean...better luck next time."

"Nat! Set up that card table in there and we can eat in the front room!"

Nathan and son immediately push the television off to one side and pull out the legs of a nearby card table. Byron bumps through the hall from the kitchen with two chairs, nods to his brother.

Perry brings two more out of their bedroom. The men sit down at the table eagerly, Perry and father talking sports, Byron half-listening, bored.

"I'll bet you five bucks the Giants won't be able to go all the way!"

"Long as Frank Mays can keep that streak goin' and ol' Vitamin Blue keeps a lotta stuff on the ball, they'll go all the way! Mark my words!"

Diane Holt trips in with three bowls and spoons, returns with a large uncovered serving bowl brimming with savory gumbo. Conversation ceases as the men get down. Diane brings in another brew to her husband and a large bottle of red soda pop for herself and the boys...sits briefly, and remembering returns to the kitchen for a king-sized box of saltine crackers. Something operatic spools itself in from the AM-FM radio in the kitchen.

"Hey baby...what's he sangin' about?" Nathan asks his wife, winking to Perry.

Diane pauses with a spoon halfway to her mouth, cocks her head to the sound expertly and announces grandly.. "He's singin' 'bout a lot of things."

"So is Muddy Waters...why don't you listen to him...at least you'd be able to figure out what he's singin' 'bout!"

Diane Holt rolls her eyes at her man, shakes her head fiercely... "I been listenin' to Muddy Waters all my life, and all the rest of 'em all my life, and you know it! I think we need to get into a higher, different level of things!"

"Cain't go no higher than Muddy, baby..."

"Not only that, Momma," Perry breaks in, "Muddy is Black Culture Nationalism, and today...especially today, we need all that we can get."

The table is momentarily stricken, Nathan Holt looks at Perry as though he had poured a glass of ice water over his head. Mrs. Holt, looking vaguely puzzled, starts away from the table. "Anybody want anything while I'm in the kitchen?"

"Man, you know somethin'?" Byron points an emphatic forefinger at his brother. "That's all you and Abdul, Ojenkasi, Kwendi and the rest o' you dudes be talkin 'bout...Cultural Nationalism, Black this, and brother that, and all the rest of the trips y'all be goin' on, but I don't see anybody doin' anything but talkin'...just talkin', that's all I hear is talk, y'all got a slogan for everything! I get tired of hearin' it myself!"

"Awww com' on, bruh! I wonder where your head is sometimes... if you'd come to yo' True Self and really recognize where Blackness really is..."

"Dig it! I hear y'all talkin' 'bout Blackness, Black Unity, Black Love, Black-us and all that...but you know yourself that...uh... Momma, or any other woman in this neighborhood, can't even walk 'round the block by herself without runnin' the risk of bein' knocked in the head, or worse! If y'all really meant what you were sayin', none of us would ever have to be afraid of gettin' ripped off, not in any Black neighborhood, anyway...if..."

"Shut up you two! And eat your supper! I didn't fix gumbo for y'all to sit up here 'n argue over it!"

Perry, anxious to get his point in, ignores his mother. "I bet you one o' those integration minded brothers...'brother'...who'd like to see Whitey remain in control...it's Uncle T..."

Father Holt's jaw muscles freeze as he stares huge daggers through Perry's head. His words are even and cold. "Your mother said shut up, son, didn't you hear her?"

The eating is resumed in strained silence.

"By'...did you say you wanted to go to the concert with me?"

Byron glares fiercely, defiantly at his brother.

"Yeah Momma...I'm goin' with you."

Nathan Holt slurps a happy spoonful of good gumbo through his jibbs, good nature returned... "You all better hurry if you don't wanna be late. What she do, Diane? Give you some more of them music appreciation concert tickets?"

"Mrs. Rossini *did* give me some concert tickets, and they are not music appreciation tickets. They're real tickets to a real concert... and furthermo', if you ask me, I think we *all* should be goin'."

Nathan Holt checks his wife out with a sarcastically raised eyebrow. "I went with you over to St. Luke's First African Pres-bye-terian, to listen to them Saddidy niggers sing spirituals like they had sticks up they butts...that was bad enough, I'll be damned if I'll go listen to the 'real thing.' You gonna have t' wait awhile longer for *me* to start playin' White folks. I ain't been a nigger forty-six years for nothin'...hahhhhah! I sho' as hell wouldn't want to let all that hard trainin' go to waste."

"Nathan Holt! I swear t' God! Sometimes you just..."

"You better git on, baby! It's 'bout eight now, and i know the daggoned thing probably starts at eight thirty, the way all them things do. It wouldn't do for two boots to stroll in late."

Diane Holt's look at her husband is devastating. She crumbles a final cracker up in her gumbo, gives her spoon a neat twist and flicks it into her mouth, gets up in a rush.

"Hurry up, By'! Your Daddy's right for once! Why don't you wear that tie Aunt Iris gave you for Christmas?"

Perry and his father exchange knowing smiles as they watch Byron squirm away from the table, a frown creasing his face. Diane Holt disappears into her bedroom, Byron into his. The Holts, father and son, sit at the table, lounging. Father Holt pulls out a pack of cigarettes, stifles a belch and passes the pack to his son.

"Go on boy! I know you smokin'...Momma found a pack in your jacket pocket the other day. You gotta be careful with tobacco though...it'll cut your wind if you smoke too much."

Perry, with a sheepish little grin, takes a cigarette and lights up. They sit at the table, bellies full, smoking, talking sports talk.

"If you could've seen Sugar Ray in his prime! I'm tellin' you, he was somethin' else! Used to lay 'em out dancin' backwards, with his left hand! Closest thing they've had come to 'im in Muhammad Ai-lee!"

"Yeahhh...I've seen some old fight films of Sugar Ray...he really was a bad dude."

Diane Holt reappears, a bizarre little hat tilted off to the side of her head, gives Perry's cigarette The Disapproving Look and pecks her old man on the cheek.

"I got a peach cobbler in the stove if you want some dessert. Oh...and Nat, don't leave those dirty dishes on the table, you know how bad these roaches is. Perry, you hear me? Put 'em in the sink and run some hot water on 'em...oh...and...uh..."

"Gon' woman! Git outta here and go to yo' concerto!"

"All right! All right! I'm goin'! I'm goin'! Just thought I'd..."

Nathan Holt, turning smoothie, curls his arm around his woman's waist... "Gon' honey...y'all have a good time listenin' to them White folks' music...us niggers'll stay home and clean up... don't worry 'bout a thang."

"Nathan...I don't know what to do about you sometimes. By'! By'! Com' on boy! We gonna be late as it is."

Byron slouches out of the boys' bedroom, a vulgar, out-of-fashion tie knotted around his neck and a pair of new, unbroken-in shoes on his feet. He waves coolly to his father and brother on the way out. Brother gives him an exaggerated Black Power salute. Father Hold simply shakes his head from side to side, looking theatrically sad.

The two of them sit quietly at the table, listening to the concertgoers footsteps going down the stairs and then, uncontrollably, they begin to snicker softly to each other, and finally, unable to hold it down to that, Nathan Holt lets loose rib rattling laughter.

"Hahhhh! hahhh! hahhh! hahhhhhhhhahhaa! There go... hahhhh! our...hahhhha! hahhha! Our...Black rep-presentatives to the...hahhahhha!...the White arts! Hahhahhahhah!"

They sit, chuckling away for a few seconds...the laughter slowly fading...Father played out, wiping tears away from the corners of his eyes.

The last bit of humor in the situation drains. And then replays itself for a few more spontaneous hah hahs.

"I got to go do some homework, Daddy. I'm fallin' a lil' bit behind in my math." "Yeahhh...hah! hahhhh...coff! coff!...you got to keep those grades up! You could be battin' a thousand and they still wouldn't give you a scholarship or nothin' else for that matter... not if you can't crack them books."

"Right on! Well...I'm off into it."

Perry goes to the kitchen for a glass of water, wanders away to his shared bedroom, puffing on the fag end of his cigarette. Father Holt takes the dishes into the kitchen, turns the radio off with a quick, vengeful twist, takes another brew from the refrigerator and returns to his easy chair. He sits, sipping his brew and thumbing through the sports page...half reading, half dozing, and then, half listening, after awhile, to weird sounds seeming to come from several different directions at once.

Father Holt looks up from the paper to the kitchen, puzzled... pads into the kitchen to reassure himself that the radio is off, checks it, leaves the kitchen frowning...tiptoes over to Perry and Byron's bedroom door and listens closely for a minute.

"Perry?"

"Yeah Daddy?"

Mr. Holt opens the door a cautious six inches, wrinkling his nose up at the heavy smell of sandalwood incense.

"Uh...what's that you listenin' to, son?"

"Oh...that's Shuwaab Dusplib playin' a thing called *Interplanetary Discussions."*

"Who's doin' what?"

"It's a C.D. by Shuwaab...called *Interplanetary Discussions."*

Father Holt slowly closes the door, his lips forming a large... "Oh."

He returns to his easy chair, sipping his brew, looking puzzled and frowning, as he mumbles savagely to himself... "Ain't that a bitch! A damned C.D. named Interplanetary Discussions!" He shakes the crinkles out of his paper and reads on, squinting at the words slightly more than necessary.

Out with the Old, In with the New

CHAPTER VII
POETS IN REVOLUTION

Dig 'er brother...!
lil' Miss Nitty Gritty...
high steppin' in her shiny pink, patent leather
mini-coat...
strollin' up 7th, tryin' t' hook a trick...

Dig Sweet Mouth Johnny and Slickhead Sid,
off in they late model rides,
goin' to collect they dues from the ladies...

Dig 'em brother...they members of the Ghetto Jet
Set.

Dig young Bam (must be 'bout twenty, look like he thirty)
and Baby June too...fiendish, enslaved junkie hypes,
runnin' 'round sinnin' all night for the sake of
some shit

in a fuckin' spoon...
check 'em out, my mannnn...
yeahhhh...they members of the Ghetto Set.

There go Jive Ass Jean the Beauty Queen and Emo the Dealer.
Big Bo the Boxer and Old Gimps, the crippled thief...
all of 'em sittin' on they asses sayin'...
better thangs is got to come...yeah Brother...!
right on! They members of the Ghetto Jet Set...

Rest your bloodshot eyes on Highslidin' Slim,
Mayflower the Sissy, Butterball Joe and
Miss Rabbit Lee Ann,
the hoodoo-high john, the conjur' root lady...
signifyin' 'n sippin' they first short dogs of the day...
yeahhh...go 'head brother...
check 'em out...see what they got t' say...
they part of the Ghetto Jet Set...

There go Militant Mose,
his woman Black Angel and a whole bunch of
other righteous Bloods...
members of the Ghetto Jet Set...
Brothers 'n Sisters who are giving Whitey his
greatest threat...

Flesh out your eyeballs on Miss Sweet Momma do right!
Sweet Momma do right...
new hair gone Afro...lookin' really outta sight!
(touch 'er if you dare and you might have the
whole Ghetto to fight!)

Check 'em out, brother...
the window clerks, artists, musicians, salesmen,
revolutionaries, lovers, warriors, prophets and others...

the community relations dudes, college students
and grass roots hustlers...
they all members of the Set...

We *all* got to be
'cause Mad Ass Whitey is circlin' the whole area
with a giant motherfuckin' Net!

The workshop, 8:15 p.m....Monday evening...milk crates, thrift shop chairs and a beat-up sofa... Lubertha and Kwendi stand in the center of the large, shabby, storefront room, tenderly kissing. Eyes. Earlobes. Lips.

"I hope my old man didn't get to you."

"Uh hah hahhh...no, no way, not really. Don't forget, I got a father too."

"Like mine?"

"Well, not exactly...to be honest about it...but they sure as hell have a lot in common.

Chiyo Mungu and Johnny Fox tip into the workshop, stand quietly watching Lubertha and Kwendi swaying in each other's arms. "Awright Bro' Jones! Unhand that beautiful sistah and leave us be gittin' down t' business!" Chiyo calls out in a mock-serious voice.

"Looka'here, brother Jones," Johnny Fox adds, slyly, "I thought this was...uh...'sposed to be a writin' workshop?"

Lubertha and Kwendi drop their arms from each other's waists sheepishly, look at the two intruders in surprise.

"Right on! What it is, brothers?"

Johnny Fox folds his arms across his chest and leers deliberately. "You got it, Blood. If I had yo' hand, I'd turn mine in."

"Awright Johnny Fox!" Lubertha says to him gaily, a childhood between them. "Keep it clean."

Chiyo leans over to smack Johnny's palm... "Let's just keep it in the family."

Kwendi and Lubertha exchange offside winks. Other members of the writing group trickle in...Ojenkasi Williams, Nici Miles, Maisha, Charlie Tucker, Abdul Aboud.

Maisha, a small, dark butterfly of a girl-woman, with a small, lean-lidded face and a close-cropped natural, flutters about gossiping.

"Hey...did you all hear about what happened to Buddha?" she asks the room at large.

"To Josie, you mean!"

"To both of 'em. Yeahhh, that's old news," says Nici Miles, tall, slender, brown and critical. "You hear about Rina, Taco, Fred Lee and a couple other dudes gettin' busted today?"

"Fred Lee? Oh wowwww! Bessie must be goin' out of her mind!"

There are almost as many conversations as there are people in the room...they break off, redevelop, bob, weave, shimmer, gleam, explode, settle down...volume up. Kwendi perches on the edge of what was a social worker's tin cabinet desk. He booms out over the talk.

"Hold it down everybody! All right everybody! Hold it down! Let's be gittin' it together!"

The group cools itself out, casually sprawl around the room, on the crates, the floor, holding small notebooks bristling with pencils and flicking ash from fast-burning cigarettes into butt cans.

"First of all," Kwendi begins, "before I say anything else, I'd like to say that it's been a groove to have been the first...uh...well, I can't call myself the president, 'cause that sho' nuff has bad connotations, or the leader...or..."

Ojenkasi, his ace, calls out humorously from behind his hand... "How 'bout H.N.I.C.?"

Kwendi smokes a tolerant, amused glance at Ojenkasi. "Well... whatever the title was...I forgot it...but the point is, I'm not goin to be able to be a part of the group anymore." The small group seems to tighten itself into a smaller knot. Kwendi becomes the heart of it.

"What happened, Kwendi?" Maisha asks him, with a sly hook to her words. "You got tired of us gettin' down so hard on your work?"

The group shares a little contagious smiling at the thought of past critiques, but then becomes serious watching the lack of humor in the situation.

"You really serious, Kwendi? I thought we were supposed to be tryin' to get material together for a book?"

"I know, Ojenkasi...I know, brother...but something a helluva lot more serious than a book has come up. I mean, like it's something I have to deal with and words won't really serve the purpose."

"What's the deal, Kwendi?" Charlie Tucker, usually so quiet, asks.

The bristling pencils recede, find pockets to stand up in...a cigarette is lit, the momentary quiet is expectant, Nici Miles, nudging Lubertha in the ribs... "You ask him what's happenin'... he doesn't seem to want to answer us." Lubertha purses her mouth to speak, but Kwendi beats her to the punch...his words come in a soft, well felt-out drawl, almost as though he were talking out loud to himself.

"As you all know, the main reason why we got our group together was because each of us felt, obviously...that we had somethin' to say, and he way we had chosen to say it was in writing. Besides that, I think...well, I don't think, I *know* we all want to speak out, to fight the shit that's goin' down in our streets...right now...right outside this door. A lot of people try to pretend that things are cool 'cause they got a little bread, or a car or somethin' that cools 'em out...but if you have any sense in your head at all, you can check things out all around you and see that things definitely ain't cool."

He pauses, reflects...and then, with obvious heaviness, goes on, looking closely into the faces of his friends. "I'm not goin' into a long, drawn out thing about what's goin' on in my head. I think everybody here knows about my brother. I didn't really believe he was hooked 'til last week... I opened the toilet door...and..."

"How old is he, Kwendi?" Abdul Aboud asks, a mean look carved on his permanently scowling face.

"Fifteen. Fifteen years old and he's a dope fiend! Ain't that a bitch! When I found out, that did it for me. My mother is goin' to pieces...well...mmmm...anyway, I know I can write about it, might be able to sell the story of my brother's addiction to some jive magazine..."

Ojenkasi pops in, thumbs down. "No way, brother...they only buyin' stories about little White, middle-class junkies these days, ainchu heard?"

"Dig it! You got a point, 'Kasi, you got a point. At any rate, due to the way things have been goin' down, I mean...like, I could stand around and rap with Rudy and the rest of the dudes who *talk* about wantin' some changes all day long and, far as I can see, it ain't gonna get me or any of us anywhere, so...I've decided to join the Blood Circle.

Lubertha's back straightens as she beams proudly at Kwendi and announces... "*We* have decided to join them."

Kwendi studies Lubertha's face for a moment, surprised and pleased to see her devotion to him so openly expressed. "Right on, baby!"

"That's right! Stick with your man, sister!" Maisha exclaims. "That's where Unity is 'sposed to start."

Ojenkasi stands, strolls thoughtfully around the group with his chin in his hand, turns to Kwendi. "Why join them, brother? Why not get our own thing together?"

The members of the group, responding to positive vibrations, to the idea, reflect their approval with a quick surge of urgency.

"Yeahhh, bruh Kwendi," Chiyo slurs, "why join them?"

Kwendi looks deeply into the faces ringed about him. "Well... one of my big reasons is that I dig the things, the way they takin' care business. I mean, they seem to be the only ones doin' somethin' for themselves, everybody else is just talkin' and beggin'."

"I still say," Ojenkasi pops back in, "why join them? I think all of us here feel about as strongly as you do about what's happenin'. Why don't we form our own group?"

Kwendi probes the faces, notes the heads bobbing in agreement, speaks coldly. "I can dig it...but I think everybody should be made to understand one thing, from the git go...there will be no bullshit! If we come together as a group to solve some of the problems we have to deal with in our community, then let's work out ways to solve them...right here, in the workshop, and then put theory to practice."

Lubertha takes out a pencil and begins to scribble furiously, seriously.

"I think the first thing we ought to do is make up a list of things that need doing..."

"Who gon' be the leader?" Johnny Fox asks, a shrewd brow raised at Kwendi.

"Why don' we all consider ourselves leaders for a change," Kwendi answers him. "That way everybody has equal responsibility for whatever is done."

Abdul Aboud, standing, his arms crossed, scowling more than usual, "Let's vote on it. Is that cool with everybody?"

Everybody in the workshop quickly tears pieces of paper, writes a name, balls it up and tosses it into Charlie Tucker's cap. Lubertha shuffles the cap around and begins reading a name from each scrap of paper...Kwendi's name appears on all nine scraps of paper.

Ojenkasi, jokingly, to Kwendi... "Don't tell me you voted for yourself, home?"

"Why not? We wanna make this a free country, don't we? Best place to start is with ourselves. Now then, let's start tryin' to work out a program."

Hope, Hope Steps…

CHAPTER VIII
UHN HUH

Uhn huh! uhn huh! uhn huh!
huh? unh huh uhnnn huh.

uhn huh uhn huh uhnnnhuh
huh? uhn uhnnnnhuh.

uhnnnn huh uhnnnnnnn huh...

uhn uh uhnnn huh...uhn huhn uhn huh...

Naw!

Fergy, dressed in a tattered, horse blanket bathrobe, stands at the west wall of his apartment building shouting... "Goddamnit, Milfred! Why don't you stop blowin' that damned thing in the middle of the night!?"

"Come on back t' bed, Fergy. You know how inconsiderate that fool is? The best thing we can do is complain to the landlord again. It's really a sin 'n a shame we got t' listen to that weird shit damned near every night and 'specially on Monday, it just starts my week off wrong, period."

Fergy comes back to sit on the side of the bed, looking disgusted. "You know somethin'...I saw him in the hallway the other day and I said to him...I said...say looka here man! We all know you hung up on that funny ass horn you playin' and all...but you start blowin' that stuff in the middle of the night when folks got to get up in the mornin' and we can't get no shuteye. How come, I asked him, how come you can't play in the middle of the afternoon? You know? When folks is at work. You know what he said to me? Dig bruhhhthaarr, he said... I plays when my Thang comes down on me. Sometimes it'll happen in the afternoon...but usually it happens at night, and when it does, I just have to gon' 'n deal with it. Well... behind that, I just looked at him hard, like he was crazy, or worse... and opened the door and came on in the house."

Lucille laces her hands behind her rolled up hair, stares pensively into the ceiling for a moment.

"Baby...do you think...do you think he's playin' anything worthwhile? I mean...every now and then he'll hit a pretty note for a minute or two and then he'll go back off again."

"I don't know if it's worthwhile or not! He could be the next Lester Young, for all I care! All I know is that it keeps me from sleepin'!"

"What is that thing he's blowin' on anyway?"

"Damned if I know...heard him tell Lubertha one day that he needed a new reed for his bass-soon."

"What in the world is that?"

"Hmmmm...I can almost see it in my mind's eye but I can't quite describe it...somethin' like a super-clarinet. No...no...not quite. One of those ol' weird foreign horns."

The eerie, wailing sound from beyond the wall dies softly.

Lucille, unlacing her hands from behind her head in surprise... "He stopped playin'!"

"Uh huh...he'll do that sometimes, you ever notice? He'll play for 'bout ten minutes straight, stop for a bit and start in all over again. See! There he goes again! Sounds a lil' bit like a rattlesnake pissin' up 'gainst the wall, don't it?"

"Ferguson Smith! You oughta be ashamed of yo'self!"

"Well...I remember you sayin' somethin' yesterday evenin' 'bout it being so quiet, for a change, that could almost hear a mouse piss on cotton. How do them apples grab ya?"

"Awright honey," Lucille answers, scooching her ample hips around in bed, "you win. Come on, get back in bed, my feet's gettin' cold."

"I guess I'm gonna hafta see that madman again tomorrow... seems like every Tuesday mornin'..."

"Yeah...talk to 'im again...from what I hear, he's about to get put out anyway 'cause he ain't paid no rent for the last month."

"Yawwnnnn...good! Well...yawnnnnn...I'll see him in the mornin' anyway...just to make sure we have some kinda peace 'till he gets booted out."

Fergy drapes his bathrobe across a nearby chair, squeezes himself in beside his wife and they both lie there, their eyes squeenched shut, trying to blot out the skirling sounds from next door.

XXX XXX XXX

Milfred Hawkins, baggy skivvies, a t-shirt two sizes too large for his bird-like frame, a three-yard long, red-black-and-green colored scarf wound around his neck, a Norwegian ski cap with pompom perched on his uncombed Afro, lies tangled in a pile of bedding, in a corner of his room...dreaming of his great work to come.

Ferguson Smith, standing on the other side of the door, swallows hard a couple of times and knocks on the door. The response from inside, after a full minute, is negative.

"Go 'way! I already got one!"

"It's me, man...Fergy!"

"Whatchu want, Fergy? It's...it's...seven motherfuckin' thirty in the mornin'! What the fuck you want this early in the mornin'?"

Fergy swallows hard, again...adjusts his belt buckle... "I gotta talk to you, Milfred. Open up...it won't take but a minute!"

Milfred gleams one fierce, bloodshot eye at the door... "Goddamn, man! Can't you talk to me later? I'm tryin' to cop some zzz's."

"Nawww man," Fergy replies, reluctantly, "I got to talk to you now. It won't take but a minute."

Milfred untangles himself from his bedding covers, muttering obscenities and scratching his crack all the way to the door. "Well? What is it?" he asks, the door opened only wide enough for his bloodshot eye to shine through.

Fergy, jolted a bit by the fierce look of the eye peering out at him, jacks his courage up. "Uh...hey brother Milfred...I hate to wake you up 'n all, but...I...uh...we..."

"I'm awake now," Milfred growls through the door, between gritted teeth. "Git to the point! I just got in the rack a few hours ago and I'm beat! Now tell me, quick! What do you want?"

"That's what I wanted to talk to you about, Milfred...about you being up so late."

"What about it?" Milfred asks, as he wanders around inside his left nostril with his little finger.

"Well...nothin' man. I mean, it's just that...well, when you stay up late, you keep everybody else awake."

Milfred strolls away from the door, still fingering the inside of his nose and scratching his crack, calls over his shoulder. "Come on in, Fergy!"

"I ain't got no time to...well, I just wanted to say what I just said."

"Come on in, man!" Milfred commands. "There's a damned breeze blowin' through this drafty-ass joint!"

Fergy edges into the apartment hesitantly, casting surreptitious glances at the piles of crumpled paper, chicken bones and cigarette butts scattered around, and Milfred scratching his crack as he urinates into a milk bottle. Mildred shake-splaps the last bit of liquid from his penis tip, places the bottle down in place and walks over to his window, still scratching...stares at the crumbly, red brick wall facing him.

"Brother, you know something?" he asks Fergy, quietly, with his back to him. "I told myself when I first moved into this joint... what was it? Four, five months ago?"

"Uh...three months ago," Fergy mumbles at him, trying not to wrinkle up his nose at the bad smells. "You moved in in March."

"Three months!" Milfred exclaims. "Ninety long, hard, cold cruel fuckin' days and nights. Three months and five years of tryin', tryin', to get this goddamned thing together!"

Fergy, looking at a small regiment of roaches march across the foot of his shoes... "Uh what thing?" he asks.

Milfred turns from the window to a table piled high with banana peels, dirty socks, chicken bones and music sheets. He digs his hands into the whole mess and starts flinging it into the air.

"This! This! This!" he screams. "Goddamnit! This!" Milfred flings the sheets of music up, again and again, as Fergy pins him with a carefully controlled but scared expression on his face.

Milfred flings the last sheets of paper into the air, bats them around a bit, crumbles down onto his bedding and begins to shed massive tears.

Fergy bends to pick up a couple of the sheets, puzzled. "What is this, Milfred? All these sheets...?"

"Sniffle! sniffle! sob sobbbbbbbbb! sobbbbbbb! It's ... sobbbbbb! It's...the...sobbbbbb! sobbbbbbb! sniffle!... *First Jazz Concerto...* sobbbbbb!...*For Bassoon*...and...sniffle! sobbbbbb! and I can't get it together! I just can't...sobbbbbbbbb! sobbbb!...get it together!"

Fergy, staring alternately at the sheets and at Milfred's tear-streaked face. "Anything I can do...to help you brother? Anything at all?"

"Sobbbbbbbbb! sobbbbbbbb! nawwww! sniffffffle! snifffffffle! Nawww! It's on me, it's on me."

Fergy gently releases the music sheets onto the floor. "Well, you know what they say, that's the way the cookie crumbles sometimes. My old man used to tell me you couldn't raise nothin' 'less you plowed up the ground first. Keep on workin' on it, it'll come t' you... watch 'n see. Well...I gotta begittin' on, I'm late as it is. You take it slow, Milfred. Be cool, okay?"

Milfred looks up gratefully to Fergy, wiping his snotty nose on the end of his scarf. "Sobbbb snorrrrt! snifffffle! snoorrrt! snifffffle! Yeahhh...right on, bruh Fergy!"

Fergy eases out, shaking his head sadly, compassionately, at the sight of a grown man sitting in a corner...

XXX XXX XXX

Stairway to the Stars

Lena Daniels, trying to take advantage of the early evening shadows, rap-taps furtively on Miss Rabbit's back door.

Miss Rabbit ushers her in, both of them check each other out with puzzled expressions. "How you been, child? How you 'n Jim doin'? Or is it too soon t' say? And where's my cobbler?"

Lena twiddles her thumbs and stares at a pattern in Miss Rabbit's worn kitchen linoleum.

"Everything's awright...I guess."

"Well...if ever'thang is awright, whatchu doin' here? Don't none o' you women come t' see Miss Rabbit 'lessen you got problems or somethin'."

Lena, her watery eyes wandering hesitantly up to Miss Rabbit's face... "I...uh ruh...I really ain't got no problem, not exactly what you could really call a problem exactly. What I mean is...uh...I haven't had time to fix that cobbler 'cause...well, I just haven't had time."

Miss Rabbit cocks her salt-and-peppered head at an understanding angle, beckons to Lena. "Come on 'n sit down, honey...come on tell Miss Rabbit all about it."

"I ain't got but a minute! Jim is takin' a nap right now and he'll be wakin' up directly."

"What?!" Miss Rabbit exclaims, an immense number of creases slicing across her forehead. "Grown man takin' a nap?! Never heard 'a such...what in the world are you talkin' 'bout?"

"Well...that's what I wanted to see you about. I did everything you told me t do, just like you said, you know, 'bout puttin' that stuff in his coffee 'n all."

"And he came home feelin' po'ly, right?"

"Yes'um," Lena nods eagerly. "He came home 'n all, laid down, and while he was sleepin' I tossed those bones you gave me under the bed and sprinkled that powder 'round, just like you told me t' do."

"Well...so what's wrong now?" Miss Rabbit asks, lighting a cigarette. "Gon'...let it out, honey...let it all out."

"Miss Rabbit...Jim done gone crazy! Every time I turn 'round he's got his arm around me and I'm just about wore out! I don't know what to do with that man! He wants to do it every five minutes! Yesterday he sent the kids..."

"Lawd a'mighty!" Miss Rabbit interrupts, holding her jaw in amazement. "If this ain't somethin'! Lena, when you tossed them bones under the bed, did either of 'em land crossways the other?"

"I...I don't know, Miss Rabbit. I didn't look, I just chunked 'em under there like you said for me to."

"Quick honey! Run home if you wants a good night's rest and uncross them bones...hahhhh hahhhhahhah! That's what happened. Them bones landed crosswise and ha! ha! ha! I betcha a fat man Jim's main bone got stuck in between somehow."

"Miss Rabbit," Lena breathes gratefully, "I'll brang you that cobbler on the weekend for sure. Thanks a heap. I was really beginnin' to get worried."

"Hmf! If you had any sense, girl" Miss Rabbit nearsightedly checks a nearby calendar, "today is just Wednesday...if you had any sense, you wouldn't uncross them bones 'til tomorrow, or the next day...if I was you..."

Lena reacts in a pleasantly scandalized fashion. "Missss Rabbit!"

"Hahhhh! hahhhh! Well...anyway, brang 'em on back when you uncross 'em. Bessie Mae looks like she gon' be needin' somethin' whenever Fred Lee gets his railass outta jail. Ahhheemmm...how's Suki-Boy's foot?"

"It seems almost well...got better almost overnight for some reason. The doctor thought..."

"Boy musta stepped in some o' that powder you sprankled 'round Jim's bed," Miss Rabbit announces, suavely flicking her cigarette ash into her apron pocket.

"You right! You right! You know somethin'? He sure did! When Jim got in the other evenin' Suki-boy hopped in to see what was wrong with his Daddy and...that's right! That's what happened! He had to step in it! What kinda stuff is that, Miss Rabbit? You can tell me, I won't tell nobody else."

Miss Rabbit smiles indulgently, pats Lena on the shoulder. "You better gon' carry yo' narrow hips on home, girl...'fore Jim wakes up. And stop worrin' 'bout Miss Rabbit's powders 'n thangs. Don't forget that cobbler, my sweet tooth is just achin' for the first bite. Go on home, now. I'll be lookin' for you."

"Don't worry 'bout a thang. I'll have it over here...first thing on the weekend, probably on Saturday."

"And don't forget to brang them bones with you...not 'lessen you want to keep 'em 'til next week?"

"Don't worry...I won't forget...hah hah hah hah. Goodnight now...thanks again for everything, Miss Rabbit."

"You take care, Lena...take care," Miss Rabbit says to her, letting her out the back door into the alley.

CHAPTER IX

BLUE VEINS

Miles Davis blew here

Somewhere Miles Davis is blowing a lovely old cut called Blue Haze. The sound of his horn is sharp and bell-like...but soft and deliberate as it snakes through the swarming streets, curling about the worn shoulders of ancient grandmothers carrying Northside-downtown shopping bags in gnarled fingers... trails hip Zulu ladies, unnaturally beautiful in their glistening, oil-shadowed faces, with their flaring nostrils and flanged behinds. And even seems to spur on the darting business of grimy little Afroid faces in sloganed t-shirts who swoop, bird-like, in and out of the moving crowd.

Masai warriors plant themselves rhythmically in front of darkened, cavernous stick halls, pool cue-spears resting easily in their manicured hands... as they fish and attempt to pull in the Zulu women and...now and then, send one of the grimy faces off on a coded errand, worth at least a quarter.

Somewhere Miles Davis is blowing...and from another place, Coltrane is too, and Lou Rawls, Aretha, Ray and the Count and always the Duke and a slew of others, both old and avant-garde, are mingling themselves with the swarm of the streets, unselfconsciously...naturally.

The music is secular. And religious. It is soft and low in parts... or high and screeching. As mad and as sane as any day in the Black ghetto can be.

The euphoria of the Black holiday, *Saturday Night*...that refused to recognize reality and of the Sunday that was equally guilty. Or innocent...is over now, and the needles, herbs and bottles that held holiday dreams are now a part of the existing, everyday reality.

The reality brings the snake of Miles' horn blowing through the crowd, fills the steamy avenues with the cry of the tortured, the yells and moans of the oppressed and the silent screaming of the stomped-down junkie. Somewhere Miles Davis is blowin...

XXX XXX XXX

Lena Daniels walks quickly past the small circle of men in the alley, glancing at the agonized looks on the faces of the two men in the center of the circle. Kwendi, Johnny Fox, Chiyo Mungu, Ojenkasi, Charlie Tucker and Abdul Aboud have Bam and Baby June surrounded.

Kwendi stands in close to Baby June, presses a .45 into his belly.

"Please Kwendi! Please! Please man! Don't be this cold-blooded, man! Don't kill me, man! Please! I wanna live. Please man. Please!" Baby June looks around pathetically at the group. Bam leans against him, nose dribbling blood, holding the side of his face.

Kwendi pops Baby June across the face with his pistol. "Shut up! You jive ass...!"

"Be cool, Kwendi," Johnny Fox cautions Kwendi, "I think you broke his nose."

"I oughta kill 'im!" Kwendi says between gritted teeth. Baby June sinks to his knees, holding his face, moaning with pain.

"Get off your knees, motherfucker! Stand up! Now either you or Bam is gonna tell me who the motherfucker is that's sellin' dope to my lil' brother, or else I'm gon' leave both of you worthless bastards dead! Right out here in this alley!"

"Please Kwendi! Gimme a break, brother," Baby June pleads. "Gimme a break! Sobbbbbbbbb! I'm gettin' sick...pleassse!"

Kwendi pops him upside his head. "Don't call me brother! You chickenshit sonofabitch! How the hell you gon' be anybody's brother, dope fiend!"

Bam pulls at Baby June's coat sleeve with trembling fingers. "Go 'head 'n tell 'im, Baby June! Go 'head..."

"I can't tell...you tell...I..."

"Johnny, Chiyo," Kwendi motions with his piece, "move aside, I'm gonna blow this motherfucker's head off!"

"It's Sweet Peter D.!" Baby June blurts out, trying to wipe his bloody nose with his coat sleeve. "Don't kill us, man! It's Sweet Peter D. ...he's the one! He's the one!"

Kwendi pushes his piece down into his belt, and without a signal, he and the others begin pounding Bam and Baby June with fists and feet.

XXX XXX XXX

Black-eyed peas, ham hocks, corn bread, ale and a sliced onion and tomato salad sprinkled liberally with vinegar graces the dinner table of Mr. and Mrs.. Ferguson Smith, hot sauce on the side.

"So I told 'er, I said, lissen here Mrs. Bernhammer, you can fire me if you want to but I'll be gotdamned if I'm gon' iron your uncle's shirts too! I just came straight out and told 'er, enough is e-nuff! She got me cleanin' the whole damned house, waxin' the livin' room floor, fixin' lunch for them spoiled-ass kids... I ain't ever seen no kids act sassy as them kids! I wouldn't've lived to be ten if I'd done *one* of the thangs they do every day...just *one!* My Momma would've killed me dead!

"To give ya an example, Timothy, the oldest, 'bout twelve, come walkin' 'cross the floor yestiddy, right after I just waxed, and had nerve enough to go tell his mother after I damned near whammed a new crack in his tail for steppin' on my floor. Mrs. Bernhammer creeps up on me later on in the day, while I'm downstairs ironin'... and says to me, Uh...Mrs. Smith...we went through an earlier thing about that Lucy bit...Mrs. Smith, she says, oh so politely, I can certainly appre-ciate your not wanting to have Timothy walk on your freshly waxed floor, but...uhhh...don't you think spanking him is a little severe? I mean, he's almost gotten to the point of being afraid to be anywhere near you. Good! I told her and kept on pushin'...and that's how that jive 'bout her uncle's shirts came in. Come to think of it, they probably her little old pimple-faced boyfriend's shirts anyway."

"Lucille"...Fergy leans back, picking his teeth, "I've told you a hundred times, if them White folks start buggin' you...quit! I don't need to be sittin' here every night, hearin' you complain about no White folks! Ain't nobody but the two of us, so ain't no need t' take no bullshit from nobody!"

"I ain't complainin', baby...I'm just tellin' you what happened. You know I ain't gon' take no crap! I did that for the last time down home...I got some more peas in the pot if you want some?"

"Mmm...Lawd no! I'm full as a tick now. What's this I hear 'bout them dope fiends gettin' busted the other day? I know you got all the latest from Big Momma 'e nim."

Lucille, leaning on the table, excited by gossip... "I didn't hear everything. Diane called me a few minutes after I got home 'n told me they all got taken away, with about fifteen pounds 'o that dope they all shootin' in their arms."

"Hah! hahhhhhhh; hahhhhhhh! Fifteen pounds! Hahhhhhhah! hahhahhhhh! hahhhhhh! Fifteen pounds!"

Lucille frowns at her old man belly-laughing at the information just laid on him.

"What's so funny?"

Fergy slows his laughter down to a little chuckling, content to keep the catalyst for his amusement to himself. "Mmmhah...

ha! ha! ha!...uh, nothin', sweetness. Nothin'...I'm just feelin' good, that's all."

He stretches himself luxuriously. "I just passed my probation period today and that means I'll be in the union, and I got a permanent spot in the plant now."

Lucille pops a quick, lush kiss on his cheek. "That's really good, Fergy...really good. Hard as jobs is to find these days."

"Yeah...I didn't think I'd make it, what with Milfred keepin' us awake at night."

"I meant to ask you last night what you'd said to that fool, it just skipped my mind, what happened?"

Fergy just is chin out aggressively, takes a deep breath. "I saw 'im...talked t' him so bad, like he was a thief, that he broke down 'n cried."

"Hmf! I guess you must've said somethin' that made some impression, come t' think of it, 'cause we didn't hear him carryin' on last night."

"I told him to stop makin' all that racket and a whole lot of other things. Well, he said he was sorry, and that he hadn't realized he was keepin' other people wake 'n whatnot and that he wouldn't be doin' it anymore. That actually saved him...'cause I was just about ready to pounce on his lil' skinny ass."

"Good...here...lemme take yo' plate to the sink. I sure am glad to hear that! He was just about to drive me in-sane!"

Lucille Smith takes their plates to the kitchen and bustles back to the front room where she and Fergy have been eating dinner. He pulls her down onto his lap. "Ferguson Smith!" she exclaims, coyly diggin the feel of his lap, "whatever in the world is on yo' mind?"

Fergy hugs and kisses his wife slowly, with feeling. Lucille asks him, teasingly, "I thought you was gonna watch the boxin' matches tonight?"

"Not tonight, baby," Fergy winks meaningfully at her, "not tonight."

"I got to do the dishes, Fergy."

"Leave 'em! They ain't goin nowhere!"

"But you know how bad these roaches are! They'll overrun us if I don't wash..."

"Stick 'em in the stove."

"You really *do* feel good, don't you?"

Fergy gently releases Lucille with a light, brushing kiss on the mouth and walks toward the bedroom, unbuttoning his shirt. "I told you...stick 'em in the stove...they ain't gonna rot."

Lucille Smith, appraising the emotional scene, quickly... places the dirty dishes in the stove. She prances into the bedroom, where Fergy sits on the edge of the bed, unlacing his high topped, workingman's shoes.

Lucille moves past Fergy, and goes into their small bathroom, motel-style, off the bedroom, humming a quiet, sensuous little tune.

"Lucille? Lucille?" he calls to her in the toilet. "Baby...didn't we have some of that rum left?"

"Yeah, yeah," she answers, preoccupied with her own concerns, "it's in the cabinet up under the sink, behind the milk bottles."

Fergy smiles at the bathroom door, pads to the kitchen in his stocking-clad feet, searches behind milk and pop bottles under the sink, and finally pulls out a half fifth bottle full of Bacardi rum, dark.

"Lucille? You want some o' this stuff straight? On some ice? Or some coca-cola with it?"

Lucille answers a few seconds later, coyly. "Just gimme a tee-nincy bit o' rum 'n a lotta coca-cola!"

Fergy, smiling his ass off, pulls a couple water glasses from the cabinet above the kitchen sink, goes into the refrigerator for ice cubes and a coke and makes strong drinks for them both. He surreptitiously takes a big, long swallow straight from the bottle before replacing it under the sink. Fergy pads back to the bedroom to find his wife propped in bed, sexily done up in a sheer black negligee. "Here y'are, baby...let the good times roll."

They clink glasses and drink.

"Uggghhh! O my Gawd Fergy! You musta put half that bottle in this glass."

"Now come on, Lucille...you know I wouldn't do no such thang as that."

He places his drink on the bedside table and sits down anxiously on the side of the bed to pull off his socks. "Fergy?"

"Yeah...yeah, baby?"

"You need a shave."

Fergy scruffles his hand across his chin, feels his grizzled jaws. "Uh...yeahhh...that's what I was just gettin' ready to do...before I climbed under these covers with you." Fergy leans over to peck his wife on the mouth, takes his drink and walks a little unsteadily to the john...he hummmms a bit while shaving and drinking.

Lucille clicks off the wall light, and turns on a small, intimate bedroom lamp just before Fergy returns to the scene, a swallow's worth of rum in his glass...a bath towel saronged about his waist. The bedroom is dim, softly lit, late evening sounds filter up from the neighborhood below.

"Lucille?" Fergy whispers. "You want another one before I lay down?"

"Uhn huhn...naw baby...I done had enough," Lucille murmurs. Fergy finds the bed in the half-light, they snuggle together under the covers...breathing hard.

"You know...I almost cut my chin in half, shavin'."

"You did? Here, lemme kiss it...that might help."

Lucille holds Fergy's head in her hands and tenderly kisses his chin...he holds her head in his large, rough, work-hardened hands and gently kisses her mouth, neck and the hollow of her shoulders and begins to nibble at her breasts...caresses her wide buttocks, snuggles up closer...begins to get off into their number.

And then, from beyond the wall...a strange, strangulated series of slithery sounds begin to slide through. They freeze for a few long seconds.

"Goddamnit Fergy! I thought you told that crazy ass nigger to stop blowin' all that...that...!"

"I did see 'im! I talked to 'im yesterday mornin'...just before I went to work."

"Well...if you talked to him, it sure as hell didn't do too much good! What's he doin' now? Blowin' air bubbles? I'm tellin' you, Fergy...we gon' have t' do somethin' about him! You know I go to work sometimes with that funny ass shit ringin' in my ears?!"

"I done already complained to the landlord a half dozen times." Lucille sprawls over on her back, arms and legs crossed. "Hmf!"

"Aww...come on, baby...I told you I spoke to 'im already...see there! He stopped! We wouldn't even be able to hear 'im if the damned walls wasn't so thin."

"You hear that? There he goes again! We got to do somethin' about him! I'm fed up listenin' to that crazy stuff! What did he say when you told him to stop playin'?"

"Whatchu mean? What did he say?"

"Fergy...I bet you ain't said nothin' to that fool!"

"I told you I spoke to him, didn't I? I said...looka here Milfred, we all know you a musician 'n all, but that don't give you the right to be keepin' folks up all night...every night! You just gonna have to pick a decent time a day to play that thing or just don't play it al all!"

"What did he say?" Lucille asks, her tone dripping skepticism.

"Uh...he said he'd stop."

"Does it sound like he's stopped t' you?" She points at the wall. "It sho' as hell don't sound like it to me!"

"Awww baby," Fergy nestles closer, nibbling at Lucille's evasive earlobes, "can't you forget about...?"

"I can't forget a damned thing!" She pushes him over to his side of the bed, "listenin' t' all that off the wall crap...besides, I'm kinda tired. We got any more o' that cotton left? I guess I'm gon' have to plug up my ears in order to get some sleep?"

"Awww...it ain't all that bad!"

"It's all that bad to me," she says, and rips out from under the covers, goes into the toilet and returns, stuffing cotton into her ears, her hair harnessed now by an old-fashioned hairnet. She brusquely settles herself back under the covers, gives Fergy a quick consolation peck on his freshly scraped cheek and turns her matronly hips to him, and...within minutes...begins to snore...

softly...melodically. Fergy remains awake, listening to Milfred and looking up at the cracks in the ceiling in disgust.

XXX XXX XXX

Fergy stands in front of Milfred's door, checks his watch and raps hard on Milfred's door, about ten times.

"Go 'way! I already got one! Go 'way, I don't want none!"

"It's me man...Fergy!"

The irritated quality in Milfred's voice is cutting enough to make Fergy wince. "Whatchu want, Fergy? It's...it's 7:motherfuckin' 30 in the...what the fuck you want this early in the mornin'? Go 'way...I'm tryin' to sleep!"

"Open up a minute, Milfred!" Fergy manages, in his best basso voice. "I got somethin' to say to you."

Milfred untangles himself from his bedding, carefully treads his way across his bone-strewn floor, and abruptly snatches his door open a few inches.

"Yeah...what it is?" he asks in a sour voice. "Whass happenin'?"

"Now looka here, Milfred! I don't mean to be wakin' you up every other mornin' but..."

Milfred walks away from the door, motioning with the pompom on his ski-capped head for Fergy to come in. He sits-slouches down at his writing table, rubbing sleep from his eyes, yawning and scratching his balls...unscrews the top from a half gallon jug of red wine and pours himself a Mason jar full of it.

"You want some breakfast, man?" he asks Fergy, jar halfway to his lips.

"Uh...naw, naw Milfred," Fergy replies, with a slight frown of disapproval, "Im on my way to the yoke."

"Well...if you don't want to drink no breakfast with me," Milfred says, graciously, "you can at least join me in a toast." Fergy reluctantly accepts a half-filled Mason jar of red wine. Milfred holds his jar high, grandly.

"A toast to us, or rather a toast to you, brother...for helpin' to pull me out of a dark, heavy place the other mornin'... I sat down after you left, dig? After you laid that heavy drama on me about gettin' my thang together...and that's exactly what I did. I got it together! Almost! Dig it! I re-worked that whole first section of the piece, the second fell into place...and I'm halfway through the third part now."

Fergy, his enthusiasm warmed by the wine... "That's really beautiful! Really beautiful! But...well...now don't get me wrong, Milfred!"

Milfred pops the jug over Fergy's glass for a refill not needed yet.

"I can dig your music, but Lucille...my wife...you know...she... she...uh ruh..."

"I been fuckin' your thang up, huh, Fergy?"

Fergy looks down sheepishly at his half empty glass, takes a bolstering swallow.

"All right, brother," Milfred says to him, "I can dig where you comin' from. You know...sometimes you get so locked up into one of them heavyweight thangs with *your very own thang,* that you sort of forget that other people got they thangs goin' on too."

"Well...like I said, Milfred...before you can play. I mean...I know what it is you goin' through...tryin' to get it together 'n all. I used to try to blow a lil' tenor sax myself, years ago."

Milfred, pouring more wine into Fergy's glass... "Really?"

"Uhn huh...yeah...that was before I got married. They tell me I was pretty good too...anyway...what I was gonna suggest...again... is this, why don't you play, practice in the afternoon? That would really be better for everybody!"

"Fergy...I'm not jivin'...I really would like to, man. I really would... But, like I told you once before, I just don't seem to be able to righteously get off into it 'til after the moon is out. But...dig... tell you what...a broad I used to mess 'round with in 'Frisco just shot in...and...from the looks o' things, we'll probably be shackin' before the end of the month? It'll probably take that long for me t' sew the bitch up."

"Well...well," Fergy adds, killing the corner in his glass, "I hope everythin' turns out okay...for you, Milfred. I really do. Like I said,

I know a lil' bit about that music bag...I used to blow a lil' tenor sax myself."

"Yeah...well, you know how it is then," Milfred shrugs. "I'm gon' git on my job and stay there 'til I take the thing somewhere... can you dig it, bruh Ferg'?"

Fergy stares at Milfred's outstretched palm for a second, realizes why it's there and then slaps it lightly, awkwardly.

"Uh...yeah...right! Right on! Well...take it easy, man. I gotta run, talk to you later."

"Awright good brother, later on."

Milfred shows Fergy out with smiles and strokes of good fellowship on his back.

Fergy hurries down the stairs, not quite as sober as the proverbial judge, hits the bottom step of the front stoop, heading for the great b.s., and almost bumps into Mr. Nolan, the building manager, going out of the door.

"Hey, Fergy! What's goin' on? Runnin' late, huh?"

"Yeah...I'm a lil' bit behind. Nolan...I thought you were gon' send a plumber over to square my toilet away?"

"I called Mr. Brownstein yesterday and he told me he was sendin' a man out. Ain't nobody come yet?"

"Hell no! Ain't nobody come! And damned near every time we flush the damn thing it flows over...I'm sick 'n tired of stickin' my hand down behind there to make the fuckin' thing work!"

"Well...hey man...like I said, I told Mr. Brownstein, and he said..."

"I don't want to hear all that bullshit! All I want is to get my toilet flushin' right! I'm fed up with stumblin' 'round in my own doo doo every time I flush the toilet!"

"Okay! Okay! Okay, Fergy... I'll call him again..."

"When?"

"Uh...this mornin'...I'll call 'im back this morning'...is that crazy horn player upstairs?"

"Yeah...Milfred's upstairs...be sure 'n tell that honky to send somebody to fix my toilet if he wants his rent...me 'n my old lady is gettin' tired o' stumblin' 'round in..."

"Awright Fergy! I told you I would and I am...!"

Lubertha walks down the stairs as Nolan goes upstairs, Fergy glaring hatefully at his back.

"Hi, Mr. Smith...kinda chilly out here this mornin', isn't it?"

"Yeah...sure is nippy. How's that scribblin' comin' along?"

"Okay...we've started a..."

Fergy checks his watch... "Wow! Gotta run...see ya later, Lubertha."

"Okay...'bye, Mr. Smith," Lubertha smiles after him, as he hurries off to the bus stop.

XXX XXX XXX

The day before the eagle flies...

A blind guitar player, dark shaded, with tin cup and a beautifully tuned tin guitar, and a little boy with four-hundred-year-old eyes leading him, strolls the length of the street singing the blues... America's only cante jondo.

Big Momma graciously plunks a few coins into the cup that the little boy holds out, and he wanders on...a lost, murky figure in a dim, cruel world. On the other side of the street, Mr. Chickens is doing his effervescent thing...for the benefit of a few pre-school age children and a clot of amused, leftover grownups.

Mr. Chickens...a tall, thin, goat-whiskered, Ras Tafarian-headed dude with obsidian eyes, striped at the corners by ghetto squint lines, huddled in an overcoat that looks, at first glance, like an ancient Afghan rug, but is, in actual fact, a heavy, once well-tailored camel's hair, at least fifty years old, straight out of Hart, Schaffner and Marx. He recites a monotonous line of sheer poetry as he puts six mangy, scroungy, toothless, dirty, funky chickens through their paces.

"One dime one show!" he calls out. "One dime one show!" With a patient little baton he helps two of the chickens up onto a length of rope he has attached to a grill at the edge of the sidewalk.

He pulls the rope taut and suddenly the chickens are doing a Wallenda across the abyss of half a sidewalk, as he clucks constantly to them with a secret stream of poultric love signals.

"One dime one show! No dime no show!" he sings out in a rich monotone.

He eases the chickens down from the high wire, squatting on his Fakired heels as the chickens huddle around him...quick pecking at carefully placed bitlets of corn kernels.

"One dime one show! One dime one show! No dime no show!" he sings out periodically, totally involved with the ways of his chickens.

One of the adults, attracted by the call, drops a dime on the ground. One of Mr. Chickens' chickens quickly waddles over to peck the dime up and bring it to Mr. Chickens. He takes the dime and gives the lucky chicken a couple more bits of seed...all done in a quick, smooth way.

"Make 'em dance, Mr. Chickens!" one of the children calls out to him.

"Yeah, make 'em dance!"

"Just the females," one of the adult adds...

"How you gon' tell the diff'rence?" a fellow adult asks...

"Bro' Chickens knows the diff'rence...hah hah hah!"

Mr. Chickens stares briefly, opaquely, at the comedians around him, and then coolly, suavely, above banalities, he taps his baton, clucks to the hens and they assemble into an almost straight chorus line. The other three jump up on his knees and one, a bolder spirit, makes it to the top of his head, as the chorus line shuffles a bit... back and forth...while Mr. Chickens calmly clucks a guaguanco tempo to them. The "show" lasts a red-hot two minutes.

"One dime one show! One dime one show! No dime no show!"

Another thin dime hits the pavement...an instant chicken scoots over to peck it up. This time, for a "show," Mr. Chickens has the other three chickens roll over on their backs simultaneously and scratch out at the air with their crusty talons.

"One dime one show! One dime one show! No dime no show!"

After a few more plaintive cries, Mr. Chickens gives up, moves on, clicking and clucking to his chickens who follow him in single file...satisfied that he has given the public one show for one dime. The cheapest "show" in town.

CHAPTER X

THE DAY THE EAGLE FLIES...

The Door of No Return

Lucille Smith lies propped up in bed, sipping a large rum 'n coke, reading Ebony magazine and looking seductive as all get out in a flimsy, low-cut, hot pink nightgown. Fergy sits on the side of the bed trimming his corns, his bath towel wrapped Sabu-style around his bulging middle. He turns, from time to time, to tweak Lucille's toes playfully...they are both in an obviously groovy state.

"Ferguson Smith! Will you stop that! Now just stop! You worse than a kid sometimes! You see me readin' and you know how ticklish I am! Teee heee! Teeee heeee teeee heeee!" Fergy stops tweaking at her toes, reaches over awkwardly to the night table and pours another drink into his glass from an almost empty fifth bottle of rum.

"Fergy," Lucille coos to him. "Why don't you put that light out and come to bed?"

"That's the way you women are on a man's payday, too bad the eagle don't fly every day."

"I'm glad you reminded me that you got paid today... I told Diane I was goin' shoppin' with her tomorrow."

Fergy turns for a long, slow, hot look at the seductive pink nightgown, swallows the last of his drink hurriedly, and scrambles into bed.

"Honey...you gonna turn off the light or leave it on?"

Fergy, smiling seductively, struggling to retain the towel around his waist, tippy-toes over to the wall switch...stubs his toe against the bedstead on his way back to the bed in the dark.

"Ooooowwww! Shiiiiiii-it!"

"Heeeeee heeee! Teeee heeee! Tee heee!"

"What the hell you laughin bout, woman?! That hurt! I coulda broke my toe, or crippled myself for life!"

"Awww Fergy...com'mere...po' baby...po' bay-beee." Lucille holds her arms out to him as he climbs clumsily back into bed. They lie...locked in each other's arms.

"Fergy...you know somethin'? We ain't heard hide nor hair of that crazy man next door for...for..one whole night. You think he might be dead or somethin'?"

"Nawwww," Fergy replies arrogantly, "he ain't dead. He just keepin' quiet like I told 'im to."

They kiss, a long, lush, lingering kiss, and begin to make love... the intensity of their action ignoring, momentarily...the slurring, softly muted lyricism that begins to accentuate, fit the rhythm of their coupled movements.

XXX XXX XXX

Down the street, Sweet Peter Deeder, waiting for Idella, late as usual, is confronted by Kwendi, Ojenkasi and Abdul Aboud.

"I got a bone to pick with you, 'Sweet Peter'."

"Later on, young blood," Sweet Peter D. shines him on, "I got some business to take care of..."

The young brothers grab him by the collar and armpits. "Not tonight... 'Sweet Peter'...you ain't got no business to take care of tonight!"

"Heyyy...wait a minute! Git yo' motherfuckin' hands off me!"

Kwendi pushes his piece into Sweet Peter's mouth. "Say another word, you sonofabitch! Just one more and I'll make you chew this up to the trigger! All of it!"

They pull Sweet Peter D. from the fender of his hog, silently, efficiently.

XXX XXX XXX

The horn and Lucille and Fergy both seem to rise to a crescendo, and then, for a moment, both blend...the loving, lovely love action stops, but the music plays on...softly...tenderly...soaking Lucille and Fergy's sleep with the First Jazz Concerto for Bassoon, by Milfred Hawkins...played for the first time, from beginning to end, minus full orchestra.

CHAPTER XI

WHAT'S GOIN' ON?

Bessie Mae Black steps out onto the front stoop, a brown laundry bag of dirty clothes clutched to her bosom...sighting around the barrel of the bag at the Saturday crowd, gathered on the steps already, determined not to let a minute of their day off go to good waste. Spring heat and a breezeless day fill the street with an all-pervasive funkiness.

"Where you off to, daughter? Wid that sack o' stuff in your chest?"

"Oh, hi Big Momma...I'm just goin' down to the laundromat." She sits the bag down and looks up and down the street, frowns across the street at Phyllissine Evans and the young dude everyone calls Chu-man. Chu-man has his arm around Phyllissine's back, feeling the edge of her breast with his fingertip on the q.t.

"You'a be passin' the store, won't you? Would you brang me a can o' Garrett's snuff when you come back? Here's a dollar. If that Ko'rean done gone up, don't git it! I'd rather do without... them Ko'reans just charge us anything they wants to... Oh...what's happenin' with Fred Lee?"

Bessie fidgets with the drawstrings on the top of the laundry bag... "Looks like he's gon' have to do some time, Big Momma. I didn't have any money to bail 'im out with...so..."

"That's really too bad...boy done served his country 'n all, the way he did. Seems like they oughta give 'im some kinda break for fightin' those Viet'nese. Well...I'm gon' say some prayers for him."

"Thanks, Big Momma...that'll help. He needs all the help he can get. I'll bring your snuff when I git back."

"If ya have to add a couple more pennies, go 'head 'n get it... I'll pay you when you get back...Lawd ha' mercy! Thangs is so high these days."

"Ain't it the truth!" Bessie replies, and lifts the bag back up into her arms.

Milfred Hawkins treads his way up the street, avoiding collisions by the use of some kind of internal radar, strolls past Big Momma and the group, his bassoon, neatly swathed in a leather carrying case, in the other hand...his ski cap slanted above a blissful smile.

Mayflower prances by in the opposite direction, proudly swinging his purse, enjoying the attention given.

"Hi Big Momma," he sings up past the snigglers on the stoop, "ain't it a beautiful day?"

"For some folks it is...sho' is a pretty handbag you got there."

Sherman and Chico Daddy look meanly at Mayflower... their -we-hate-sissies-look.

"Ain't it somethin' else!" Mayflower says, defiantly staring back at the two Afro-Lords. "I was strollin' through Mickum's the other day and spotted this, and I thought to myself...girrrlll! That's just... too...too! You have just *got* to have that! You just *got* to! So, I bought it! Right then 'n there!"

"Hmmf! Musta cost you a pretty penny," Big Momma comments, with acid on her tongue.

"You can say that again! A pretty penny indeedy!"

"I'll bet it did," Sherman mumbles to Chico Daddy as they watch Mayflower switch away, swinging his purse gaily.

John 15X eases up to Bam and Baby June farther up the street, on well conditioned welterweight feet.

"How come you brothers ducked out on me Sunday? I thought you all were serious about goin' over to the mosque with me?"

"We was serious, man," Baby June mumbles between swollen lips, as he tries to focus on John 15X with his two black eyes. "We was serious...we just had to get away from Kwendi and them other young fools."

John 15X takes a long, compassionate look at their discolorations, swellings and painful looking cuts...adjusts his bow tie suavely.

"Don't look like you got too far away, brothers."

"Heyyyy...don't rub it in, brother...I'm sick as I can be."

"Me too, man."

"I know what you two brothers are goin' through...believe me, *I know*...like I told y'all before...when I had a Jones...I sho' nuff had a Jones.

John 15X stands straight and pencil slim, nourished on positive thoughts about himself, rappin' to Bam and Baby June about the virtues of life in the Nation.

XXX XXX XXX

Lucille and Ferguson Smith sit at their kitchen table, leisurely sipping their Saturday-morning-ain't got-to-go-to-work-coffee.

"Fergy?"

"Huhnnn??"

"Fergy?"

"Yeah baby?"

"Fergy, put your newspaper down a minute."

"Uh huh...what is it?"

"Did you hear Milfred playin' last night?" she asks, stirring more sugar into her coffee.

"Umm huh...yeah, I heard 'im...sort of," Fergy smiles back.

"That thing he blows didn't sound too bad, did it? Strange as it is, I mean, well...it sounded kinda nice, in a way, don't you think?"

"Might be 'cause neither one of us had t' get up to go to work this mornin'..."

"Maybe...maybe..."

"It doesn't matter anyway, now...we won't be hearin' 'im anymore anyway...I don't think."

"What do you mean? What!?"

"I saw 'im walkin' down the street a lil' while ago, with a bobtail suitcase and that...that...bassoon. First time I'd ever seen him out in the daytime since he moved in. I guess Nolan must've given him notice."

"That figures, rent day is Monday...so I guess if he is gone, he picked a good time. Ooooops! Lemme get outta here! Diane'll be waitin' in front of her house, tappin' her foot by now."

"Don't spend all *my* money!"

"Our money, you mean! Don't worry...hah hah hah...I'll see you later. You goin' out?"

"Might...in a lil while."

"Well, before you do, don't forget to fix that toilet... I'm gettin' tired of hearin' that thing run all the time."

"Uh huh...uh huh...all right."

"Don't forget now, Fergy!"

"Yeah...okay baby...don't worry 'bout it, I'll take care of it."

Lucille leans over, behind Fergy's already re-raised newspaper, and sticks a warm kiss to his mouth.

"Fergy...I love you, honey."

Fergy looks surprised and pleased as she hastily departs.

XXX XXX XXX

John 15X continues spieling...watching closely as Bam and Baby June lean against each other in pure misery, seek the mercy of someplace to sit, rest, be sick...they wander around the corner and into the alley as John 15X follows them, persistently.

"Give us a try, brothers...what have you got to lose? A dirty rotten stinkin' life of crime and time...that's all. I'm tellin' you I know what that blue-eyed devil has hooked you up on. I was there, deep in the heart of all that devil-caused misery you goin' through right this minute... I'm tellin' you brothers...I was there, believe me! Bam, you remember when I was in that bag!"

"Yeahhhh," Bam moans. "Yeahhhh John...I remember."

"Awright then, brothers...how 'bout it? If I managed to do it, messed up as I was, you can too."

"Goddamn! I'm sick. . .shiiii-it! Motherfuckin' cramps...come on June...we go to go...do...somethin'."

They move away from John 15X, ashamed to look in his eyes as they accelerate to their familiar wolfish trot. John 15X stands watching them go, tears running down his cheeks.

XXX XXX XXX

"All right everybody!" Kwendi shouts above the buzzing of the people in the workshop. "Let's have a little order about ourselves! Thank you! As you all can see, I've invited Brother Rudy, Brother Sherman, Brother BoBo, Brother Woods and Chico Daddy."

"Hey, Kwendi! I'm a brother too."

"Hahhh hah! Sorry 'bout that! And...Brother Chico Daddy."

"Right on!"

"Anyway, I've invited these brothers in, in line with our policy, to hear our program and...uh...maybe, if they can dig where we comin' from, they might want to join our group...each one of these brothers has been vouched and spoken for, so I'm not goin' to waste a lot o' time shuckin' 'n jivin'... I think we've done enough of that already."

Chiyo Mungu raises his fist to be recognized. "I got one question. Why do we have to have this meetin' on Saturday night... I was 'sposed to be goin' to..."

Kwendi cuts into him sharply. "Can you think of a better time than Saturday night for niggers to get anything together? Maybe if we gave up a few more of our Saturday nights, then it might be Sunday for a lot more sisters 'n brothers, dig it?"

"Right on!"

Kwendi looks around fiercely at the group...Abdul and Ojenkasi at his side, Lubertha behind him, studying the group with dancing eyes.

"We got together the other night, for the information of all those who were not here at the time, and drew up a list of things we think need doin' in our community, right now! Not tomorrow or next week, or when somebody finally begs Whitey into doin' it, but right now! The program ain't really been completely laid out yet... but we think we can make a good beginning' by just working' on these things as a start. You can change the order of things around as you see fit. I'm gonna just read 'em as we come up with 'em..."

Kwendi opens up a notebook in front of him. "Number one...we want an end to the robbery that the merchants in our area practice every day; whether they be food merchants, clothes merchants, or whoever is selling us somethin' rotten, or that we don't need, for too much..."

"I bet Sweet Peter D. won't be sellin' anything else when he gets out of the hospital," Abdul interjects.

"If he ever gets out, you mean," Johnny Fox reaffirms, slapping Abdul's palm.

Rudy eases through the sudden hubbub with a question mark on his forehead. "I heard about that...did you all...?"

"You damned right we did," Kwendi reaffirms, vehemently. "But we can talk about that later...lemme finish this first." Rudy looks away sourly.

"Number two...we want decent housing, fit for the shelter of Human Beings. Number three...we want, we demand, textbooks and courses in *our* schools to be relevant to who we were, what we are, and what we might become...if international Whitey ever starts actin' like a human being. Number four...bear with me now, I've only got two more to read...number four...we want an end to police cruelty and systematic murder of Black people. That means, to put it another way, we do not need to be over-policed and under-protected by people who hate our guts to begin with."

Rudy raises his fist urgently...

"Hold it a minute, brother...number five...we want the people of our community, the Black community, to be brought to trial and dealt with by a jury of their peers. If we have to be tried for anything at all!"

"Whatchu mean by peers!" Chico Daddy asks, innocently.

"Peers, man!" Sherman tells him, scornfully. "People like us, like the people in this room."

"Awww...I thought...uhhh huh...yeah, I can dig it."

"And number six...but not last, or least, we want freedom. We want the power to determine the destiny of our community."

"Which means," Ojenkasi adds, "that we want the White boy to stop tryin' to tell us what to do!"

"Hey man," BoBo calls out. "You didn't say nothin' 'bout jobs. Me *and* my Daddy is outta work!"

"We can put that in," Kwendi says, closing the notebook. "We don't have a lotta things written out, but we know about 'em, everybody knows about 'em, we can add those later. Well, what do you think, brothers? Have we got a beginnin' ...can you dig where we comin' from?"

"I can dig it all!" Rudy says. "And I could maybe add some things...but how do you plan to go about doin' all this?"

"By whatever means necessary!" Kwendi answers, jaws clenched.

"Like beatin' heads?"

"If you talkin' 'bout Sweet Peter D., Rudy...I'll say this...you don't see him out there on the corner kickin' LuLu and Idella in the ass tonight, do you? Settin' the worse kind of example for our young brothers...or pushin' heroin off on our lil' sisters 'n brothers!"

"Yeah man...I can dig that. But that ain't really gettin' to where all the shit is comin' from. Sweet Peter D. is backed by..."

"We don't give a damn who he's backed by...if he brings his ass onto one of these corners, we'll off him too! Sweet Peter was just a start in the right direction!"

"And if we ain't got the means to deal with whoever, we'll get the means!" Ojenkasi calls out.

"That's just what I'm talkin...the methods I think you all plannin' to use! Violence breeds violence!"

"Awwww bullshit, mannnn!"

"Sho' is outta pocket, Rudy!"

Kwendi holds up his hands to cool out further comment. "No... no... I think you're wrong, brother. I really and truly do. I've thought about it for quite awhile now...quite awhile...and I'm damn near certain that I'm livin' in a place where violence, 'specially Black violence, can stop violence! The kind that they killin' us with every day of the week and twice on Sunday! What you got to realize, Rudy, is this one thing, that the people who rule this country...Whitey don't really understand but one thing, violence! That's his strength and his weakness! And if you don't go to that, you'll be runnin' 'round tryin' to be White, beggin', tryin' to fit in and do a whole bunch o' thangs that won't really matter...'cause the only thing Whitey understands is death and destruction, that's his heritage, dig it?"

The workshop is momentarily stricken with silence.

"Hey, I can dig the program, brother...what do I have to do to get in the group?"

"You already in it, Sherman," Nici Miles assures him. "You were born into it."

Rudy looks around, disturbed at the vibrations aroused by Kwendi's answers.

"Dig Rudy," Kwendi says to him. "You're a good brother 'n all, but it's time to go to some other places. We've argued with each other a helluva lot, up 'n down the streets, 'n I have a lot of respect for your ideas, but, like the sister said to us on the corner the other day...it's time to struggle...are you with us?"

XXX XXX XXX

Lena Daniels walks hurriedly, apprehensively, up the back steps to Miss Rabbit's apartment...checking the shadowed spaces carefully as she goes, a peach cobbler held out like an altar offering.

Miss Rabbit, hip to the Saturday night drama, opens her back door cautiously... "Well now, Mrs. Daniels, what have you got here?" Her eyes measure the deep, aluminum-covered dish.

"It's a peach cobbler, and I hope you enjoy it, Miss Rabbit."

Miss Rabbit politely takes the cobbler from Lena's hands, sits it on her checkered kitchen table, slowly folds the foil back. "I know I'm gonna enjoy this, honey...sho' is a beautiful light crust on it."

"And it's still pipin' hot."

"You wanna stay and have a taste of it with me?"

"No...thank you... I got to be gettin' back... Jim promised me he was gon' take me downtown to the show tonight."

"Ahhemm...how is Jim?"

"Fine"...Lena responds with a blissful smile. "Jim's just fine."

XXX XXX XXX

Saturday night...fire, water, ice, revolution from necessity... patience worn out, an invasion.

Deep Saturday night, a discussion, an argument, the wound festering, decisions made by the Decisive, an invasion...an invasion, anything smelling of independence. Well...the fucking communists were supposed to be telling Black people they should have human rights in the '60's...so what's new?

XXX XXX XXX

Rappin' Rudy, surrounded by fewer followers, leans into his favorite stance...a sad expression on his mug, a direct contrast to the brightness of this particular Sunday.

"Well...actually...in a sense, it don't really make too much sense to be runnin' this whole thing down to you. Y'all know what happened last night? Pigs busted in, actin'...as usual, wild 'n crazy, messin' with people, pulled all of us out...one o' 'em started feelin' around on Lubertha like he was searchin' for a weapon or somethin' and Kwendi went off! First time I'd ever seen him that way! Anyway, by the time all the shit got unscrambled, Kwendi had snatched that little bastard's piece, what's his name?"

"Jonesy?"

"Yeahhh...that's the one! Kwendi snatched his piece and burned 'im!"

"Oh wowww!"

"Right in the gut! When that happened, a whole bunch o' shit started...some more pigs showed up and the whole scene got wilder still...Ojenkasi, Tucker and Abdul started a hassle with the other pigs that gave Lubertha and Kwendi a chance to get away...it was a wild scene. We all did what we could...they cracked Nici in the head, Sherman got shot in the hip...tryin' to get away, and everybody else got carried off...pigs talkin' about conspiracy or some shit, whatever that's supposed to mean!"

"What happened to you, man," one of the groups asks him.

Rudy opens his mouth to sow four bottom teeth missing. "You see I'm here...don'tchu? And I'll say this right now...Kwendi was right! The only way to get the shit squared away here is to do it with sticks, knives, guns, any fuckin' thing you can get your hands on, 'cause Whitey has no respect for anything but violence, with a capital V!"

"What's gon' happen to Lubertha and Kwendi?"

"Better hope they get away...to begin with..."

CHAPTER XII

GOD BLESS THE CHILD...

Hattie Evans and Thelma Edwards peer over the window ledge, down onto the street.

"Who is it? Which one?" Hattie asks, squinting.

"It's just the one they call Rappin' Rudy out there...flappin' his jaws off about Lubertha and Kwendi."

"Yeahhh! I heard the police broke in on that workshop thing they had last night, while they was makin' bombs or somethin'... and arrested a bunch of 'em. Lubertha and Kwendi got away...that's what I heard."

"Uh huh...I understand they holdin' old man Adams in connection with the whole business. Can you imagine how upset Charlotte and Ed must be now?!"

"Yes indeed...I certainly can," Hattie answers, her mouth curled in a wry smile. "Yes indeed...but go on...what were you sayin', before Lubertha and that boy came up?"

"Oh...anyway, you *know* the way they are, Hattie! The minute they begin to smell hey britches and they lil' ol' pee-pees start gettin' hard, you can't tell 'em a blessed thing."

A two-man police squad car slowly wheels through the block, police calls ringing out, somehow, above the rest of the noise on the street. Rudy dips and slips down behind his group, dashes through a urine-splattered passageway leading to the back alley.

The policemen spot him briefly, rev up and whip around the block, lights suddenly gleaming on the top of their machine, siren zoooonning...all done under the sullen, hostile eyes of the neighborhood.

Hattie and Thelma take a quick, complete look at the squad car speeding through and return to their conversation without comment.

"Noooo...you can't tell 'em a damned thing. Ain't that the truth! But it ain't him I'm worried about, it's her I got to watch. She came sneakin' in here the other night, headin' straight for the bathroom, but somebody was already in there, so she didn't get a chance to rub out the stain on her dress. If I'd followed my first mind, I woulda knocked her ass back down the stairs, but well...I don't know...I started thinkin', I guess, 'bout some of the things we used to do and..."

"What did she say to you, Hattie?"

"Ain't so much what she said to me...it's what I said to her...you wanna 'nother can? It oughta be cold by now."

"Burrrp! No thank ya, Hattie...you know how I get after a brew and I've already had two already. What did you say to her?"

"I just came on out 'n told 'er...I said, Phyllissine, people been talkin' about you and Chu-man all hemmed up in these hallways 'n whatnot. Bessie Mae told me just the other day that she'd caught 'em in the hallway."

"What did she say?"

"Well...I could tell I'd hit a nerve 'cause her eyelids drooped all the way down to her kneecaps. I ain't been doin' nothin' wrong, Momma... I ain't been doin' nothin' wrong. That's what she says to me...but you know how children lie these days."

"Lie faster than a cat can lick his ass! Hell! I don't know! Whatcha gon' do with 'em?"

"I don't rightly know, Thelma... I don't rightly know. I've told her a thousand times, if you go out there and git a big belly, it'll be your lil' red wagon. I ain't about to become nobody's babysittin' grandmomma...uhnn unhnn...not me! Much livin' as I got to do yet!"

"I know whatchu mean! I know just whatchu mean! Hmf! Ohh...'fore I forget...almost slipped my mind. You know 'Nita is gonna have a bingo game tonight, don'tchu?"

"It's about time. We been havin' games all winter at everybody's house but hers...it's 'bout time she broke down. What she gon' have?"

"Chit'lins, cole slaw, 'tater salad and monkey bread. She's tellin' everybody to brang their own, we might play a lil' sniff 'n sip whist."

Hattie peers anxiously out of the window for a second, checking out the back of a figure that resembles her daughter's. "I'll try to make it if I can...but...well...I gotta stay pretty close to home these days. The minute I leave here Chu-man is blowin' smoke all over the doorknob... Lawd only knows what's happenin' while I'm at work."

"I know how it is, Hattie...me 'n Mathew ain't never had none, but we've helped brang up a few. If you need any kind o' help, you know where my door is."

"I really 'ppreciate that, Thelma...I really do. I 'member somethin' Earl used to say to me a lot...before he...uh...went away. Baby, he'd say, having a girl baby is a helluva lot harder than havin' a boy baby...all you have to worry 'bout is one lil' ding-a-thing when you got a boy...but when you got a girl, you got to worry 'bout all the ding-a-things on the block!"

"Ha! ha! ha! hahhh! That Earl was always sayin' somethin' like that. I heard him tell Matthew one day...man, you know what Confucius said? 'Virgin just like balloon, one prick, all over!' Hahhhh hah! Hattie...you ever...hear from him?"

Hattie responds with studied casualness. "Ooo...every now 'n then I catch sight of 'im slippin' 'n slidin' 'round one o' these corners...or he'll pop in for a hot minute with a lil' money for Phyllissine and be hot to get a piece. That woman is really runnin' that man into the ground...last time I saw 'im he was thin as a rail."

"Yeah, I know. Mathew told me he saw him down at the Dew Drop Inn the other night. Well...you know what the say... 'the Lawd works in mysterious ways' sometimes. Hattie...listen, I got to run... we'll be sittin' up here runnin' our *mouthes* all afternoon. Mathew'll be home in a while, actin' like a grizzly bear."

"He workin' on Sunday?"

"Just a half a day. They had a heavy shipment comin' in this mornin' and old man Bugosi asked him if he'd come in and help unload, for time and a half. We sho' could use the money. Where's Phyllissine?"

"She was gone when I got up. That's the kind of thing she's doin' these days...'specially on the weekends...leaves at eight or nine in the mornin'. You know how I like to sleep late on Saturday 'n Sunday, and sometimes I don't see 'er again 'til that time in the evenin'."

"Tsk! Tsk! Tsk! Hattie...you gon' have to chastise that child!"

"I done damned near wore out her Daddy's razor strop on her behind. I don't know too much else to do...at fourteen, she's almost as heavy as I am. Like I said, I told her...Phyllissine, if you get a big belly, you gon' be in trouble in mo' ways than one."

Thelma Edwards struggles to her feet, swaying a little from arthritic stiffness. "Well, I know you doin' your best," she says. "Like I said, if I can help in any way, just let me know."

"I sure will, Thelma. Are you sure you don't want another brew before you go?"

"If I do, I never will be able to get outta here, and Lawd knows I got things to do. Try to make 'Nita's game tonight, Mr. Jackson's gonna be there."

"That old geechee!"

"Well...you know how much he loves bingo...and ever since his wife passed..."

"Thelma Edwards! Hahhhah...hahhh...you git outta here, talkin' that trash!"

"Man has a nice little business, Hattie...and he ain't the worst lookin' man on the block."

"Ha! And he ain't the best lookin' one neither!"

"Burrrrp! I...uh...I guess you got somethin' there, but I know for a fact that he's got eyes for you."

"I guess beggars can't be choosy, huh?"

"Now come on, Hattie! You too good lookin' a woman t' be talkin' like that. Anyway...come on over if you get a chance."

"Okay...I'll try."

"All right...talk to you later on." Thelma Edwards weaves to the door, tipsy after a midday brew sip-gossip session.

Hattie Evans returns to the small table nestled at the window's edge, a half-empty can of warm beer cradled in her work-worn fingers. She sits...listening to the thum and hum of the street, staring pensively at the brand label on her beer can. The sudden loud noise of children playing a game jerks her head around. Phyllissine and Chu-man stroll up the street... Chu-man staggers a bit, loaded on reds. He lets his hand drift from Phyllissine's waist to her buttocks, brushes, feels, rubs, caresses, 'til she knocks his hand away playfully. Minutes go by as Hattie waits, slowly turning the beer can around in a wet ring on the table, impatiently.

Phyllissine, lithe, lush brown, slightly bovine, pops into the room, slamming the door behind her, looks quickly and evasively at her mother and heads straight for the refrigerator. She peers inside intently, "What we got to eat, Momma?"

"Where you been, Phyllissine?" her mother asks, in a hard, flat tone.

"Oh...up 'n down the street," she answers, snatching the last piece of salami from the under stocked 'fridge. "Over at Mary Jo's for awhile and then..."

"Up and down the street where, Phyllissine? Me and Miz Edwards been sittin' right here in this window just about all afternoon and we ain't seen hide or hair of you in all that time... and the first time I do catch sight o' you...you come strollin' up the street wit that no-count bastard Chu-man...with his hand all over yo' rump!"

Phyllissine stands awkwardly, posing with one leg bent to the side, popping gum and switching stances as the mood of her mother's lecture goes from light logic to heavy drama. Mrs. Evans' temples bleed with repressed anger and her right eye twitches as she goes on. And on. And on.

"Now Phyllissine! I've told you a million times not to be rippin' 'n runnin' up and down these streets with boys hangin' all over you! Especially Chu-man! You know he ain't no good! Boy ain't but fifteen years old and got two babies already."

Phyllissine, tired from a full day of rippin' 'n runnin' up and down the street with Chu-man, nods listlessly, sighs slightly with boredom between gum chops.

"Now Im tellin' you, Phyllissine! It's gonna be your lil' red wagon! Chu-man ain't got no job, ain't got a pot to piss in or a window to throw it out of!"

As her mother rages on and on...Phyllissine's attention wanders so completely that it appears she has mentally blotted her mother out.

"Phyllissine! Phyllissine! Damnit! You hear me?!"

Mrs. Evans suddenly springs from her chair, enraged by her daughter's lack of attention. "After all I done for you! And you run around like a common hussy!" Mrs. Evans screams the words out, hitting at Phyllissine's head with the beer can, slinging a sparkling stream of warm beer across the room.

Phyllissine casually dodges the can and her mother's flailing fists, at first...'til the full weight of her attack lands. She stumbles backwards, shielding her face and head with her arms as her mother hits wildly at her with open palms, and then her fists, and finally with a hairbrush snatched from the dresser.

Her anger is a grunted, disgusted, mad, savage, primitive one... between the two of them, Hattie Evans' angry grunts and the deep-throated screams coming out of Phyllissine, the small room rocks with a feeling that can only be called madness. Phyllissine, bruised, too hurt to scream any longer... Finally, her mother's anger and her attack slow down, 'til she is just simply pounding at her daughter's body with no strength in the blows, the handle of the brush broken off on Phyllissine's head. And then she stops, crying bitterly, along with Phyllissine...hard, cold, brutal tears...milked from her by frustrated visions and lack of breath.

Phyllissine sits sobbing on the floor, her head resting on the side of the bed, lumps, snot and tears streaking her pretty brown face.

Mrs. Evans walks slowly, woodenly, away from her, to the refrigerator, pulls another can of beer out of a six-pack and moves heavily past her daughter, back to the open window. She sits, looking tired, angry, and blue.

The room and space between mother and daughter is filled with spent tension, but not private tension. Below them the sound of a blasting car horn, from the next room the sounds of a man and a woman making drunken, loud, careless love...and from other places an El train rumbling by, the gravelly sound of Rev. Tilly, Aretha, Ray, Pharoah, Sun Ra, Ornette, Cecil, Mongo, the screams and yells of a group of playing children.

Phyllissine crawls up over the side of the bed, swollen, hurt, in a state of shock...crying bitter, sporadic tears. Hattie Evans sits, quietly sipping her beer, tears running over her cheeks and down into the corners of her mouth. Phyllissine sobs herself off to sleep, while her mother remains in place, shaking her head slowly as though trying to rid herself of evil thoughts.

The two of them remain in place, as though in a state of suspended animation...the daughter beaten and worn...the mother worn and beaten...almost.

XXX XXX XXX

"Phyllissine? Phyllissine?! Wake up, baby...let Momma talk to you."

Phyllissine jerks backward on the bed involuntarily as her mother reaches out to pull her into her arms... "Don't be afraid, honey...Momma's sorry...I guess I just lost my temper, I'm sorry."

They sit, in a warm silhouette, framed in the half-light of early evening, mother and daughter with their arms around each other, crying quietly.

Hattie Evans holds her daughter's tearstained face in her hands, trying to blot out, in some way, the noise, the filth, the rats, roaches, poverty and meanness of their lives.

"Baby...listen to me, please... Momma don't wanna be beatin' on you, but that's the only way I can teach you what you have to know in life. Life is hard and men ain't nothin' but dogs and that's a lesson you got to learn early in life! Men will sweet-talk you and jive you 'til they get what they want, and after that, they don't wanna have nothin' else to do with you. Now don't get me wrong!

Some men ain't like that...but most of 'em is. And 'til you learn the diff'rence between the two, you got to really be on guard...or as y'all say nowadays...you got t' be on your job."

"What it is..." Phyllissine says quietly, and she and her mother look at each other openly, with affection for the first time since she entered the room.

"Phyllissine...you gettin' to be too big a girl for me to be throwin' you around this room the way I'm doin'..."

They both stare suddenly, fearfully, at the door as several bodies in the hallway wrestle-bump through it, the sounds of men arguing come through and then fade as they go on.

"I know what I think you really need, probably more than any advice I can give," Mrs. Evans continues. "You know what that is?"

Phyllissine shakes her head slowly, negatively, from side to side, as she wipes her nose with the back of her hand.

Mrs. Evans gently removes her hands from her daughter, a determined look in her eyes, begins to bustle about the dingy little apartment, assembling herself. She pulls a blood-red dress with fringes around the hipline from a small collection of outdated dresses in her closet, shakes her head negatively and pulls another one out, weights the merits of the two dresses carefully and finally decides to stick with the red fringe. Mrs. Evans, totally caught up in the dress selection thing, temporarily forgets her daughter, who sits up in bed watching her mother's actions with a puzzled expression.

"Momma?"

"Huh?"

"You never did tell me what it was you thought I needed."

Mrs. Evans pauses in the course of greasing her legs and gives Phyllissine a secretive little smile... "I got it in mind, sweetheart... got it in mind, if it works out okay, I'll tell you about it later on."

Phyllissine continues staring at her mother quizzically. "You goin' out somewhere?"

Mrs. Evans, in her best nylon slip, putting on makeup in the mirror, mumbles, "To a bingo game at 'Nita's." And goes on to her hair, strugglin a bit with the handle-less brush. Phyllissine hops from the bed to help her mother, beads of perspiration on her forehead and top lip, zip up the slightly-too-tight red dress.

They manage, with a joint effort, Mrs. Evans sucking in deeply, Phyllissine pulling the zipper up, to get the dress on.

"Well, how do I look?" she asks, making a couple turns in place.

"It looks nice, Momma...it really does."

Mrs. Evans sways rhythmically a few times, suddenly caught up by the music from someone's radio being played weekend loud down the hall. She bounces over to a cheap mahogany jewel box for a piece of costume jewelry to set her dress off with, hummmmmming a bit as she does so.

Finally, satisfied that her thing is together, she turns to Phyllissine. "Now listen...I may not be in 'til late... I want you to stay inside the rest of the evenin'...a girl can't do nothin' but get herself into a whole bunch o' trouble bein' out in the streets late at night, okay?"

"Okay, Momma...what we got to eat?"

Mrs. Evans re-powders the moist places on her face, digs down into her purse and hands Phyllissine five dollars.

"Take this and run down to Pop's Place and buy yourself a couple hamburgers. I'll bring some food home when I come home. 'Nita's cookin' chit'lins 'n stuff."

Phyllissine folds the three dollars into a neat square and balls her fist around it. Momma gives her daughter a quick, urgent peck on the cheek and a tender hug.

"You be good now! I shouldn't be out too late...run on down to Pops and come right on back, don't be lollygaggin' 'round, you understand? You got your key?"

Phyllissine nods yes stiffly, silently showing her mother the apartment key on a string around her neck. Mrs. Evans pauses at the door to see if she has her own key and, without another word, leaves...her jaws set for bear.

Phyllissine stands, as though rooted to the spot for a moment, slowly wanders over to her mother's last beer can, shakes it for proof of content and then downs the dregs. She wanders listlessly, aimlessly, about the room, sits staring out of the window at all the people on the street for a couple of minutes and finally, impulsively, decides to go for her hamburgers.

She trips through the hallway of her building, pausing to be curious at each door, starts downstairs and meets Chu-man lounging on the second-floor landing with Billy Woods and BoBo, killing a pint of White Port. They make a sudden move to run before realizing who it is...settle back into their groove, seeing that it's only Phyllissine.

Chu-man, thin, hawk face shadowed under a big hat propped rakishly on his bulging Afro, suavely reaches for Phyllissine's arm as she walks past him.

"Where you goin', girrrl?" he asks, in his best Sweet Peter voice.

"Ohhh," she answers, grinning, love flashing, "nowhere in particular...just walkin' out..."

Chu-man pulls back up the steps a bit, whispers loudly, "Come on, go up on the roof with me...I wanna show you somethin'."

"You want this corner Chu-man?" BoBo calls up to him as he and Phyllissine start back up the stairs.

"Naw...go 'head, y'all kill it," he calls back, making an obscene gesture behind Phyllissine's back.

On the rooftop, filled with as much garbage as any of the alleys below, they spot...over in one corner, behind a crumbling chimney, two glowing tips going around in a circle.

"Must be Willie and some o' the fellas gettin' loaded," Chu-man says, trying to make out all the faces in the dark.

He leads her by the hand to another section of the roof, behind a chimney. They stand, leaning against the waist-high roof edge, staring down, fascinated by the sight of the swarming people on the street below doing so many different things at one time...and by the glistening lights from the tall buildings downtown, throwing a spectrum of colors on low-lying clouds.

Chu-man edges behind Phyllissine, aligns himself to the shape of her behind, locks his arms around her waist and begins to nibble on her earlobe and kiss her on her neck.

"Stop, Chu-man, don't do that! I got to go."

But Chu-man doesn't stop, his hands go on...to cup her breasts, to reach and to push his slender fingers into the elastic top of her panties.

She turns to face him as he attempts to pull her down onto the gravel surface of the roof. "Ooooh Chu-man...I love you so much," she says and kisses him, her eyes closed and trusting, his open and cynical. He crudely pulls her dress up, starts yanking her panties down and off, and trying, in the same motions to unzip his fly.

"Chu-mannnn...Chu-mannnn," she whispers to him as she permits herself to be stretched out on the roof, "you know I think you wrong about my period! I don't think I'm just irregular...I've missed three times in a row now...I think I'm pregnant. I don't think those red devils you gave me work."

Chu-man shows the slightest possible interest in the information Phyllissine lays on him. He begins to make hard, forceful motions inside her. "Move," he whispers abruptly. "Move over this way a lil' bit! This damned gravel is hurtin' my knees..."

Three large silhouettes ooze into view, freezing Phyllissine's motions with fear...towering above the two of them.

"Whassamatter?" Chu-man asks, breathing hard. "You don't dig the way I fuck or somethin'?"

"I don't think that's it, young blood," one of the figures says, the joint still glowing in his fingers, "I think she's just waitin' for a real dick, that's all."

Chu-man looks over his shoulder with fear and the shame of knowing what is about to go down.

"Go 'head and finish, lil' bruh...I'd wait an hour for a shot o' that tender young pussy."

One of the figures nudges Chu-man in the side with the toe of his shoe and asks, in a cold-blooded voice... "We ain't don' have no trouble outta you, are we, young blood?"

Phyllissine holds her face in her hands, trying for a scream that won't come, as Chu-man's body rolls off of hers, exposing her nakedness to the night air.

CHAPTER XIII

AFRICANTHROPUS ERECTUS

Africanthropus Erectus

Deep...deep in the guts of shadowed back steps...
shrouded by piss-stenched hallways, fumbling rats and
benign neglect...
The dark baby boy screwed his slender face into a criss-crossed
knot,
tightened the cord on his bubbled vein...
and impatiently waited his turn...
The thin, flayed arm, traced to the wrist with sullen
bites from the angry needle...
slowly settled itself by the side of his slim dark body...

stung by the Horse...
There were no grass bound lawns, romping dogs or
indulgent parents shedding social tears over his dry little frame...
no concerned society to mourn him...
no informative pieces in Life or Look...
Just a mean clutch of men from downtown...
bending stiffly to snatch the smoking spike from his silent limb...
smiling secretly at the thought of another nigger gone...
Bam.

XXX XXX XXX

Bam and Baby June look around anxiously at Mayflower's back door...knock timidly. Baby June gives Bam a sharp look and motions for him to knock again, harder.

Mayflower, inside the apartment, in the front room with drawn shades, practicing exotic steps to exotic music for an exotic, sometime-to-be-performed dance, finally hears noise at the back door...skips through gaily.

"Better say who, quickly...else you gon' stay out there!"

"It's me, baby lady," Bam answers, in a mustered up macho voice. "Me, Mr. Bam Lovestick."

Mayflower peeks out at the two of them on her back steps... ignores Baby June after a glance.

"Bam...are you drunk or somethin'? What's this lovestick business?"

Baby June drives on him quickly, urgently. "Dig Mayflower... you been pretty nice people to both of us and we thought...well... you go 'head 'n tell 'er Bam." He nudges Bam in the ribs to get him started.

"Well you see...it's like this, Maylady...we got some stuff and we wanna take off and we ain't got nowhere to go. The streets is red hot...some rotten niggers raped that lil' ol' Evans girl..."

"Yeahhh, I heard 'bout that! Niggers is sho' nuff changin'... never used to commit suicide and rape."

Baby June nudges him again, harder. "Uh huh...right on! Anyway, the streets is smokin'...ever since that shit with Kwendi, we really been in a bind...we ain't sure but we think Sweet Peter might put out a contract for our asses, and if that ain't bad 'nuff...there's a bunch o' crazy motherfuckers who raped that girl."

Mayflower, left hand placed saucily on hip. "Ain't gon' make my house no shootin' gallery, no suh-ree!"

Bam, turning up his sweetest, most appealing choir-boy face. "Awwww...come on Miss Maylady...don't be that way, all we wanna do is spend one night, we can git on in the daytime...but you know how it is, we apt to sho' nuff get busted lurkin' 'round on Sunday night."

Mayflower opens the door, stands in it, his look going from hard to soft, taking in the two pathetic figures drooping on his doorstep.

"Well...come on, one night ain't gonna make all that much difference, I guess. Bam...I remember lookin' at you in high school thinkin', he could be the sweetest thing since Baby Ruth, if he'd stop hangin' out with...Baby June." The two men rush in gratefully as Mayflower carries on a non-stop conversation with them and himself.

"Baby June...why don't you go home and stay with yo' Momma?"

"Hey May...you know I would if I could, but Momma barred me from the crib...only way I can get in is to break in."

"Uh huh...I can dig it. Go on in the front room and take care your business, I'm gon' make some coffee, anybody want some?"

Bam and Baby June slouch through the small apartment, checking, subconsciously, for anything of value.

"Uh...nawww, Maysister...we don't want no coffee."

Mayflower removes his stash of money from his hiding place, stuffs it down in his panties, makes instant coffee and walks in smiling...sits sipping coffee watching Bam and June cook and shoot.

"Damn! I missed! Com'mere May...hit me, will you?"

Mayflower sits his coffee cup down with a clatter... "Hell no! I said you could come in here and take care of it if you wanted to! I didn't say shit 'bout playin' nurse."

Mayflower grimaces as Baby June takes the hypo from Bam and hits him, expertly, in the neck.

"Listen...y'all gon' 'n do what you got to do, my thang is weed, cigarettes and men...and right now, damnit! I ain't got no cigarettes. Bam, June...either one of y'all got any?"

They both nod softly...no... already on their way ***Out There***. Mayflower with one lithe move, snatches his pants from a nearby chair and pulls them on over his leotards, whips the shoulder strap of his precious Sicilian purse over his shoulder and announces to his drugged guests:

"I'm goin' out to get some cigarettes...if I come back here and find one single goddamned thing missin' ...both o' you niggers can hang it up, dig it?"

Baby June, his head dripping down between his knees, answers for both of them... "Righttttt...onnnn..."

Mayflower looks at Bam, his head tilted back, his mouth dropped open and smiles. "Okay...be back in three shakes!"

Mayflower walks quickly through the slowed-down, Sunday night streets, digging, as usual, the attention paid him. He prances into the Dew Drop Inn, clangs cigarettes from the machine and suddenly, impulsively, decides to sit at the almost empty bar and have one.

"What'll it be, Henry?"

"Mac! I tol' you to stop callin' me Henry, either call me Mayflower or else I'm gonna take my business elsewhere."

"Sorry 'bout that," the bartender apologizes and lights his cigarette. Mayflower takes two petulant puffs before ordering.

"Do you have Champale, cold?"

"Yeah, baby...we got everything you want."

Mayflower looks carefully across at Mac the Bartender, sixty-three years young, pot-bellied and bald, and snorts derisively. "Hmmf! Shiiii-it! I'll bet you have. Lemme have a *cold* Champale in a champagne glass, that's one of those round shallow ones, and stick a cherry off in it for me, will ya, lover?"

Two couples, dregging through the weekend, sniggle-giggle at Mayflower. She burns them into the wall with an icy stare. And turns to sip delicately from his glass. Another couple, two men with thick necks and lumpy shoulders, check him out closely without a change of expression...hunch themselves over their beers.

Mayflower, enjoying the casual notoriety of being the only one of his kind in the bar, sashays over to the jukebox, plays three records and slithers back to his seat at the bar, bumping and grinding slightly, all the way.

"Mac...could I have another one of these...and would you please make it cold this time?"

Mac, with a slightly exasperated sigh, reaches down into his refrigerator-bar, feels several bottles and finally pops the cap from what seems to be the coldest one, pours up.

Mayflower, sighting himself in the bar mirror for the first time, primps his hair, studies the angles of his face carefully and exchanges a brief, knowing glance with one of the thick-necked men at the end of the bar.

Mayflower, conquest-positive...sips a few more swallows from his glass, exchanges another significant look with the gent at the end and prances past the sniggling couples, rolling his eyes in bitchy fashion on the way out.

Mayflower stretches luxuriantly outside the bar, glances back through the window to check to see if he is being followed...and smiles with ego-pleasure to see that he is.

He walks slowly, seductively, on the shadowed parts of the streets, waiting for her man to catch up. Goose pimples break out on his neck to hear, on a darkened section of the sidewalk, a hard, rasping voice.

"Hey...wait a minute...wait up, I want to talk to you!"

Mayflower wheels around, high fashion model style, and with a slender, well-manicured nail, points into his own chest. "Who? Me?" he asks, eyelashes blinking coyly.

The man strolls up to him, a rolling, weight-lifter's walk. "Yeahhh...you! I was in the bar a few minutes ago...and...uh..."

"I saw you. You and your buddy, what happened to him?"

"He decided he wanted to stay and drink beer...I decided I wanted to talk to you."

"What about?" Mayflower asks, slowly moving along, overjoyed at the boy-meets-girl strolling aspect of the situation.

"Oh...a whole bunch o' thangs...uh...why don't we sit in my car and talk about 'em? I'm parked across the street."

Mayflower throws his nose up in a huffy way. "I think you must be confused, honey! I don't know what gave you the idea that I make it my business to get in strange cars with strange men."

"Awww come on, you know me and I know you, how come we can't sit and talk a lil' bit?"

He graciously lights a cigarette for Mayflower, and he, with a moment's hesitation behind him, consents to the talk. "Okay...but just for a minute."

They cross the street, the man guiding Mayflower by the elbow to a brand new Chevy...he opens the door for Mayflower and on his way around to the other side of the car, unzips his pants and jumps in.

They sit for a long moment, and then the man uncorks his member from his opened fly. "You ever see anything this big?" he asks, waving it back and forth.

Mayflower glances quickly and then turns away, disgusted. "Don't be so vulgar! That's disgustin' the way some men act!" The other thick-necked man is suddenly at Mayflower's door, pulling him out of the car roughly as his partner, behind the wheel snatches with ham hands at Mayflower's purse.

"Oh my God!" Mayflower screams, trying to prevent himself from being snatched out of the car without his purse.

"Go 'head, man! Rip it off his arm!"

"She's holdin' on too tight!!"

Mayflower, screaming hysterically now, is hit several quick, methodical jabs in the mouth and nose, but still tries to escape clutching his purse.

With the man on the sidewalk blocking Mayflower's exit, his partner reaches down, stuffs his thing back into his pants, and pulls out a knife from his coat pocket and begins to saw at the strap of Mayflower's purse. Mayflower reacts by striking out blindly, courageously.

"Well...I'll be goddamned! This motherfuckin' punk got nerve enough to be hittin' me! You punk ass..."

The man behind the wheel thunks his knife into Mayflower's chest up to the hilt, pulls it out, and with the full power of his arm, slams it in, again and again.

"Pull this bitch outta here, Moose!" he calls out urgently to his partner on the street.

The occasional pedestrian has now become a fearful group of six, standing a safe distance away...trying to become brave enough to edge up to the car and ask what is happening.

Moose drags Mayflower from the car, throws him on the sidewalk, tries to pull the purse from his grasp one last time, fails, and kicks him in the face in exasperation. He jumps in the car, disgusted at the blood on the seat and the situation.

"Goddamn! Ray! Since when did you get so fuckin' weak you can't even pull a goddamned purse out of a sissy's hand?"

Ray, deliberately taking his time to back up and pull out, answers..."Didn't see you do no better! That punk really wanted to keep that pocketbook."

Moose, lookin out at Mayflower on the sidewalk as they begin to pull away... "Wait! Hold on a minute! If that sissy wants to keep that purse that fuckin' bad, he's got to have somethin' worthwhile in it. Wait!"

"Mannn! You crazy! You see all those people startin' to come out!?"

Ray accelerates in time to avoid having his car hit by a couple bricks, thrown by members of the group who've finally realized that they were watching an attempted robbery and the fatal stabbing of Henry Mayflower.

XXX XXX XXX

Baby June stretches himself into a long, fierce yawn...checks the daylight streaming through the lace-curtained window and creeps through the house looking for Mayflower.

"Guess the old girl musta gotten into somethin'," he mumbles to himself and pads to the kitchen to raid the refrigerator, scratching at his ribs, body beginning to feel the urge to nourish its Jones.

He wanders thoroughly through the apartment, his promise not to burglarize forgotten, nibbling on crackers and cheese. He strolls over to Bam. "Bam...wake up, man...you want some cheese 'n soda crackers? Just like a punk to be havin' somethin' like cheese"

He shakes Bam by the shoulder, jarring him from his head-back, mouth-open position.

Bam keels over onto the sofa cushions and down on the floor, stiffly.

"Bam?" Baby June speaks to him in a tiny, faraway voice, dropping cheese and crackers. "Bam...wake up man! Please wake up!"

Baby June stumbles over to a corner of the couch, too stunned for tears. He sits, staring at his friend, curled up on the floor, head held back stiffly, mouth frozen open...unable to move.

XXX XXX XXX

Big Momma drags her favorite chair and spittoon can out onto the front stoop...scans up and down the street for signs of anything unusual and, finally satisfied that there is no such animal, settles on her seat, trying to circulate the already humid air with a rolled-up newspaper...prepared to make a report on a bluer Monday than some of them have been.

Later in the day, Baby June makes it past Big Momma's post, half held up by John 15X... "I need help, brother...I'm sicker 'n anybody ever been...no bullshit!"

John 15X helps him along, pauses with him for a drawn-out session of the dry heaves into the gutter.

"I know you need help, brother...most Black people do, even if they ain't on drugs...'cause they still hopin', secretly...a lot of 'em, that the blue-eyed devil is gon' help them solve their problems. If they ain't learned better by this time...well..."

They struggle on up the street...Baby June's arms wrapped around Brother John 15X's shoulders.

Big Momma watches the two of them reach the corner and turn it... Her eyes sweep back to a big, black lettered group of words sprayed onto the side of the corner building. She pulls her glasses from her apron pocket, cleans them and leans forward slightly to read:

FREE LUBERTHA - FREE KWENDI
FREE BLACK PEOPLE, NOW!

Finally, she got what we needed!

It started here y'all…

ADDENDUM – "GHETTO SKETCHES, 2021"

This piece of writing came from "Brother Saul" in Yazoo City, Miss'ssippi. "Brother Saul" is one of Odie's Daddy's friends. He's about 100 now, full of piss and opinions.

He's an ex-share cropper and a felon – "I been framed twice 'cause they needed somebody to grow some cotton on the jailhouse plantation."

"Brother Saul" read "Ghetto Sketches". He thought about "Ghetto Sketches, 2021". He thought about what is going on today and he thought about what the future looks like. "Brother Saul" wrote the following thoughts. . . . **"Is Y'awl Craziii?"** is his first typed work.

"Is Y'awl Craziii?"

Y'awl **must** be crazy to think that we are goin' to allow y'awl to prevent us from voting?

After we have gone thru all of what we've gone thru to get to the vote.

Y'awl **<u>must</u>** be craziii to **even** think that we would drop down to where you once put us, to be where you once had us, to prevent us from voting.

We understand, we know, with all of your Inco-herent mis-understanding of our history, that you might be freaked into misunderstanding that you can prevent us from doing what we've bled to do, what we've died to do.

Y'awl **must** be craziii to even think that we are goin' to allow y'awl to prevent us from voting. After we've been thru the bleeding and the dying, all of the lyncinging, the daily tortures, all of what you've put in front of us to prevent us from being citizens of the greatest nation on Earth (made with our enslaved labor)...

Y'awl **must** be craziii.

Pick up an un-redacted history book quick, don't get tricked out by racist rhetoric, don't wind up on the wrong side of your own his-story.

Y'awl **must** be craziii to even think that we are goin' to allow y'awl to prevent us from voting.

Open up your eyes to American history, not racist notions

That's all I'm sayin', y'awl **must** be craziii.

You know what I'm saying?

Printed in the United States
by Baker & Taylor Publisher Services